SLAVE OF THE SPARTANS

'But there's a small service you must perform first,' Lefthera drawled to the young waiter, lighting another cigarette by striking a match on the sole of her foot. 'My servant here has been very naughty. While I was eating breakfast, and I was unfortunately without my clothes, I know he was looking at my naked body, and masturbating. You know you were masturbating, you smutty young snail. Don't deny it, Ben.'

Ben blushed.

'I . . . I can't deny it,' he blurted.

'So this young man of mine needs a caning. To get your tip, you must cane him a dozen strokes on his naked bottom, in punishment. I am far too lazy to do it myself. Ben, select a cane, and give it to our visitor.

'And there's just one other thing,' she said, turning to the waiter. 'I want you to be naked when you cane my servant. One naked boy caning another is a spectacle that pleases me. As you see, I'm quite wet already, and excited at the prospect of my servant's bottom squirming.'

SLAVE OF THE SPARTANS

Yolanda Celbridge

This book is a work of fiction.
In real life, make sure you practise safe, sane and
consensual sex.

First published in 2006 by
Nexus
Thames Wharf Studios
Rainville Rd
London W6 9HA

www.nexus-books.co.uk

A catalogue record for this book is available from the
British Library.

Typeset by TW Typesetting, Plymouth, Devon
Printed and bound in Great Britain by Clays Ltd, Elcograf S.p.A.

ISBN 0 352 34078 9
ISBN 978 0 352 34078 8

Contents

1

Caught Smoking

'Smoking?' drawled the matron, Miss Elena Ramsey, her own Dunhill king-size recently and discreetly extinguished. 'It's a disgusting habit and stunts your growth. You are a big boy now, Ben, and you don't want your growth stunted, do you? And you were smoking with Louella Potts, a senior girl. Both of you are supposed to set an example. Not only that, you were ... well, you were kissing her and groping her. I have the report here, and it's all written down. You had your fingers up her school-uniform skirt – inside her panties, I think. Feeling her bottom, and in all likelihood her private place, making her wet down there, and her tongue was certainly in your mouth.'

'I admit that we were kissing, yes,' the boy blurted, 'and that I was feeling her bottom, but not her, you know, her other private place. I'm no dirty beast. But it's my fault! Louella is a fine person. Perhaps I was just a little bit dirty, and lost control of myself.'

'I have to tell you that you are not the first boy Louella has allowed to grope her, or do more to her. Her thighs, as I'm sure you noticed, are most firm and muscular. She's over eighteen! It must be all the skiing. That young lady has quite a history. Skiers are lascivious people, you know. In a way, you are quite lucky you were caught by Miss Dodson.'

Ben Fraunce was crimson with shame.

'Well, Matron, I'm over eighteen,' he blurted.

Good, thought Elena. She had always fancied the pretty boy, and there was just a tinge of jealous fury in her reaction to his groping Louella. This, the last day of term, was her last chance to indulge in some unmatronlike pleasure.

'I'm terribly sorry, Matron.'

'Sorry isn't good enough. You should know that.'

'I do know it, Matron. But, please, it's my last day at school . . .'

'It's precisely for that reason that I must make an example of you. *Pour encourager les autres.* You've been sent to me because smoking and gross venery are considered medical problems, by the powers that be. In earlier, easier days, you'd have just been sent to our dear headmistress, Miss Gray, for a swift whacking. I mean, that was done in the time of our grandparents. Short and sharp, a nasty little boy, found being beastly, got his trousers taken down for a good six of the best on his underpants, or often on the bare buttocks. Bare bum was fairer, because the cane on knickers would spoil his underpants, and underpants are expensive to replace. Isn't everything, these days? But now I have your file. At Hereford Hellenic, we expect our alumni to set an example. You'll be going up to Oxford and you'll probably meet all sorts of company, some good, and some bad. You might even be tempted to go to nasty places in London –' the matron shuddered '– and we want you to stay out of that and not disgrace your old school. Ben, big boys don't say please. They take their medicine like a man.'

'Medicine?'

'I think you know what I'm talking about.'

'I'm sorry, but I don't.'

'There you are, saying sorry again.'

'I'm sorry.'

'You see? You incorrigible boy! I'll have to punish you.'

Hereford Hellenic, the venerable old school, with its quaint traditions, dated back to the Renaissance, and was founded to instil classical learning. The matron of Hereford Hellenic sighed, and took a deep breath, smoothing her navy-blue nylon stockings, and tapping her throat to make sure that her white nylon tunic was buttoned correctly, up to the neck, so that she was proper in every way for what was about to happen, and what Ben was beginning to sense was about to happen. Under her nylon tunic, and her white nylon bra, Miss Elena Ramsey's nipples were hard. She was nearly at her twenty-fifth birthday, and was understandably proud of her good and respectable position, so early in life. She was also proud of her hard young body, and her 96-centimetre breasts, which she massaged and measured every day, with a steel tape measure, wrapped tightly around her bare skin.

Her voice was as stern as she could make it, as she tried to ignore the tickling in her nipples. Her big plum-crimson nipples! Like giant tingly fruits! And a slice that became deliciously, but embarrassingly, wet whenever she performed a medical examination of a naked schoolboy, frequently having to tap his unruly *membrum virile* with an ice-cold spoon to stop the stiffening, or, more rarely than she would have liked, the discreet flogging punishment of a fellow's bare buttocks for some misdemeanour. As matron, she was qualified to do that, for it was called 'treatment', not punishment. How she moistened as she whopped the boy's squirming bare buttocks! Biology was sometimes unfair to girls.

'You'll have to take a caning on your naked bottom, Ben,' she said sternly, but with sympathy in her voice. 'It's the only way to sort this problem. Six of the best, my hardest strokes, on your bared buttocks.'

'A caning? And on my bare? I ... I ... well, I suppose I must consent, but I've never heard of such a thing being done, in this day and age.'

'Oh, it's done, Ben. Hereford Hellenic has a long and honourable tradition of corporal punishment, following the Spartan doctrine of Lycurgus. Fellows were even *birched* on the bare, just as at that newcomer school Eton, who copied birching from us. Two dozen lashes with a sheaf of cruel little twigs and, sometimes, they were strung up naked by their wrists, for a bare-back flogging with a

3

cowhide whip, as in the Navy. When you get to Oxford, to read classics, you'll find that a lot of people, a lot of women, are, shall I say, traditionally minded. Young people were whipped in ancient times, as a matter of course. Whipped naked, sometimes for punishment, sometimes as a religious ritual. But, as a classics scholar, you are aware of that. I wish I'd read classics myself, but you know how it is: good jobs are hard to get nowadays, so I am a school matron with a nursing diploma.'

She smiled cruelly, as her quim moistened. He was gorgeous. Such a pleasure to beat a gorgeous boy on his naked bum. Wipe the cherubic smile from his face.

'I admit I've been stupid with Louella Potts,' Ben said, 'but ... what you've just told me ... isn't that a bit old-fashioned? Like, out of storybooks?'

'Hereford Hellenic *is* a bit old-fashioned, as you should know by now. And what are your Livy and Tacitus and Plutarch and Caesar but storybooks? What is anything but a storybook? It's your choice. Your name will go on the gold board, a scholarship winner to shine in Classics at Christ Church, or you can slink out of here in shame. But, if I punish you with a swift six, then you are still the golden scholarship boy. Do you agree to take my punishment?'

'I ... I suppose so. Perhaps I don't have much choice.'

'That's a good Stoic way of looking at it.'

'I don't think you'll hurt me too much, though, will you?'

'Yes, I'll hurt you. And supposing isn't good enough! You must ask me for your punishment, in fact beg me for it. I might refuse to punish you, if you displease me.'

'Refuse to punish me? And me having to beg for punishment?'

'Yes. And it'll hurt a lot. A bare-bum caning always does. You'll walk a bit squiffy for a few days. Down on your knees, and beg, now,'

'I don't believe this!'

'Beg.'

Miss Ramsey crossed her nyloned thighs, so that Ben saw her white nylon panties, a mere string, with a tiny

4

triangular sliver of fabric covering the swelling of her shaven hillock. She noted his glance.

'Feeling Louella's bum and panties,' she mused. 'You'd like to have her wet panties, wouldn't you, Ben? Sniff them, wank off in them, as boys do? In fact, wouldn't you like to have mine, that you've just so rudely peeked at?'

'I ... I couldn't help ... Whatever do you mean?'

'I mean, *have* them, possess them utterly. Or like to get inside them? Feel my secret place, my woman's temple, my Eleusinian mystery. Your fingers wet from me. My place like Louella's mouth, but warmer and deeper.'

Ben was erect. The matron could see it, and her eyes glinted, and the knowledge of her seeing his shame made his erection stiffer.

'No! I mean, yes,' he whimpered. 'Oh, please, Miss Ramsey, don't make fun of me.'

'And your beating will of course be on the bare bum. That won't be fun. The lash of a rod on naked skin is the oldest sound in human history.'

Ben paled.

'You really want to cane me with no trousers on? I mean –'

'I'll have clothes on. You, not. As I said quite clearly, I shall cane you, or, more accurately, beat you, with a fibreglass riding crop, bound in leather, on your bare buttocks.'

'You can't mean it! I mean, really? On my bare bum?'

'Yes. Are you hard of hearing?'

'I don't know.'

'Start knowing. Crouch. And beg.'

Miss Ramsey extended a foot. As Ben, scarlet-faced, crouched to do her bidding, she dropped the shoe from her nyloned toes, and ordered him to lick her foot, in obeisance. He took the toes into his mouth, and began to suck.

'At Oxford, you'll meet much worse, or more demanding, or perhaps much more thoughtful, than this,' Miss Ramsey said. 'I know people at Oxford. Just lick my stockinged toes, Ben. Not even my bare toes! Just my

5

sweaty, smelly nylons. This shame hasn't softened the blatant erection of your phallus, has it? Shame won't hurt you as much as the bare beating you're to get. Or would you prefer to lick my naked toes? Many men like to do that.'

'I must obey your orders, Matron,' said the boy, blushing. 'I do want my name on the gold board.'

'Lick, then.'

'Very well. I . . . I have to do your bidding, don't I?'

'A gentleman always has to do a lady's bidding, Ben.'

Ben's lips fastened on Miss Ramsey's toes, wet with sweat in her stockings, and he began to lick.

'No, not just a licking, I want you to suck,' she said. 'Take my whole foot in your mouth. Suck my stockings dry.'

He obeyed, his lips pressing hard on Miss Ramsey's toes.

'Smelly, aren't they? All sweaty and horrid?'

'Yes, if you say so, they do hum a bit, miss.'

When he had sucked the toes of both her feet for a while, she said, 'Wouldn't you like me to take off all my things, to be naked – although of course you are forbidden to touch me – and let you wear them? Haven't you ever dreamt of wearing a girl's things? Doesn't every boy secretly long for that? Especially a girl's undies, you know, bra and stockings and everything, that aren't fresh, but are scented, really humming, ponging with her body? Her smelly soiled knickers? So that he can feel like a girl?'

'I . . . I . . .'

'I think you would, Ben. What you think, of course, doesn't matter, for you are only a boy.'

'I'm eighteen! A man!'

'We'll see about that.'

As Ben sucked her nyloned toes, Miss Ramsey parted her thighs, and drew her white panties down to her knees, to display her bare-shaven hillock. Between the swollen folds of her vaginal lips, she began to rub her clito, its small pink knob glistening, moist with juice, in its tender stiffness.

'You still have an erection, Ben,' she said. 'And rather a large and impudent one, too! We'll have to cure that. I think we'll have to shame you a little bit, quite apart from the pain of my caning you. I think you'll have to be caned, bare bum of course, but wearing a girl's stockings and bra. Mine, in fact. And I'll put your hair in a braid – when did you last have it cut, you lazy boy? – so that you will look all the prettier when I flog that tasty bum. And you do have nice buttocks. I can see why Louella went for you. She likes a boy with a trim derrière. Well, most girls do. Now, get them off, Ben. You know what I mean. Bend over and spread them. Those tasty buns.'

Ben took his drooling lips from Miss Ramsey's toes.

'Yes, miss,' he sobbed.

'First, I think I'll shave you,' she said. 'Shave your balls and cock. You won't mind. In fact, you'll feel a lot cleaner, and will probably want to remain shaved. Men are such hairy creatures, like base pongoid apes! So you may strip naked. Take all your clothes off, just as in a normal surgery visit.'

Elena was renowned for her efficiency as matron. A boy visiting her for the slightest complaint had to be fully examined in the nude, often with one or two of her fingers, in a plastic surgical glove, probing his rectum. When Ben was stripped, she soaped and lathered his balls, then applied a deft razor, and soon his phallus, perineum and balls were bare. With Ben still in submissive position, she applied lotion to his chest and back, and shaved him there, too, then shaved his legs and arms, until he was totally smooth. Five disposable razors were used during this operation.

'Now you look presentable,' Elena Ramsey said, rubbing her quim, which was quite wet. 'The cost of the razors will be added to your final school battels.'

What happened to Ben was beyond his strangest dreams, and his worst nightmares. It was unthinkable, something that you read about, or pretended not to read about, in the trashy tabloid papers, about creeps and perverts. Yet it was happening to him, and he was letting it happen. Didn't it happen, too, in the ancient Greece that he longed to see, but had only read about in books? He was dressed in Miss

Ramsey's intimate garments. He had her stockings on, rolled right up, almost to his bare-shaven balls; her white thong panties, which bit uncomfortably, with strange, beautiful pain and shame, into his arse cleft; and, worst of indignities, her white bra. The high-born Minoan ladies of ancient Crete went bare-breasted, with their nipples pierced to carry golden rings, while ladies of the ordinary classes wore a bra, but could be nude at sports, and made a show of it, flaunting their naked teats as they played their ball games – battledore and shuttlecock, an early form of badminton, being the favourite, with much bouncing of naked thighs and breasts. All sports in the ancient world were, or course, played in the nude, which was also the tradition at Hereford Hellenic, except for rugby football – with girls' teams as well as boys' teams – where the boys wore jockstraps, but nothing else. It was also one of the few schools that awarded prizes for bodybuilding – Ben had won a medal for his pectoral development – that practice being also carried out in the nude, with boys and girls working out in the gymnasium side by side. But, although boys and girls swam and exercised together in the nude, there was a complete ban on any form of sexual activity – which was why Ben was so ashamed of his lapse with Louella.

Ben had excelled in swimming, bodybuilding and rugby (association football was forbidden at Hellenic) and his body was hard and trim, with firm pectorals, and these were now strapped in a girly Cretan bra! Yet his excitement made his phallus stand rock hard, and the spreading of his buttocks, almost nude in the tiny thong, smelling of Miss Ramsey's unwashed anus and shaven lady's place, with the knowledge that this young woman was about to flog him, wearing her panties, the sacred sliver of cloth having covered her shaven hillock, made his excitement almost unbearable. Miss Ramsey herself was bare-breasted, bare-legged and barefoot, wearing only her skirt, clinging to her pantiless buttocks. She was a Cretan priestess of old.

'Is this how you imagined, or wanted, Louella, Ben?' she taunted. 'What is it like to wear a bra, and stockings? You *are* pretty, you know. And you didn't really get that far with Louella. A grope! That isn't really much. Louella's a tease. She's had more than groping. She's no virgin. She's had boys' members right inside her, thrusting, until they spurt their fluid. You're still a virgin, I can tell. You've never put it into a girl, have you?'

'No, Miss Ramsey.'

'Ever been naked with one?'

'Not really.'

'What does that mean?'

'No.'

'Just playing wanky games with other boys.'

'No, miss! I mean, I haven't done that for years.'

'I know. It's a normal phase young boys go through. Still, I think it's rather sweet. Girls aren't so forward, and have to be a little more discreet in their wanking. I expect you'd like a smoke before I cane you.'

'What? But you're beating me for smoking!'

'No, I'm beating you because you have a pretty bottom, which begs for the crop. Work it out, Ben.'

She lit two Dunhills, and pressed one between Ben's lips. Hungrily, he sucked smoke, while Miss Ramsey flexed her riding crop, and allowed her cigarette to dangle from the corner of her mouth.

'This crop is a corker,' she drawled, drawing the pluming smoke into her nose. 'I got it from the saddlery shop in Hereford. Not too many people have horses these days, but they still like to buy crops. Makes you think, doesn't it? You see, as if you probably haven't guessed, I've thrashed other naughty boys on the bare. I like it. I like the way their naked bums squirm, and they get all soppy and sobby, and the skin reddens so nicely. It's a bit like having a flower garden, and growing nice red roses or peonies. And, by the way, just an hour ago, I thrashed Louella on the bare, made her lift her skirt and lower her knickers, and gave her four strokes of the crop, for having her beastly tongue in your mouth. Her bum squirmed quite satisfactorily, and the poor little thing was in tears. Now I think we'd better start your treatment. But you must give

9

me the word, Ben. It could go beyond a sixer, if we're to cure that erection. The word, Ben?'

'I . . . I don't know . . . I'm so confused . . .'

'Your hard phallus is not confused. When you go up to Oxford, Ben, you'll have to know. The word a gentleman always uses to a lady?'

She lashed the air with the riding crop, making a fearful whistling sound, and Ben's arse clenched.

'Please, Miss Ramsey,' he blurted.

'Yes, that's the word,' she said, spreading her legs in an athlete's stance, for the bra-clad boy's caning. 'But a little bit more wouldn't go amiss.'

'Oh, please, miss, cane me. Cane me on my bare bottom. Make me . . . make me wriggle in pain. I deserve it.'

As he spoke, Ben's phallus throbbed, rock hard, in the skimpy girl's string.

'Thank you, Ben.'

Contented, the matron lifted the riding crop, swished it in the placid Hereford air, and began to flog the boy's bare. *Vap! Vap!* The crop made a satisfactory dry sound on the boy's naked buttocks, which squirmed, clenching, at each stroke. She took him beyond the six, to a full ten, because she said his stiff phallus, bursting his girl's thong, was still a disgrace, while he gasped and sobbed, his eyes moist with tears, and, when his clenched and writhing buttocks were striped red, Miss Ramsey delicately and discreetly masturbated herself to a shuddering orgasm; after her spasm had ebbed, she said that he had behaved well, had taken his punishment like a man, but that he must now add the other word that gentlemen said to ladies.

'Thank you, miss,' he stammered.

'But you are still erect.'

'I'm sorry, miss.'

'That word again.'

Miss Ramsey placed a fingertip on his swollen glans, and he groaned.

'I don't think this will take long,' she said, as she gently rubbed his stiff penis.

'Oh, miss . . .'

'I expect you do this all the time. Boys do, don't they? Wank yourself off. But girls do it too, you know. In ancient Greece, wanking off was quite a normal practice. People didn't wear many clothes, and sometimes they just walked around quite nude. If you felt like it, by the roadside, you just, I suppose, obliged your body.'

Her touch on his penis made him squirm.

'Oh, yes, please, thank you, yes, oh yes . . .'

When Ben had spurted his sperm into the matron's soft palm, and she had cleaned herself by licking up and swallowing all of his creamy ejaculate, glistening in the Hereford sun, she said that the gold board, and Miss Gray's accolade, awaited him. She stripped him of his girl's raiment, all except for the thong panties, which left his reddened buttocks fully visible, and fastened him in a leather halter, also from the saddlery in Hereford, in fact an ass's harness, tethering his buttocks, breasts and balls. That was one of Hereford Hellenic's quaint traditions. Then, herself prim in her matron's uniform (although she was nude under her skirt, with no panties, for they were worn by Ben), she led him through the school corridors, while his fellow students, boys and girls, laughed and cheered, none more heartily than Louella. This, too, was an ancient school tradition, dating back to the founder's time in the fifteenth century, when Hereford Hellenic was one of the pioneers in the new Renaissance study of Greek, as well as the traditional Latin.

Miss Gray the headmistress also laughed, and, dressed in sandals and a flimsy straw-coloured peplos, with a garland of black olives on her head and breast, said, in her oration in classical Greek, that Ben was a good sport, possessed of a fine English gentleman's sense of humour, which was just like the lusty humour of ancient Greece, and he could see a good joke, although he was no Lucius, the Ass of Apuleius, and presented him with his scholarship certificate. She said, in Greek, that he would bring honour to the school when he was up at Christ Church, and must never forget that Hereford Hellenic was his home, and that, wherever his travels took him, all the school would continue to love him. Especially Miss Ramsey. It was a sunny day in Hereford, and his humiliation and punishment, his shameful nudity itself, seemed unimportant, merely part of some antique ritual, and perhaps doing him honour in some obscure way. In his harness, Ben bowed to the ladies, in their Grecian dresses – delicate fingers of their applause were heard, like a whispered echo of ancient sibyls, as he unwittingly presented his whipped bottom – and, in perfect classical Greek, though with a slight West Country accent, said 'thank you' to the ladies.

2

Freshers' Fair

It was Dr Rosalynn Demande's practice to rise at four in the morning, don a purple tracksuit and leave her rooms in Christ Church College, with a cheery nod to Perkins the night porter, then proceed to Christ Church Meadow, where she would run circuits until dawn. Once in the bosky privacy of the meadow, she would strip off her tracksuit, stow it neatly folded under her usual tree, and run in the nude. Her preferred time was under a chill bright moon, but she made her circuits even when it was raining, and relished the cooling droplets of water on her pumping naked body. She finished her run with a naked swim in the cold waters of the Isis, near the rowing stations, where, later, beefy young men in shorts and singlets would be sweating at their oars.

At that time of the early morning, the landscape was usually deserted, hers alone, although occasionally she would espy a pair of drunken lovers, trousers down and skirt up, at their amorous task. They would exchange complicit and encouraging glances: each to his own. She approved: it was classical, Dionysian, and the offering of a man's seed into the womb, or perhaps the anus, of a girl, helped the flowers and trees to grow. After her swim, she would perform a hundred press-ups, then grasp a tree branch and perform fifty pull-ups. A second cooling swim, and then she would hang upside down by her heels from the tree branch, her naked thighs parted wide, her long raven tresses brushing the ground, and the rain or the moonlight washing her opened sex, and intone a prayer to the fecund earth beneath her face, while she rubbed her clito, feeling her juices trickle down her body, and masturbate herself to orgasm – her sacrifice to the earth.

On occasions, her friend and sister classicist, Dr Sarah Mountjoy, from neighbouring Oriel College, would accompany Rosalynn on these expeditions, and the two nude girls would vie to see who could take the more punishment, do the more press-ups and pull-ups, sweat the more. At 25 and 26 respectively, both were at the pinnacle of physical, mental and career development, and both were serious bodybuilders, their built bodies swollen with ripped muscle. Rosalynn was particularly proud of her long legs, and superbly built thighs, which attracted lustful glances wherever she went, and especially if she chose to wear a short skirt.

Where Rosalynn was dark of mane, Sarah was blonde. Running around the meadow was only a prelude to the serious workouts at the Phiditia Club. Whether Rosalynn ran alone or with Sarah, they were bound to meet at the Phiditia, just off Turl Street, after Rosalynn had returned from her run, with another cheery greeting to Perkins, as the sun's rays began to gleam, and taken time in her chambers for a breakfast of lambs' kidneys, olives and goat cheese, followed by bread and honey, and washed down by copious, well-sugared tea, the meal prepared by her scout, the kindly Mrs Lord.

In her room, in the presence of servants, Rosalynn preferred to wear a simple Greek peplos, although, at college or university business, she was every inch the English lady, sumptuous in court shoes, cashmere, tweed or tartan, silk or ten-denier nylon stockings, with lace suspender belt and garter straps, although the latter items were of course known to her alone. Sometimes she wore a quite unnecessary satin and bone antique corset, in a sky-blue colour, which Rosalynn claimed, or fancied, had once belonged to Lewis Carroll's Alice Liddell, when she had grown too old for the Christ Church don's chaste but voyeuristic attention. She had bought it from an antique

14

shop in St Aldate's. The corset pinched her pencil-narrow, muscled belly to even further slimness, and thrust her hard young breasts into melons, for her own secret pleasure.

Early breakfast left time for a brisk walk up to Turl Street, as the dawn light glimmered, and a couple of hours in the gymnasium, before her first lecture or tutorial of the day. The Phiditia, for girls only, was a true gymnasium, that is, a naked place. All members, upon entering, doffed their clothes, and the staff, too, were nude. Thus could Rosalynn, Sarah and their friends, academics all, sweat at bench presses, work on their abs and pecs and lats, and gossip about the wondrous changes effected by muscle-ripping on their young bodies, and the glory of the Greek sun on those same bodies, during the summer vac. Like all bodybuilders, they despised mere weightlifters, usually sweaty young men with unsuitable accents, and covered in unseemly body hair. In the afternoons, they would take a punt at Magdalen Bridge, and pole themselves up the Cherwell, tributary of the Isis, to Parson's Pleasure, the nudist enclave formerly reserved for male academics, but today, of course, occupied by women too.

Rosalynn and Sarah were friends and rivals. Rosalynn had published the definitive book on the poet Tyrtaeus, of ancient Sparta, whose surviving work consisted of only a few fragments, yet how wonderfully she had brought the poet to life! Tyrtaeus preached the manly virtues of the strange Lacedaemonian military city-state, where no tyrant had ever taken power, because all citizens were required to dine communally, and naked, in the Phiditia, or public mess, separate messes being reserved for males and females. Failure to pay your mess bill resulted in loss of citizenship, and Rosalynn impishly suggested that this was the same as being sent down from an Oxford college for failing to pay your battels, so ancient Sparta was a bit like Oxford.

Sarah had published on the role of ritual flogging of male and female Spartan youth, and the importance of bodybuilding; Rosalynn, on the Spartan obligation of nude female wrestling, as well as male wrestling; Sarah, a

15

seminal book on Lycurgus the lawgiver, and institutor of flogging both as punishment and as a source of civic virtue, the spectacle of whipped naked malefactors inspiring the citizens, male and female, to their own virtue; Rosalynn, a daring but incontrovertible book on buttock worship in the ancient world. Her thesis was that the ancients regarded both male and female buttocks as sacred, representing the fruits of the earth, or perhaps various stars and moons, and that, accordingly, those buttocks must be whipped naked, in ritual sacrifice, with the victim tied to a tree.

She drew some interesting parallels with the traditions of ancient English schools, and, indeed, the Royal Navy of old, where cadets were whipped on the bare buttocks, and, moreover, expected and desired such treatment, as a matter of honour. Perhaps the English were in some way the modern Spartans. Sarah had countered with her own paper on Tyrtaeus, in which she suggested that Tyrtaeus – as with everything Spartan, very little was really known, for there were no Spartan historians like Thucydides – was in fact a woman, which would explain her obsession with male buttocks, and apparent love of both witnessing and receiving whipping on the bare nates with a scourge of olive branches, and that Sparta, far from being a male-dominated fascist society, was in fact dominated by women, themselves bodybuilders, who kept the males naked, flogged, muscular and subordinate, to use them for their pleasure.

That thesis caused some controversy, with pursed lips and creased brows throughout the scholarly world. Rosalynn had published a slim volume on the importance and history of masturbation in the culture of the ancient Mediterranean. It was considered a sacred rite for male and female youths to masturbate together, naked at dawn by a crossroads, 'the place where four roads meet'. In the corrupt modern world, people masturbated from fantasy, an erotic picture of some kind, but, at the dawn of civilisation, they needed no pictorial stimulus, and masturbated at the sheer joy of living, in worship of the earth.

That thesis, too, caused scholarly eyebrows to rise. Sarah had added to it with a monograph on the sacredness of the crossroads in ancient Greece, like Oxford's Carfax, and drew a parallel with English ley lines. It was agreed in academe that, however controversial, neither Rosalynn nor Sarah could be ignored.

That morning, a fresh autumn day, was the first morning of the Michaelmas term, and Rosalynn, nude and sweating in the sauna with Sarah – who was saying she would kill for a hot cup of tea – grumped that she had some freshers to see.

'There's a young man called Benjamin Fraunce, from Hereford Hellenic,' she mused. 'I'm to be his tutor.'

Rosalynn's idle fingers stroked Sarah's sweat-soaked bare bottom. She tapped the firm globes, brushed her manicured fingernails inside her friend's cleft, as an aid to thought. Blonde Sarah's buttocks were dusted with golden downy hairs, and while both women were earnest about shaving their bodies, with perfectly clean pubic mounds, Rosalynn made a point of shaving her legs, armpits, anus, perineum and of course pubic hillock, to complete gleaming nudity every day. When she was cross with Sarah, she would accuse her of laziness, and not shaving to perfect smoothness, then playfully spank her bare bottom a couple of dozen slaps.

'Perhaps related to Abraham Fraunce?' said Sarah. 'I mean, it would have to be, descended from. You do know his *Arcadian Rhetorike*? I was thinking of doing a paper on it. Don't you so love minor poets, especially so minor as to be almost invisible? Like our friend Tyrtaeus? Or Stesichorus of Sparta? Just a few fragments of parchment, a whole person to reconstruct from that, so yummy!'

'I don't know,' said Rosalynn, idly pinching Sarah's bottom. 'But Ben has won a brilliant scholarship, with a fascinating paper on the Peloponnesian War.'

'Ben, now that is a good name. There must be a synergy in these things. Benjamin Jowett, master of Balliol, then vice-chancellor . . . the translations of Plato, of Aristotle, of Thucydides . . . you know how much we owe him!'

17

'Of course I know. Do you think me a lump?'
Sarah chortled, and recited:

I'm Master of Balliol, name of Jowett;
There's no knowledge but I know it.
I'm Jowett, Master of Balliol College,
And what I don't know isn't knowledge.

'That's cheeky,' said Rosalynn. 'And cheeky girls get spanked.'

'I thought you'd never tell me,' purred Sarah.

Counting, Rosalynn spanked her friend 52 slaps, twice a Greek sacred number, on the naked buttocks, while holding her by her nipples. Sarah's bottom clenched delightfully and with vigour, as it always did. The next time, it would be Rosalynn's turn to squirm, for bare-bottom spanking, at Phiditia, was as much friendship between girls as religious rite. After Sarah's spanking, the girls went to the Randolph Hotel for tea and toast with proper Dundee marmalade. Sarah complained, only half seriously, that her bottom was awfully hot from her spanking, and that her nipples were rather sore, too, but in a nice, tingly way. She kissed Rosalynn's fingertips.

'Ben Fraunce,' Rosalynn said, 'has been recommended by Elena Ramsey, whom I knew slightly at school. It appears he's never even been to Greece. She says he has potential. I wonder if that means what I think it means.'

'Do let's find out,' said Sarah.

Ben was slightly nervous, as he had his first meeting with his new tutor, Dr Demande. There was such a rush of new things, as a fresher at Oxford, getting to know your corridor in College, making friends with your servant, and tipping appropriately, a new city to explore, the arcane and intricate ways of the University, the lanes and streets hallowed by centuries of quiet, contemplative history, the multitude of activities into which a young undergrad was expected to throw himself. It was more or less obligatory, although at Oxford nothing was really obligatory, to attend the Freshers' Fair, where various societies – the OU Dramatic Society, the OU Birdwatchers, the different political parties and groupings, all vied and cajoled for the custom of a new arrival. He thought he had managed quite well, so far, but the presence of Dr Rosalynn Demande, and her explanation of his status, unnerved him somewhat. He would have a weekly tutorial with her, and would have to write an essay every week, which he must read to her, and expect merciless criticism. In between, he might attend lectures, if he chose to. The beauty of the University was that you could attend any lectures at all, so that, if you were reading Mods and Greats – classics – as Ben was now doing, you could nevertheless equip yourself with the latest studies in zoology or post-structuralism.

If it all seemed a bit much, then the person of Dr Demande herself was overwhelming. Ben thought he had never seen such a beautiful, dominant woman, long dark curly tresses garlanding her head like whips. She wore a grey cashmere skirt, daringly short; white silk stockings, and black court shoes, with a white silk blouse, under which her braless, muscular breasts, and the big jutting cherry nipples, were clearly, but somehow innocently, apparent. Dr Demande's muscled body exuded power – her thighs, like Louella's, rippled so invitingly, dangerously so – and her friendly, twinkling eyes glittered towards Ben's growing erection, as if she knew exactly what was in his mind.

He wanted to wear her clothes. Wanted to know what colour her panties were, wanted to sniff and kiss them. Wanted to kiss her stockinged feet, lick the smelly juice from her toes, suck the juices from her panties, and have her whip him for those guilty urges, and his beastly impudence. The thought made him giddy, and, when Dr Demande dismissed him, after giving him the title of his first week's essay – 'Some aspects of the ritual punishment of boys in ancient Sparta' – he treated himself to a pint of beer and a meat pie in the Bear Inn. That made him feel better, and he went to the Freshers' Fair.

There, he was bewildered by the cacophony, the elaborate stalls and importuning young men and women, with their strange and varied enthusiasms, their piles of documentation, brochures and leaflets, none of which enticed him, until he came to a table at the end of the vast hall, which was occupied by a solitary bare-legged girl, dark-haired and olive-skinned, seemingly uninterested in the hustle and hype of the rest of the fair, for she had her bare brown feet on the table, and was meticulously painting her toenails purple. A cigarette, in this no-smoking zone, dangled carelessly from her lips. Her very short dress was what Ben recognised as a simple Greek peplos, and she was evidently, and unconcernedly, almost naked underneath the white shift, which clung to her ripe buttocks, pantied in a small and apparent brown thong. Her long legs, topped by meaty, perfectly sculpted naked thighs, caused Ben's phallus to rise. He had a longing to masturbate, just looking at this girl's thighs. She had a scalloped brown bra, which did little to conceal the ripeness of her full jutting breasts, with big domed nipples, like luscious sponge cakes. And those nipples were adorned with golden nipple rings, pierced through her flesh. Her lips were painted with purple lipstick.

Her skin was tan, her hair long, olive-black and curly, brushing her lightly brassiered breasts under the skimpy shift, and Ben thought longingly of Dr Demande's hard muscled breasts. This girl's were softer, fuller and more rounded – like her full buttocks and massive thighs, vessels of milk and honey. A sign, in the Greek alphabet, said 'The Lacedaemonian Society', Lacedaemonia being the name of ancient Sparta. There were no leaflets or any other paraphernalia of selling, just the single indifferent girl, painting her toenails, and, beside her bare feet, a coiled hippopotamus-hide whip. He knew it was hide of hippopotamus, for that was the favoured, hardest and most expensive instrument of correction among the tyrants and schoolmasters of ancient Greece. He wondered where she obtained hippopotamus hide for her whip. Wasn't that an endangered species? He lingered. After a while, the girl became aware of his gaze.

'Yes?' she snapped, her white teeth sneering under purple lips.

'I'm sorry . . . I was wondering . . .'

'Oh, you're sorry, are you? Perhaps you have something to be sorry for. Like wearing an ass's harness.'

'No . . . I just . . .'

She stroked her bare thighs for a few moments, quite close up to her apex, and Ben knew she was taunting him, and had seen his erect phallus, then went back to painting her adorable toenails, on her adorable feet, and Ben wanted to lick every one. He wanted to kiss those thighs, rip the slim brown thong from her loins, and wear it himself, to cradle his balls and phallus with the scent and tightness of her girlhood; he wanted to strap her bra over his own breasts, and beg for her to flog him in punishment, then suck her feet, as he begged for her forgiveness. He wondered what the brown bra and panties were made of – silk, nylon? – and yearned to be properly and severely punished for that thought, too.

'Are you still here?' she said.

'Well . . . the Lacedaemonian Society,' he blurted.

'It means ancient Sparta. I don't suppose you'd know that. You're some sociology type, I expect, but too young to grow a grotty beard. The sort that in fact deserves to wear an ass's harness.'

Ben haltingly explained that he was reading Mods and Greats, and that he did, in fact, know it, knew about the Peloponnesian War, and Helen of Troy and her husband King Menelaus of Sparta, and that he was at the House, and his tutor was Dr Rosalynn Demande. The girl raised a momentary eyebrow, then yawned, flicking her perfect pink tongue against her perfect white teeth. Her purple lipstick made her look like an exotic wildcat.

'We don't accept just any ignoramus,' she drawled. 'For a start, Helen of Troy was not really Helen of Troy: she was Helen of Sparta. She was *taken* to Troy, by Paris. She deserted King Menelaus. Then she betrayed Paris, and married his younger brother, then betrayed him. She dominated and betrayed every man whom she captivated, and went back to King Menelaus eventually. And she is worshipped as a goddess. In fact, I'm writing my book, not

21

on Helen, but on the bucolic poet Stesichorus, who wrote a poem in the Doric dialect condemning her, and was struck blind as a result. But when he composed the *Palinodia*, in apology, he got his sight back. He invented the triadic stanza, divided into strophe, antistrophe and epode, but some fools outrageously say he didn't, and I have to beat *them* to a pulp. Less than a hundred lines of the work of Stesichorus survive, so you see how tough it is to get at the truth. And you see why I have little time for fools.'

'I do see,' Ben said. 'Yes, you're right.'

'I don't think you really do see,' the girl said. 'But you seem willing to learn. I suppose we might have a vacancy. If you can pass the initiation rite. Turn round.'

'What?'

'Turn round, so that I may see your buttocks. Hold your trousers tightly, yes, like that. Hmm, I suppose you might be all right, as a helot. You're a virgin, aren't you?'

'How . . . ?'

'A girl can tell. Helots must be virgin. We don't accept filthy beasts as Spartans. We're not talking about beastly boys' wanking games, and groping a girl, and feeling her thighs and quim, and putting your tongue in her ear, and other noxious things, but you must never have put your phallus inside a girl. That's an absolute. Virginity is the first requirement.'

'I . . . really! Well, yes, since you put it so bluntly. Yes, I'm a virgin.'

'Thought so. Knew so.'

'There is no shame in that, surely? But what is it you do? The Lacedaemonian Society, I mean.'

'You don't ask,' she hissed. 'You learn.'

She uncoiled her whip, and kissed it, then coiled it again, with a devilish leer. Then, she flipped him a hand-painted card, which gave her name simply as Lefthera, under a portrait of a wrist-strung boy's bare buttocks squirming and red under a girl's whip, and an address in the Iffley Road.

'Two o'clock sharp, Thursday afternoon,' she said, yawning again, and patting her muscled, adorable brown thighs, as though they were sleek pets. 'That gives us time to organise your initiation. If you are a moment late, Ben, your initiation will be far worse than it is already destined to be.'

She looked at Ben's erection, smiled, stroked her bare thighs, getting her fingers right under her skirtlet, and touching the gusset of her thong panties, then removed her hand, and licked her fingers, which were glistening with moisture. Disdainfully, she flicked her painted fingers, dismissing him.

'By the way, Ben,' she said, 'the Spartans wear traditional Greek costume, so do kit yourself properly for your initiation. Get a decent panties and bra. Stockings, too, if you like, and a matching skirt. Sky blue, I think, would suit. Go to Stygia's boutique on the Woodstock Road. Our friend Stygia will know how to take care of you. And, Ben, you mustn't masturbate at any time from now on. Boys are filthy creatures, but you now have a chance to remain pure. You mustn't rub your phallus. Awfully sorry, but it's the strictest rule.'

As she spoke, she caressed the smooth brown skin of her superb naked thighs, letting her skirtlet ride right up to her apex, so that he could see her panties gusset, delicate and beckoning with a film of moisture. She leered maliciously.

'Yes . . . I see . . .' he stammered.

'You don't see yet,' drawled Lefthera, 'but, if you are lucky, you shall.'

Ben went back to the Bear Inn, and had two pints of beer, and two meat pies with rather large helpings of brown sauce, but his feast did little to quell the stiffening of his phallus, and his fear and desire of his initiation ceremony in the Iffley Road. It would be difficult not to masturbate, on the peremptory and rather unfair order of this girl. He had not introduced himself by name, nor had he spoken of an ass's harness; how had Lefthera known to call him Ben?

23

3

Stygia

'When I was younger,' said Dr Rosalynn Demande, 'my brothers and sisters and I used to walk around naked in the garden of my grand-uncle, in his mansion near West Looe, in Cornwall. He was very rich, an amateur archaeologist, and had a fascinating collection of Minoan pottery and solid hide artefacts, which I used to play with as a little girl, until I grew up, and was forbidden them, for I recognised that they were dildos. They were mostly bulls' pizzles. He paid us to do simple gardening tasks, weeding and flowerbed arrangement and so forth. That's where I got my love of gardening. Gardening in the nude, or indeed nudity in general, Ben, is one of life's simple pleasures, because you are in touch with Mother Earth. We lived nearby, closer to Looe proper, in quite a large house, though not as big as Grand-uncle's mansion, but we had ample grounds, so there was no need to wear clothes. Our family were nudists, and, as I grew up, we would spend glorious naked afternoons romping among the dunes, and in the Atlantic surf, on the beach at Cawsand, or Crafthole.

'In the summer, we would take the car ferry, and drive down to holiday in Montalivet, in southwest France, where the nudist beaches are perhaps the best in the world, rather like the Cornish beaches, for it's the same ocean, but with bigger dunes and a bit warmer. I don't think Mummy and Daddy were nudists by conviction. I mean, they weren't fanatics who belonged to clubs and things. They just found it simpler not to bother with clothes, when, of course, the weather permitted. Some nudists, who are fanatics, will freeze in winter, rather than put on a woolly sweater!

'Daddy was a professor of marine biology at the University of Plymouth, and he would take his students on nude scuba-diving trips! I loved him very much. He was quite happy for any of us, girls or boys, and we were quite a large family, to do naked gardening for Grand-uncle. I learnt to dive, and of course the sea is warm down in Cornwall, thanks to the Gulf Stream, but I got tired of all the fiddly apparatus, oxygen tanks and everything, and never really took to diving, until I went to Greece. There, where the Aegean is shallow, you dive naked, without equipment, just holding your breath, like the pearl divers and oyster gatherers of ancient times. You are a fish in the sea.

'Grand-uncle was very old, I'm not sure how old, but I suppose he liked the sight of a young girl's body. Men do, don't they? Menelaus did. Agamemnon did. It's part of their power, and reminds them of their youth. My grand-uncle was nude himself, an Agamemnon sitting in a wicker chair. I knew I was his favourite. He watched me wobble my bare bottom, just to please him, for I secretly hoped he was masturbating his phallus, to get himself some pleasure, although he probably wasn't, for the sight of naked young girlflesh is pleasure enough. I suggest you read my book on masturbation in ancient Greece, Ben. At any rate, he paid for my trips to Greece, and my fees to go up to Oxford, and now I am your tutor. I expect you to read me extremely good essays. Wobbling your bottom is, ah, optional.'

They both smiled.

'Yes, Dr Demande,' Ben said.

'I gather you've joined the Lacedaemonian Society.'

'Well, not exactly joined . . . I mean, I have to go to the Iffley Road, for a sort of initiation. And before that to Stygia's boutique in the Woodstock Road for my kit. I'm not sure what it's all about, but I'm sure it's all good sport.'

'Let me know what happens. And don't forget your essay for next week. Punishment of boys in ancient Sparta, I believe. I hope you've been in the Bodleian Library, gnoming away. Now I have important people to see, Ben, so go away for the moment. Please say, or gasp, hello to Lefthera for me.'

'Gasp?'

'You'll learn.'

Stygia was a tall woman from Bolton in Lancashire, almost two metres high, with a prominent bosom, and a mane of bright-red hair. She was perhaps thirty years of age. She laughed quietly at Ben when he entered her shop in the Woodstock Road.

'Another one for the Spartans?' Stygia said. 'Well, you're choice, and I can't say fairer than that. And a virgin, I suppose, too.'

'You *must* be a virgin, for the Spartans.'

'A virgin boy! Yes. How rare, and how lovely.'

Her fingers fleetingly stroked his bottom.

'You've the bum for Sparta, or Lacedaemonia, as they call it, but rather you than me! Let's kit you, then, virgin boy. We'll eat first, and you can pay. I trust you're not a whinger about money, as so many people are these days.'

'No . . .' Ben said.

'Good.'

They went to Aunt Alice's Café across the road, where they had giant mugs of sweet tea, and Stygia ate a Melton Mowbray pork pie, with chips made of Bintje potatoes, imported from Flanders by a nice Belgian man from Knokke-Heist, who currently lived in Headington, and Ben and Stygia had their pies with lashings of brown sauce. And they had Lancashire hotpot, with mushy peas. Stygia was most insistent on the correct boiling, saucing and consistency of mushy peas. Just a touch of mint and garlic, she said. Ben ate the same as the statuesque red-haired lady, for it seemed the gentlemanly thing to do. The pies and hotpot and mushy peas were good. Ben paid, as a gentleman does.

'Lefthera wants you in blue, does she?' Stygia said, once they had returned to the shop, and she had locked the door, and was scanning Ben with a practised eye. 'I'd have thought pink, or mauve, perhaps, myself. Mauve, in fact, is just that little bit more decadent. It's purplish, without being too purple. Let's try mauve, shall we? Don't worry. It's all the same price. I don't take those beastly plastic cards, by the way, just old-fashioned cash. You have cash, I suppose?'

'Yes, I have – whatever you say, miss,' Ben replied.

'Strip off, then, so that I can measure you. I have to measure your bum and bollocks.'

'You mean –'

'Strip off means strip off.'

'Oh! I . . . yes, I see.'

'You're not embarrassed, are you? Don't be. I've seen more nude boys than you've had meat pies. Some virgins. And if you get an erection, as you probably will, I promise not to be embarrassed, me.'

Ben took his clothes off and, indeed, he did have a massive erection, as Stygia measured his breasts, buttocks and balls with a steel tape measure.

'Nice big cock,' she said. 'Good body, good meat, and pretty with it, like a girl. Sort of Grecian. Good big balls, too. Lots of sperm, I'd guess. A heavy creamer. When you wank, I expect you really spurt lots. So when you stop being a virgin, the chosen girl will be happy enough with that package inside her. I'll just . . .'

She took control of his wallet for safe keeping.

'I think I have your size all right,' she said. 'In fact, I have a lot of nice things in stock that could have been made for you. You're the perfect Spartan size, the bum and tits I mean, and, heavens, that is a corker, that cock of yours. I hope it's not going to stand up all the time when you're properly robed. A thong gusset can only stand so much pressure. Those girls in the Iffley Road, they don't allow you hand relief, do they? It's awfully cruel, but, then, it's their job to be awfully cruel. Each to their own. My job is to make you look pretty.'

Ben looked at himself, blushing and erect, in Stygia's looking glass, as each stage of his robing took place. The redhead rolled mauve nylon stockings up his legs, tucked him into a lacy mauve suspender belt and fastened the stockings; then fitted his breasts into a tight bra of mauve nylon. The strap stung his back.

'You need to keep working on those pecs,' Stygia said. 'They are superb, lovely and hard, and your nipples are almost like a girl's, and to keep up that quality you must work on them. Don't bother with lipstick and powder and scent, that's for girly men, and you're certainly not a girly man. Quite the opposite, in fact. Now, a nice white petticoat, it's second-hand, belonged to Margot Asquith, and I think a corset would suit you, I have a lovely whalebone one in stock, it's not quite mauve, but it's nearly mauve, that belonged to King Edward the Seventh's Queen Alexandra, and then the panties, *they're* new, from Paris . . .'

Ben looked at himself in the glass, and did gasp, for he looked very beautiful, looked like a female twin of himself. He thought, for a fleeting moment, that he looked like his tutor, Dr Demande! Although she didn't wear mauve, and he thought obscurely that mauveness made him one up on her. He was kitted in mauve, with skirt, blouse, brassiere, stockings, panties, corset and petticoat, his longish hair fastened back with a silver pin. It all hurt. Girls' clothing seemed designed to hurt. All the straps and pins and zips and buckles and things! But it was a lovely, glorious hurt.

'You don't need shoes,' said Stygia, inflaming a cigarette with a gold lighter. 'The Lacedaemonian girls up in the Iffley Road are all barefoots, so they wouldn't appreciate shoes. Anyway, I don't do shoes. The people in Northampton, who made the best shoes in the world, went out of business. It's the way of things, isn't it? Also, when you shred your stockings, trudging up the Iffley Road, then you have to come back to me and buy some more.'

Cigarette dangling from her lips, Stygia stripped to her pink bra, stockings, suspenders and thong knickers, and posed in the looking glass beside Ben. She put her arm around his shoulders.

'I'm more of a pink person, myself,' she said. 'You know, up in Bolton, pink is the favoured colour for girls, but I thought it would be nice to show you how pretty a man can be. Mauve suits you, Ben. That skirt is so nice, and – you don't mind, I hope –' as her fingers delved beneath the skirt '– that corset, and that petticoat are just *you*. Don't worry about payment: I've already taken it from your wallet, to spare you the embarrassment. Now, I need a big hot cup of tea, and I dare say you do, too. You're wearing girl's clothes, and you have a stiff phallus! Whatever next.'

She laughed, not unpleasantly, but with sympathy.

'I can't help it, Miss Stygia,' said Ben rather lamely.

'Of course not. You see, boys really want to be girls. That's why they like to fuck us, pardon my French. They are trying to get into a sweet haven, the womb, which they never wanted to leave in the first place.'

Stygia served sweet tea, and, gratefully, he swallowed the whole cup of hot Darjeeling. His erect cock expanded the area of his white petticoat and mauve skirt. Stygia put a finger to her lips. Her feet entered the area of Ben's skirt, and touched his balls, but did not stimulate his penis.

'You have lovely big balls, Ben,' Stygia declared. 'Nice and tight. I mean, a boy doesn't realise how lovely his balls look to a girl, he's perhaps rather ashamed of them, but they are the most ducky things, and you have a lovely bum, and a lovely cock – well, I'm blushing, just to say that – but of course I can't help you with your erection, because you are forbidden to masturbate. I suppose that must make you terribly frustrated, because I know how hard it is, in every sense, for a boy to endure an erection that won't go away.'

'I'm sorry,' Ben said.

'But you are dressed as a girl.'

'I suppose so.'

'As a rather beautiful girl.'

'Thank you.'

'So, if I licked your rather lovely balls, under your panties and petticoat, and sucked your stiff penis, while I spanked your pantied bottom, and I do love the lovely crimson helmet of that big penis, and made you come, and swallowed your seed, while you sucked my toes – like for like, and I do like a boy to suck my toes – and I rubbed my own clito, then you wouldn't have masturbated. Oh, lummee! I've never seen just a big phallus! It makes me all giddy and tingly just to look. Perhaps I myself would have masturbated, but it wouldn't be against the Spartan rules.'

'I suppose not.'

'Well, then, let's do it. God, you do look beautiful in mauve. And those bum buns! I like to masturbate, while a ladyboy with lovely trim buns sucks me. Get down, Ben.'

'I'm not a ladyboy! Please don't call me a ladyboy!'

Stygia took Ben by the nipples, under his bra, and bent him over, while she raised her palm to spank his arse, almost bare under the mauve thong.

'You are a ladyboy. I'm glad to see you shave, although the Spartan girls will probably want to shave you extra-finely. Body hair is so disgusting. All men are ladyboys, you know. Why do you think I sell so many goods from my shop, and men come from London and New York and Paris and Rome and Edinburgh? And I'm going to show you why all boys are ladyboys. God, you look so gorgeous, properly dressed in skirt and stockings and panties, you look so lovely in mauve, Ben, and that's a delightful bare arse – a boy's bare arse, those dimples, so wonderful, and those gorgeous globes demand whipping, and I'm going to enjoy whipping them, while you suck my sex. My stiff clito. All hard and wet for you. See how I'm juicing, just looking at your girl-pantied mauve bum, Ben? And I'm longing to spank you. I've been longing to spank your lovely girlish bare bottom ever since you walked into my shop. I could die for those beautiful globes! I have to spank them, just a little. I hope those Furies in the Iffley Road won't mind too much. They'll give you more than spanking.'

Ben did not cease to be erect, as he took Stygia's vigorous spanking, of over a hundred slaps. His skirt was up, and panties down to his knees, he was bent over her powerful thighs, and her palm was hard on his buttocks, but she took care only to slap his bare flesh, and not spoil the clothes she had just sold him. As she spanked him, Stygia's thighs were parted, and she discreetly masturbated her clito. Then, she instructed Ben to take her whole cooze into his mouth, and suck, and, furthermore, to swallow her salty juice. Salty as the Aegean Sea, she said. After his spanking, which excited him, without really hurting him very much, Stygia squatted over him, her buttocks crushing his face, and he felt her lips enfold his penis, lick his frenulum and peehole, while his tongue was inside her quim, and he spurted his sperm almost at once into her mouth, as she swallowed his cream, and masturbated herself to orgasm, her fingers brushing his probing tongue.

Ben had never heard the sound of a girl's orgasm before, except perhaps with Louella, and he had not been sure how genuine her gasps and moans were. Stygia's did seem genuine, businesslike, a woman who knew her body, and knew what she was doing to it. Moreover, she knew what she was doing to his. She told him that his spank marks wouldn't last long, although his bum was lovely and pink for the moment, so that, when he presented himself for his Spartan initiation, he would have fresh cheeks. Like most young men, Ben had wanked off frequently, and now he sensed that the gorgeous flood of sperm, the honey flowing from the balls, to be really satisfying, had something to do with being spanked by a girl, and wearing a girl's clothing. The shop doorbell tinkled; Stygia dressed quickly, and hurried to deal with her new customer, after blowing Ben an air kiss.

Ben got a bus to the Iffley Road, and Lefthera welcomed him to the premises of the Lacedaemonian Society, if welcome could be called the right word. Ben carried his girl's clothing in Stygia's shopping bag; he did not yet dare to be robed in public. Lefthera was barefoot, wearing a purple peplos, which did not hide her magnificent naked body beneath: no bra or panties. The body of a wild beast. A cigarette dangled from her purple lips, and she looked at Ben with disdain.

31

'Ah, the sociology student. And carrying a shopping bag.'

'I'm not –'

'You're a minute late, worm,' she drawled. 'Your horrid little arse will have to pay the price.'

'But, by my watch –'

'New worms are always a minute late,' she said. 'You have your proper kit?'

'Yes! It's in the shopping bag. I went to Stygia's, as you told me.'

'Well, strip off, worm, and we'll get you cleaned up.'

She took hold of Ben's bag, looked inside and guffawed.

'Mauve! By the balls of Zeus! Stygia sold you this?'

'Why, yes . . .'

'We'll see how you look, after your cleansing. Stygia's a greedy Boetian cow, and cheeky, too. Did she spank you, after she robed you? Speak honestly, or it will go the worse for you.'

'Just a little.'

'Yes, she does that. How many slaps?'

'Well, a hundred or so.'

'Not enough for a worm, though. But I suppose you had an erection, and she sucked your *sperma*.'

'I . . . well, yes, she did.'

'Was there a lot of it?'

'She . . . she said so.'

'A heavy creamer, then. We'll deal with Stygia in due course. She likes polluting boys. But I take it you've remained pure, apart from sperming in her mouth. No wanking. No fingering yourself.'

'No wanking, I promise, Miss Lefthera.'

'We only take boys who are nice and juicy, and full of spunk. You must be virgin, and wank off on our orders. Wanking, you see, to us Spartans, is no casual act, but a sacred rite, and your sperm belongs to us. If we suspect you've been impure, and especially if you are a heavy creamer, there'll be Hades to pay.'

'I think I'm pure,' Ben said. 'I'm certainly a virgin, although I can't lie: I admit I've wanked a lot.'

32

'All filthy worms do. That lovely feeling, as your sperm spurts. But that's not what you really want in this life, Ben. At least, you need to wank, and spurt that sperm, all over your filthy hands, on the orders of a girl. A girl who laughs at your cock, and dominates your worthless male hide! Now, what do you really want, Ben? Really, really want in this life? Tell the truth, the total truth, from your heart, because lying is forbidden among Spartans.'

'Oh, God, I don't like to admit it.'

'You say "Zeus", you filthy little snail. Now what is your heart's desire?'

'I want to be whipped by a naked girl. By you. I want to be your slave. I want to be yours. Your property. I don't know why. I want to serve you and please you. I just want it. I want my bare buttocks beaten, and I want to be completely naked for my cruel girl, to smart from a girl's whip. I want to be enslaved by a girl. By you, Miss Lefthera. By no other girl.'

'I think I want more than that.'

'I want to bend over, to present my bare bum for caning, to be completely in my girl's power, to weep and cry and groan as she flogs me. And love my girl for the sublime pain she gives me. Love the smarting bare bum she gives me. Have her – Zeus, I don't know how to say it – have her bugger me with a dildo, if she wants. To show I'm in her power, for a boy must always be in a girl's power, and want to obey her orders for ever.'

'Yes. And because?'

'Because . . . because a boy whose bottom smarts from a girl's cane is in her power always.'

'Well, that's all right. It seems reasonable. But don't call me a girl. I shall be your mistress.'

'Yes, mistress. Shall I strip off, now? I mean, if that's what I have to do. But I'd so love to wear my new clothes for you. For you to find me beautiful, mistress.'

Lefthera spat out her cigarette, and lit another.

'Of course you must strip off, snail. Are you deaf, as well as stupid?' she said.

33

4

The Furies

It was agony. Ben had never known such a strange, exotic, yet oddly seductive kind of pain. Matron's caning had been agony, but Miss Ramsey *had* allowed him a certain dignity, as she whipped his bare bottom. Stygia's spanking had been painful, but playful at the same time. The pain of a spanking, even a caning, was one thing, and manageable, but this was new, and quite another. In the pain was the humiliation of its being administered. Three naked girls – Iphigenia, Roxanna and Cybele, sibyls of Sparta – held him down in the bathroom, while Lefthera, herself also nude, laved his rectum with a rubber tube thrust to his colon. Lefthera still had a cigarette drooping from her crimson lips, and pushed the tube further and further into Ben's sigmoid colon, while he moaned. The water squirted, filling his arse, and spurting out on the floor, whose tiles depicted ancient Cretan scenes of bulls and bare-breasted girls.

'Oh, please, no more,' he gasped. 'It hurts so.'

It was the arrogant, insouciant nudity of his torturesses that hurt more than anything. Nude girls were supposed to be tender, frightened and submissive! Yet, with these women, nudity was an act of aggression.

'You dirty boy,' snarled Iphigenia, who had put down the manuscript of her thesis on Aristarchus of Samothrace.

'You must be fully cleansed before your initiation,' said Roxanna.

34

Roxanna was writing a thesis on Dudo of St Quentin, who died in 1043, the historian of the first dukes of Normandy, his chronicle a primary source. Roxanna said that his work, *De moribus et actis primorum Normanniae ducum*, was completed sometime between 1015 and 1026, and that it was very inaccurate and time-serving, which made it a lovely subject for a postgrad thesis, to take Dudo to pieces.

'A dirty boy must always be hurt,' said Cybele.

Cybele was writing *her* thesis on the Lesbian poetess Sappho. She said that it was not known how her poems were published and circulated in her own lifetime and for the following three or four centuries. In the era of Alexandrian scholarship (especially the third and second centuries BC), what remained of her work was collected and republished in a standard edition of nine books of lyrical verse and one of elegiac. This edition did not survive the early Middle Ages. By the eighth or ninth century AD, Sappho was represented only by quotations in other authors. Only one poem, 28 lines long, was complete. The next longest was sixteen lines. No complete poem had been recovered.

'Yummy for scholarship,' Cybele said. 'Less is more.'

'I think we may agree that all boys are dirty,' said Lefthera, and the others chorused agreement.

'Look at his balls!' cried Roxanna. 'They are a positive forest of filthy hair.'

'And his cock,' said Cybele. 'There are hairs there too.'

'His back, his chest,' snorted Iphigenia. 'He is a pongoid! An ape man.'

Ben wept, as his arse writhed under the cruel spouting enema, administered by Lefthera. The water was cold, with soap and vinegar added.

'I promise you, ladies, that I do shave,' he gasped, as fluid filled his squirming rectum.

'Obviously, not enough,' snapped Lefthera.

It was not the pain of the colonic irrigation that hurt Ben so, although it was extremely painful, yet strangely welcome, but the shame of his subjugation by the four powerfully muscled naked girls, treating him with divine disdain, as some kind of zoo animal. Iphigenia held his wrists, Roxanna his ankles, while Cybele sat on his head, her shaven quim warm and wet against his scalp.

'Keep the beast down,' ordered Lefthera.

And the extra shame that, as his arse writhed in the agony of the enema, his phallus was erect.

'We'll easily flog *that* away!' Roxanna chortled, and the other girls chortled with her.

'I don't know, though,' said Lefthera, as Iphigenia lit cigarettes for them all, 'this particular boy might require a bit of extra flogging. Look at that phallus, so big, and strong and stiff. It's like a donkey's.'

'Well, we'd better hurry up then,' said Iphigenia. 'I've a lecture on pre-Achaean Argos to give at five o'clock.'

'And I've a tutorial on Doric temples at six,' said Cybele.

Lefthera ripped the rubber tube from Ben's anus, and he groaned in relief, as the cleansing liquid flooded from his arse. The girls still held him, while Iphigenia soaped his private parts, then wielded the razor on his phallus and balls, shaving him clean, and Roxanna attended to his back and breasts, and Cybele shaved his legs and arms. Their razor strokes were not kind, and, when he was clean, Ben asked, 'What do you want with me, ladies?'

Lefthera laughed, and blew smoke in his face.

'We don't want anything with you, boy,' she sneered. 'That's the whole point. It's what you want from us. Now get your kit on. Mauve!'

'What a worm!' said Roxanna.

'A locust!' said Iphigenia.

'A snail!' cried Cybele. 'Probably a snail who's been masturbating! By Apollo, he'll be punished if that's true.'

Ben was released, and led to a bedroom, which contained many furry teddy bears, to robe himself for the ladies' approval. His bag was there, his mauve girl's clothing neatly laid out for him. He put on all the things he had bought from Stygia, his stockings and petticoat, bra and thong and suspenders, and the corset, laced tightly. He pinned his hair back, as he had learnt. He made sure his stocking tops were correctly gartered, that his corset was correctly laced, and that his bra was correctly fastened. He reappeared in the dining room, to face the four nude ladies, all smoking, and drinking tea, with their faces buried in learned papers. Their naked bodies gleamed, shaven and resplendent with hard muscle.

'Oh, you again,' said Iphigenia.

'That beastly boy,' said Roxanna.

'I'd . . . I'd hoped you might like me in this,' Ben blurted.

'In mauve, for the love of Heracles,' said Cybele. 'Do me a favour.'

'He does have a certain charm,' said Lefthera. 'His stockings fit quite well, his petticoat and corset are rather sweet, and his bra is just his size. He has rather big hard tits. As for his panties, I can't speak.'

Iphigenia looked at her watch.

'Well, let's string the bugger up, and flog them off him,' she said. 'I haven't got all day. You have the hippopotamus-hide thingie?'

'Of course,' said Lefthera.

'Then let's use that, with the other thingies as backup. Agreed?'

The nude ladies all agreed.

'Bend over, Ben, lift your skirts, and show us your globes,' drawled Cybele.

Ben obeyed.

'An obedient boy!' said Iphigenia. 'That's something.'

'A woman's work is never done,' sighed Roxanna, as she lifted the hippopotamus-hide whip over Ben's quivering naked bottom, his buttocks almost totally exposed by his tiny mauve thong.

'No, let's string him,' said Lefthera. 'Get him by his wrists, from the gibbet, and whip him whole-body.'

'That will take more time,' said Roxanna. 'We'll have to armlock him, and gag him and bind him and everything. You know what trouble these boys are, with the gibbet.'

'Until you get them strung, and their bare bums are striped by a strong girl,' said Cybele. 'Those lovely bare bums! Get them burning from a woman's hide, then they're begging for more whip.'

'Beaten by girls, it's what boys are for,' said Iphigenia. 'Those luscious bare buttocks, flaming under a girl's cane, under the moonlight. And, soon enough, they learn it. But they're trouble to start with, for they don't understand, at first.'

'Please, miss, I mean, mistress,' Ben stammered. 'I think I do understand. I know I want to be . . . to be whipped by women. To submit to their cruelty. To wear a girl's clothing.'

'He understands,' sneered Roxanna. 'Well, that's a start.'

Lefthera touched Ben's balls, and his erect phallus.

'Ben, your glans is swollen like a lovely big Euboeian plum,' she said. 'You are awfully excited. And you know you must be whipped, quite savagely, in fact. I mean, we are not nice ladies, the kind you knew in Hereford Hellenic. We are the Furies. We'll string you up, and whip you, on your back and your thighs, and, of course, your lovely tight bum, and your body will smart for days, with horrible whip welts. But I don't think you will give any trouble, like some filthy rotter. Will you, Ben?'

'No . . . Miss Lefthera . . . I promise I shall never give you any trouble . . .' Ben replied. 'And I'm not filthy, I must tell you, please, that I am a virgin. I have never, you know, done it, put my phallus into a girl.'

Lefthera lit a cigarette.

'Oh, we know that, Ben,' she drawled. 'But you've probably thought of it, wanted to, haven't you? Wanked off, looking at pictures of nude girls?'

'I can't deny it,' said Ben, wretchedly.

'So you see why you must be punished. For filthiness.'

'Yes! Yes, I do see.'

'And we *are* nude girls. Not pictures. The real thing. Look at us. Our breasts, our bottoms. All plain to see. But nude girls are Furies, here to punish boys, not please them.'

It was worse than he thought, worse than he ever imagined. Miss Elena Ramsey seemed gentleness itself in comparison. The enema had been bad enough. But now the cruelty of the Furies seemed to grow immeasurably. Ben was clad in his finest girl's raiment, which he had paid for, and of which he was proud, so proud that he wished to walk up the High, or the Broad, or Turl Street, strutting like a ladyboy, yet here he was strung to a gibbet by his wrists, with his panties pulled down, and his nipples, in their mauve bra, bitten by wooden pegs. His stockinged toes dangled above the floor.

'Please,' he begged. 'Miss Lefthera. I didn't know I was in for this.'

'We never know what we are in for, worm,' said Lefthera, as she flexed her hippopotamus-hide whip over the boy's trussed nude body. 'Haven't you read your Empedocles?'

All the women lifted whips, thongs of cowhide, or many-tongued quirts of rubber.

'We've time to whip those frilly mauve shreds from him,' said Cybele.

'Yes,' said Iphigenia.

'Yes,' said Roxanna.

'Yes,' said Lefthera. 'Mauve! The nerve of the boy! But, if he wants to be a Spartan, he won't cry out. You see, Ben, Spartans take their pain in silence, no blubbing or girly noises.'

It was Lefthera whose hippopotamus-hide whip, the hardest and cruellest, delivered the first lash to Ben's naked buttocks. *Vap!* The whip bit into his lower buttocks, just above his stocking tops. He gasped, as his eyes moistened, and his bare nates clenched, to try to dissipate the fearful, stinging pain. But Iphigenia's rubber quirt followed up with a four-thonged stinger to his top buttocks, just below his frilly suspender belt. Ben's body jerked, swinging helplessly in the gibbet. *Vap!* Roxanna's cowhide thong took him on the upper thighs, and he heard a slashing sound, as the whip ripped his stocking tops. *Vap!* Lefthera lashed him across the bare back, her whip cutting the strap of his bra. He gritted his teeth, determined not to cry out, as the agony of the whips seared his body. The women

39

settled to a rhythm of cruelty, Lefthera lashing his shoulders, Iphigenia his buttocks, and Roxanna his thighs, while Cybele strode in front of his sobbing, shuddering body, ripped off his nipple pegs, which brought hot tears to his eyes, and tore away his bra, so that she could proceed to whip his naked breasts, her lash striking his nipples with hideous accuracy. Ben's beating lasted nearly an hour, on buttocks, thighs, back and breasts, and, though his eyes streamed with tears, he did not cry out once. When the girls put down their whips, his entire mauve raiment of stockings, panties and petticoat, apart from his corset, was shredded beyond repair.

'Well!' said Cybele, putting down her whip. 'I think he might just about do, as a helot. But look at that erection! All the time we were lashing him, he had that most revolting and impudent stiff phallus.'

'Yes, that won't do,' said Lefthera. 'But we must admit he was quite brave, in a girly sort of way.'

'Oh, yes, he'll probably do,' said Iphigenia. 'Actually, I think his phallus is rather nice. Amusing, like a donkey's.'

Roxanna touched Ben's black-bruised buttocks.

'These welts have come up quite decently,' she said, 'so, apart from the impudent erection, I'd opine that he might be useful.'

Lefthera untied Ben from the gibbet, and the women laid him on the floor, where he wept and gasped; but his phallus still stood.

'He is making a *bit* of noise,' said Iphigenia.

'Well, it's only natural,' said Cybele.

'A helot, in his early stages . . .' drawled Roxanna. 'You know, this stiff phallus –' she kicked Ben's cock helmet with a painted big toe, and he groaned '– perhaps he is one of those helots who really *do* relish whipping.'

'Some boys are like that,' said Iphigenia.

'Most of them, I'd say,' added Lefthera. 'I suppose he could have his skirt and bra, if we're all agreed. Roxanna, will you do the honours?'

Ben was fitted with a simple white cotton skirt, and also a spanking skirtlet, a pair of sort of bloomers, which had a divide at the back, and were held up by a waist string, so that, at any moment, a slave might have his buttocks suddenly exposed for a flogging. The women applauded.

'He does look nice.'

'Yes.'

'What do you say, Ben? What does a gentleman say to a lady?'

'Thank you, mistress.'

'But you're still erect! You beastly little helot. I suppose you want to wank off.'

'I . . . no . . . I'm sorry . . .'

'Well, we might allow you to. You were quite brave under your whipping.'

'And I suppose the sight of four nude ladies is a bit too much for those sperm-heavy balls.'

'Should we let him wank?'

'Why not?'

'He'll have to, when we get him to Mílos, in the summer vac.'

'We'll want to see him perform, like a good helot.'

'Might as well put him through his paces.'

'Wank off, you snail.'

'Who gets the juice?'

'It's my turn,' said Iphigenia.

As Iphigenia knelt before his balls, Ben, gazing at the nude bodies of the girls, began to rub his glans and peehole.

'Harder! Full shaft!' barked Lefthera, herself masturbating, like Roxanna and Cybele, while the kneeling Iphigenia's fingers were busily rubbing her clito.

He masturbated in only a few strokes to a heavy orgasm, with his sperm jetting into Iphigenia's mouth. She took all of his ejaculation, but did not swallow. Instead, with cheeks bulging, she rose, and kissed each of the other sibyls on the lips, transferring a little of the precious fluid. When the kissing had been accomplished, then all the girls swallowed their portion of Ben's *sperma*.

'Now, crouch, worm, and kiss our feet,' Lefthera ordered. 'Make sure you lick all the cheese from between our toes.'

Ben obeyed, kneeling, to kiss the bare toes of Lefthera, Cybele, Iphigenia and Roxanna in turn. Their feet were dirty and smelly, and he relished the humiliation of cleansing them by mouth. He sucked hard, his tongue cleaning their toes of grime, while each girl smoked a cigarette, and masturbated herself to a leisurely climax.

'I don't believe this!' panted Roxanna. 'His beastly phallus is stiff again!'

'I suppose the snail wants to have another wank,' said Cybele.

'Ladies,' Ben said, 'I was instructed to remain pure. And I shall obey my instructions. Begging your pardons, and worshipping your feet, I promise I shan't wank off, until I have your orders.'

'Dress and go, then, you grubby helot. You'll be summoned for your next appointment,' Lefthera said.

Ben dressed in his male attire of grey flannels and sports jacket, and went to the Bear Inn, where he had two pints of ale, and two meat pies, drenched in brown sauce, and, as his stinging bottom smarted, he felt curiously proud of himself, superior to the drinkers around him. *They* had not been laved and flogged and wanked by cruel naked girls!

5

Iffley Road

'I'm not sure I like this, entirely,' said the boy, strapped to a wooden trestle, in the house of the Spartan women, beside Ben's nude body, while the nearby traffic of the Iffley Road hummed outside.

Like Ben, he was naked for his whipping, but for his white skirt, which had been turned up, like Ben's skirt, by the nakedly efficient Iphigenia, to expose the bare buttocks, while his wrists and ankles were strapped to the trestle by nude Cybele, with rubber cords. There were five naked fellows awaiting flogging, and trussed in this way, with their bare bottoms up and spread.

'I don't think we're supposed to like it,' said Ben.

'Well, we may at least introduce ourselves. Before the show starts.'

'It's not a show,' said Ben. 'I think they're serious.'

'Yes. Rotten luck. But a fellow must take his whacks.'

'We're not supposed to give names. We're just helots.'

'Of course. But I'm Wadham. Reading PPE.'

'And I'm Trinity. Mod. Lang. Touch of the Spanish and Italian.'

'I'm Univ. Psychology and Physiology.'

'I'm Corpus Christi. Law.'

'And I'm at the House, Mods and Greats,' said Ben, not without pride, for Christ Church was the biggest and richest college in Oxford. 'Dr Rosalynn Demande is my tutor, actually.'

'And, if we fit the bill, we get a trip to Mílos. That'll be fun, I dare say,' said the lawyer from Corpus.

'Fun? I heard from a fellow at St Peter's, that –'

'Pot Hall? Bit low.'

'He went to a decent school, though. Ludlow.'

'I suppose that's all right, then. What did he say?'

'These Lacedaemonian girls . . . they do things . . .'

'They . . . what could be worse than this?'

'They pierce you.'

'Pierce you? How?'

'They put hot wires through your nipples, and make holes in them.'

'But that's for grotty perverts. Sort of thing you read about in the Sunday papers, not that any sound man reads the Sunday papers.'

'It was, in fact *is*, normal in Sparta, among the Lacedaemonian women. They pierce a fellow's nipples, then adorn him with bronze nipple rings, as a sign of slavery and submission. And they pierce the bum, too, and put rings in there, so you can't sit down very comfortably, and they can hook your bum rings or your nipple rings with cords, and string you up for a whipping. The girls like to pierce a ring slot right through a fellow's bumhole, too. And some helots have . . . this is a bit awful . . . they have their cocks pierced, you know, your bell end, and a ring inserted there. It's called an albert, because apparently Prince Albert, husband of Queen Victoria, bless her, had one, to stop him getting an erection of his rather large meat, at ceremonial occasions. The ring goes through your peehole and that sort of place, and the Spartan girls can hook you by it, if they are cross with you, drag you across the sand, or drag you, I suppose, wherever they want. Chap with a ring through his bell end and his nipples and his bumhole can't really object, can he? Mind you, it's just what I've heard.'

'Cripes!'

'Lummee!'

'What have we let ourselves in for?'

'Well, I suppose all that sort of thing, it's what a fellow needs, to make him a proper slave of girls. Do their bidding, and all that. Sort of like taking a girl's whops on the bare, like a man.'

44

Lefthera, naked, and carrying a whip, entered the room, with a Dunhill drooping from her lips.

'Stop talking, you filthy little worms!'

The strapped boys froze into silence.

Roxanna, Iphigenia and Cybele followed her. All were nude, all smoked cigarettes, dangling sluttishly from their lips, and all carried whips, quirts or canes. All the nude girls wore golden hoops, of intricate design, through piercings at their nipples. Without preamble, they lifted their rods, and proceeded to flog the naked boys on their buttocks. The strokes came hard and fast, and the students, initiates to the Lacedaemonian Society, were forbidden to make a sound, as they were whipped on their squirming rumps. Nor did they. As they took their lashes, the boys looked at each other, grimacing, with tears in their eyes, buttocks clenching, and with forced complicit grins, yet unable not to gasp, at the ferocity of the nude girls flogging them. The whippings went to forty or more strokes on the bare, with hard pickled rods, or quirts, or heavy hide whips, but the flogged boys did not cry out.

'You've proved yourselves to some extent,' said Lefthera, sipping tea, and lighting a Dunhill, 'so you are permitted to attend another cleansing next week. Now you may absent yourselves. And, by the way, you will walk back to your colleges, down the Iffley Road, proudly wearing your Lacedaemonian skirts and bras.'

The flogged boys licked the toes of their chastisers, and obeyed the girls' instructions. Oxford is a tolerant and humane place, and it is assumed that a young man walking barefoot and rather stiffly, with a whipped bottom, in skirtlet and bra, across Magdalen Bridge, and up the High, has his own business in mind. Rosalynn had told Ben that Oxford's greatest art historian, John Ruskin, fainted, and was never able to consummate his marriage, when, on his wedding night, he discovered his bride had pubic hair. According to the paintings, girls simply did not have pubic hair, and nor, Rosalynn agreed, should they. Neither should boys. The marriage was dissolved, on the grounds of non-consummation, and Effie Gray later married the painter Millais. This marital impasse did not hinder Ruskin's career and renown, as a grand old man of culture.

'Hello, Mr Fraunce,' said Perkins, at the Christ Church lodge. 'Aren't you a bit cold in that kit?'

'I am a bit,' Ben said.

'Well, each to his own. Let me know if you need extra blankets, sir.'

Dr Rosalynn Demande was giving a private lecture, in her chambers, to carefully selected girl students. Her private lectures were conducted with all attendees in the nude, as was Rosalynn herself. Her subject at this time was female masturbation in the ancient Mediterranean world, and to help with her lecture she had Lucy Parvis, a golden-blonde eighteen-year-old fresher from St Hilda's, who had a special interest in the minor sixteenth-century French poet Jean de Caen Bertaut, notable as a writer of polished light verse, and distinguished for his slightly naughty collection *Recueil de quelques vers amoureux* of 1602, which was what really interested Lucy, who intended, eventually, to write her DPhil thesis on him. While praising virginity and virtue, Jean had alluded frequently to masturbation, both male and female, but especially female, as *le bel art*.

Lucy admitted cheerfully that she was intent on remaining a virgin, in fact belonged to a club of girls, the Hymen Club, dedicated to retaining their virginity, and to this end, in order to keep herself free of pollution by boys, and the danger of unwise attachments to men in general, had masturbated from an early age; she now masturbated twice or three times a day, either on her own, or with one of her friends from the Hymen Club, and adored the subject of masturbation. Lucy was delighted to explain her virginal philosophy, and demonstrate her autoerotic methods.

'See how Lucy skirts the opening of her pouch,' Rosalynn explained. 'A caress of the labium minus, and of the paraurethral duct. Ladies must never forget the sensitivity of their peeholes, when masturbating. That's right, the finger flitting between the labium majus and minus, and

46

reaming the vestibular fossa beneath. This is very good. Note that the clito remains untouched, save for a few brief, exploratory strokes, designed to titillate, before full stroking commences. Now, the clito, starting with the prepuce and frenulum, skirting the gland itself, always building the quim to a heightened sensitivity, before the real work of masturbation. Caress to the labial frenulum below, leading to the sensitive perineum, and touching the anus pucker. Finger inside, reaming the anus pucker, very good.

'Now, we get to the intimate touching, fingernails nipping the greater vestibular gland, the ragged rim of the pouch hole itself. Thumb on the clito, squashing gently, and fingers probing the entrance to the slit, now fingers inside the vulval hole, with a double action, caressing the clito. Lucy reaming her lovely little clito, round and round, with a jab at the clito bulb, now healthily swollen. And look at the juice flowing from the vulval aperture. Quite copious, and enough to wet her fingers, for further penetration, of the vagina or anus.

'I will be dealing with the specific role of anal intercourse, and intercrural or intermammary intercourse, for those girls who sensibly wish to remain virgin, in subsequent lectures.

'Good, Lucy has got a finger well inside her bumhole, and is poking herself, while maintaining attention to the clito. Note how stiff the clito has become, and very nicely extruded. Nubbin between thumb and forefinger – you can see from the squirming of the entire vulval apparatus, and the copious juicing from the quim, that the subject has reached the alpha stage of autostimulation, as we discussed last week.'

Lucy yelped and gasped sharply, as, finger in her rectum, she masturbated herself to climax, and the naked girls applauded politely.

'Thank you, Lucy,' Rosalynn said. 'The role and practice of male masturbation will also be discussed and demonstrated in my next lectures. Meanwhile, you ladies will please feel free to experiment with the techniques I have described, and Lucy has admirably demonstrated.'

The nude girls giggled, and began shyly to masturbate, less shyly, as Dr Demande strutted and approved their performances.

'Yes, Fiona, that's good. Good technique, Annabel. Nice action on the clito, Honoria. Leonora, you might shave your quim and hillock just a *little* more often. And don't forget to rid yourself of those anus hairs. A clean anus is most important.'

It was then that Ben Fraunce knocked on the door, wearing his scholar's gown, as was required, and bearing the essay he had completed for his tutor. Rosalynn, thinking it might be Mrs Lord or another servant, draped herself in a peplos before opening, but stripped off the flimsy garment, pulling it over her breasts and head, and resumed her nudity, when she saw it was only Ben.

'It's you, Ben,' she said, smoothing her long dark tresses over her nipples. 'You may as well come in. We can do two tutorials in one. Take your clothes off, be as naked as we are, in the Grecian fashion, apart from your scholar's gown, of course, which you must wear before me, and read us your essay. I think we'll all like to hear it. Punishment of boys in ancient Sparta, isn't it? Ladies, this is Ben, a prize scholar, from Hereford Hellenic.'

Ben was crimson with embarrassment. He was nude, sheathed in only his black scholar's gown, in front of a gaggle of nude girls, and his phallus stood rock-hard. His flogged bottom was blue with bruises, from the whips of the girls in the Iffley Road, and the gown did little to hide that shame. Furthermore, to his amazement and shame, the girls were actually masturbating their immodestly opened coozes, all pink and wet, and very distracting, with sucking, squelchy noises, as he read his essay.

'I'd say he's taken a flogging recently,' said Monica Trencher, a second-year student from Somerville, as she openly wanked off. 'Look at his pretty striped bum. It looks yummy in his scholar's gown. Isn't he going to masturbate, Dr Demande?'

Rosalynn smiled.

'Only on my orders,' she said. 'I know we all like to see a naked boy masturbate, but I think Ben has recently been with the ladies of the Lacedaemonian Society. His bottom is probably feeling quite sore. We'll see if his essay is any good.'

Ben read.

'The naked boys of Sparta were tethered by the women at dawn, with bright-pink, purple or green ribbons knotted around their testes, and the helmets, sometimes called the bulbs, of their male organs, just below the neck of the swelling, and matching ribbons in their long curled hair, which the girls had anointed with sacred oil. Like that, the young men were herded through the street, to the ritual whipping post, where they were to be trussed with leather cords, knotted around their breasts and balls, and flogged naked by girls, until their buttock flesh was purple with welts, and they fainted, or screamed. The chastising girls, too, were nude, and were encouraged by the priests of Bacchus and Cybele to masturbate, as they flogged the buttocks and backs of the young men with whips of hippopotamus hide, imported from Egypt.

'The priests or priestesses of Cybele instructed young girls, when they were of age, in the sacred art of masturbation, which had to accompany the whipping of young men. Whipping was an ordeal every young man had to endure, at every third full moon, before he could be accepted for the army. Failure to be accepted for the army, like failure to pay your mess bills, or battels, was the ultimate disgrace in ancient Sparta, and led to loss of citizenship. This was the doctrine of the perhaps mythical, perhaps actual, lawgiver Lycurgus, in the ninth century BC.'

'This isn't bad, Ben,' said Rosalynn. 'I think you may go on.'

'It's awfully exciting,' said Lucy, enthusiastically and blatantly frigging her clito. 'All those nude boys being whipped! You won't mind, Dr Demande, if I come again?'

'Of course not.'

'I tend to be rather noisy.'

49

'Well, you are so young. And you've been awfully helpful.'

'Thank you, Doctor. Oh! Yes! Ooh! Oh, *yes*! I want another one! Please go on, Ben. May I call you Ben? This is so thrilling.'

As Ben continued to read, about the tortures inflicted by women on the young males of ancient Sparta, he found his task harder and harder, for the entire room of nude girls were licking their teeth, and masturbating, covertly or blatantly, at his words. When he told them that the flogged youths were required to masturbate, and water the earth with their sperm, at the place where four roads meet, every girl in the room was frigging herself, wet and moaning.

'I think Ben might bend over for an extra spanking,' said Rosalynn. 'This will be an educational experience for most of you girls. You will, I hope, see, that the experience of being spanked on the bare buttocks, by a girl, causes a young man's phallus to rise, as Ben's has already risen, and remain pleasingly erect. You won't mind a little extra punishment, Ben. After all, you are almost a Spartan.'

'I . . . no, Dr Demande. I must obey, of course.'

'Good. Bend over and spread them, then. There'll be a nice cup of tea for us all, afterwards, when your bum's nice and red, over those rather beastly blue welts. I'll get my servant to organise it.'

The spanking from several hands was accompanied by giggles, and was not as painful as the brutal flogging from the girls of the Iffley Road, but it got harder, as the palms cracked on his bare, and the girls' giggles turned to gasps and sighs. Ben squirmed; the girls were really enjoying themselves, as his spanked bare bum clenched. Or perhaps it was the promise of tea, which gladdens any girl's heart.

'Zeus, he's luscious!' he heard.

'What lovely moons!'

'Look at them squirm.'

'And redden!'

When his arse had taken well over a hundred spanks, from the bare palms of the naked girls, Rosalynn said that he had had enough for the moment, and that she would

50

give him an A grade for his excellent essay, but that there was one more thing before tea.

'Now, after all, let's see you masturbate, Ben.'

'The ladies of the Lacedaemonian Society forbid us to pollute ourselves.'

Rosalynn smiled.

'You didn't know, but I am High Sibyl in the Lacedaemonians,' she drawled. 'I have the authority to overrule minor priestesses like Cybele and Iphigenia. Lefthera – well, she is another matter, but we needn't go into that now. You may masturbate for us, Ben. You may rub your lovely big phallus, and spurt your creamy life fluid, in worship of Mother Earth. In fact, please do. Then, when you've proved yourself fertile and proud, we may all enjoy our nice cup of tea.'

Ben's fingers took hold of his prepuce, and began to draw it back and forth over his glans.

'Like this?' he panted.

'It's your phallus, Ben. You should know what to do with it. I suggest you tickle the frenulum, the neck of your glans, the corona. I'm glad to see it's all properly clean shaven. Give the ladies a good show. Draw the foreskin fully down, to expose your helmet, then all the way back up. That's always an exciting spectacle. Wanking shouldn't be something you do furtively, and in private. It's not just pulling your pud. It should be shared with flowers, and rivers and trees, to gladden the earth, and make girls excited.'

'I see.'

'Do you? Then obey.'

Ben obeyed. He began to rub his erect phallus.

'Yes!' said Lucy.

'Yum!' said Monica.

He looked at the shaven bare quims and teats of Lucy and Monica, with a sly glance at the magnificent naked breasts of his tutor.

'That's right, Ben,' said Rosalynn, 'admire my breasts as you wank off. And don't forget to peek at my cooze hillock.'

She turned, and wiggled her muscled bare bottom.

'My bum, too. Now get your fingertips well up and down, rubbing your helmet. Rub your corpus spongiosum, give it a brisk thrashing. Be delicate at your peehole, just brush it with your fingertips. Caress your frenulum. Isn't that a yummy feeling? And look at the naked girls who are watching you. Isn't that what a virgin boy dreams of, Ben? Being a virgin is a good and necessary thing, until you are ready to breed, and purchase a suitable slave bride, to produce Spartan warriors.'

Ben caressed himself, as his tutor instructed, making his phallus stiff as wood, and it was not long before he panted in agonised, ecstatic pleasure, as his seed came. Business-like, Rosalynn caught his spurt of cream in her hand, while remarking on its copiousness, and rubbed it into her breasts, then licked her fingers clean of his sperm, which she swallowed, with every evidence of satisfaction. She cleaned his phallus with a tissue before telephoning to Mrs Lord for tea. The girls dressed, chattering, as they donned stockings and skirts, and Rosalynn presented Ben with a pink bra, panties and nylon stockings, a pink and white tartan skirt and a pink blouse.

'You can wear those, Ben,' she said. 'I think you look quite nice in pink. Your bum's pink enough.'

The girls chortled at Ben's unconcealed delight, and his burgeoning new erection, as he rolled on his pink nylon stockings and pink nylon thong panties, then zipped up his skirt, and fastened his blouse over his bra. When Mrs Lord brought their tea, the girls were decorously, even dowdily, clad, in the manner of Oxford girl students, and they were all enthused by the steaming hot crumpets, dripping with butter, sandwiches of smoked salmon or cucumber or meat paste, sugared pastries of every hue, and the choice of China or Indian tea. Rosalynn tipped well, and Mrs Lord did her proud. Forgetting his female dress, and any possible embarrassment it might cause, Ben tucked into the meal, with the rest of the company.

'That young man looks nice,' said Mrs Lord. 'These days, it's good to see a gentleman with dress sense. And one who appreciates his food.'

6

The Hymen Club

Ben wasn't sure whether the Spartan interdiction on masturbation still applied to him, but, despite his constant erections, he refrained from self-pollution all the same, except when in tutorial with Dr Demande, when he was permitted, or encouraged, to masturbate for her inspection, as a reward, or perhaps imposition, for reading her a successful essay. She liked to sit in silk and cashmere, while Ben lifted his pink skirt, lowered his thong panties over his pink nylon stockings, took off his bra and rubbed his phallus to orgasm, while Dr Demande smoked a cigarette, sometimes with her skirt up, and rubbing her own wet panties, on her clito. He wasn't sure, either, where Dr Demande's sibyllic authority coincided with, or overrode, that of Roxanna, Lefthera, Cybele and Iphigenia, the priestesses at the Iffley Road. He did know that the more, or perhaps the less, he was permitted to masturbate, the more he loved to wear girls' frillies, and began to buy them from Stygia, who would give him a light, friendly spanking on the bare, bent over her thigh, in the intervals of tea, hotpot and meat pies at Aunt Alice's Café, and fitting him in bras and petticoats and panties. He bought clinging black nylon nighties, too, although generally he preferred to sleep nude.

Stygia's spankings were always a prelude to tea and pies, hotpot, mushy peas and then cakes, with lots of sugar dusting, and seemed to be much the same sort of social ritual for her. She was rather fond of tomato ketchup and

53

mustard on her pies, while Ben preferred brown sauce, although he allowed her to introduce him to Dijon mustard. He loved the smell of Stygia's sweaty thighs, as her palm smacked his bare bum, and he made exaggerated yelps of pain, although they both knew it didn't really hurt much – it was more a drama – and he was not ashamed to admit he liked being spanked, although it was different from being brutally and severely whipped on the bare, with extreme pain, which he suspected and feared he needed. He dreamt of being whipped by Lefthera, or by Rosalynn.

He also shopped at the mainstream department stores, until he had quite a collection of girls' underthings, especially thongs and bras, in pastel colours. He went out in sombre male attire of grey, brown and black, and a black overcoat, for it was getting colder, as the winter drew in, but underneath, wore corset and stockings and girly underthings, suspender belts and garter straps to hold his stockings up, and he loved the silky, slithery feel, as he slid his legs into nylon stockings every morning. He was happy that Dr Demande seemed to approve of him, enjoyed his tutorial essays, and suggested that he attend the college gymnasium, and continue to practise his school bodybuilding, with weights and rowing machines and suchlike. He did so, and found that he was quickly putting on more muscle. It was not the done thing to be completely nude in the gym, unless in the showers after workout, but the briefest pink or yellow girl's thong was considered adequate gentleman's kit. He shaved his entire body every day; the muscle was handsome, gleaming and oiled, as he admired himself naked in the looking glass, before donning his girlish raiment.

Being a late riser, and missing breakfast in college, like many students, he fell into a routine of taking breakfast at White's Café in the market, where he would feast on bacon, eggs, beans and black pudding, and strong cups of tea, while reading the newspaper, amid a fug of illegal, but customary cigarette smoke. There, one day, he met Lucy Parvis, wearing a green German loden coat, over a matching tartan skirt, with white silk stockings, and a white silk scarf, and who seemed genuinely pleased to see him. She had a Marlboro drooping from her scarlet lips. He blurted that she looked divine.

'You don't look so bad yourself,' she said, accepting his offer of a cup of tea. 'Four sugars, please. You've some muscle. Been working out?'

'Yes.'

'Got a girlfriend, then?'

'No, not really.'

'That means no.'

'I suppose it does.'

She laughed. 'This is Oxford, not Cambridge. You don't suppose, you *know*.'

She offered him a cigarette, lit it herself and placed it between his lips. Ben blushed.

'You're right, it means no. I have no girlfriend.'

'However we define that,' she said putting her hand on his thigh. 'I loved your, um, performance at Dr Demande's, and I hope you liked mine.'

'I did. It was beautiful. It was ... so sincere. I've never seen anything so beautiful.'

'Thank you. Yours was, too, and I'm not just saying that. You have a lovely phallus. It's very handsome and proud and strong, but rather tender at the same time.' Lucy took a gulp of tea, and her face flushed. 'It's the sort of phallus I would want to, you know, impregnate me, when I decide to lose my virginity, and become a breeder. Ben, you're still a virgin? Answer truthfully.'

'Yes, I'm still a virgin.'

'Then come and see me at St Hilda's, sometime soon. We have a club, the Hymen Club. I hope it doesn't sound awfully silly, but we are vowed to virginity, and chaste masturbation, and, yes, we are totally sincere. There are no male members yet, but – who knows? – you could be the first.'

She laid her hand on his, and stroked it.

'Thanks for the tea,' Lucy said, as she left the café.

Ben looked at her voluptuous bottom, wiggling under her loden coat, and imagined it wiggled for him.

* * *

Dr Demande locked her door when he went to his tutorials, and let him deliver his essays in the nude, or else wearing some of her clothes, which she rather carelessly threw at him.

'Put those on, Ben,' she would say, giving him a skirt and panties and bra, 'and let's see how you look.'

Whenever he wore girls' clothes, he had an erection, and Rosalynn would permit him to masturbate in front of her, after he had read his essay. Sometimes, she herself would be nude, sometimes wearing cashmere and silk and wool, if she had business elsewhere. He could not touch her person, though, and would not dream of doing so. But he could look at her nude or clothed body, her legs in shiny nylon stockings, as he wanked off, for her pleasure, and his own great relief, for it was difficult to restrain himself from pollution, when he spent so many hours of the day wearing girls' panties and stockings, and achingly stiff. Sometimes, Rosalynn was nude, except for stockings, peach or red or cream glassine nylon, and she would cross and uncross her stockinged legs, showing her naked shaven pouch, and then Ben's thrilled and obedient fingers made him spurt all the faster. Rosalynn would compliment him on the copiousness of his ejaculation, as she briskly towelled him dry.

She encouraged him to explore various avenues of her own research, into the relation of sexuality and slavery in the ancient Mediterranean, and he found himself spending a lot of time, 'gnoming', as she put it, in the Bodleian Library. He began to form the thesis that, in the ancient world, sexuality was slavery; production slaves were automatically sex slaves. That was why there were so many freed slaves in ancient Greece, Egypt and Rome, because the freedmen were actually the sons of their owners. With some apprehension, he awaited his next summons from the Lacedaemonian Society.

'Your body is getting prettier, with your workouts in the gym, but you haven't got your nipple rings, yet,' Rosalynn drawled one day. 'I expect that will come soon. Iphigenia is a fanatic for piercing. You'll look so pretty with a slave's nipple rings, Ben.'

One evening, she invited him, as an honoured student, to accompany her on a run around Christ Church Meadow, with her friend, Dr Sarah Mountjoy. Rosalynn explained that they ran in the nude. Wearing tracksuits, the three passed the lodge, with Perkins in charge, and proceeded to Dr Demande's favourite tree, to strip off before their naked run. It was a beautiful moonlit night. Ben could not easily beat the girls round the meadow, for their calves and thighs were more muscled than his, at this stage in his development, yet he adored the sight of the naked female bodies pumping and straining before him, their bare backs, thighs and buttocks rippling with muscle, as he ran.

Soon, however, they let him outstrip them, and he ran naked and proud towards the Isis. He was the leader. But trouble came, when he was caught in a net, strung from a tree, by the girls from the Iffley Road. Lefthera, Cybele, Roxanna and Iphigenia were naked, and carried whips, coiled at their waists, as they laughed at the nude boy, writhing in his string trap, just above the earth. Iphigenia consented to release him from the net, just as Dr Demande and Dr Mountjoy arrived, panting and sweating, and their muscled breasts heaving from the exertion of their run.

'The brat will have to take a flogging,' said Lefthera, flexing her whip.

'Agreed,' said Dr Demande.

'Seems reasonable,' said Sarah Mountjoy.

'And piercing . . .'

'Yes.'

'His nipples need adornment, if he's to proceed to full helot. His bum can be done later.'

'Get down, worm, and give me a hundred press-ups,' snarled Cybele to Ben.

'A gentleman must obey a lady,' said Rosalynn.

'Yes, mistress,' Ben panted.

He had learnt that naked girls liked to be called mistress. He of course obeyed, and, as he performed the exercise, felt Cybele's hide whip lash his naked buttocks at every third press-up. He did the hundred press-ups, and received more

57

than thirty lashes on the bare. The agony of doing the press-ups, his belly and stiff penis striking the muddy earth was nothing to the agony of his simultaneous flogging by the vicious Cybele, who said that Sappho, the aristocratic poetess of Lesbos, liked to flog young naked boyslaves. And, with her intellectual girlfriends, she liked to swim in the Aegean, and play spanking games, the nude girls slapping each other's wet bottom on the beach by the turquoise sea. For her thesis, she was investigating this side of Sappho's work and sensibility, which had not been fully explored. Spanking and poetry! One was the same as the other. The air was cool, the moon was full, and Ben imagined himself spanked by the mysterious Lesbian poetess; he felt that somehow, in his pain and submission to girls, his sacrifice was wholesome.

Iphigenia decreed that he should be hung upside down from Dr Demande's favourite tree branch, while she pierced his nipples, and inserted bronze rings, four centimetres in diameter, bought that very day from Stygia's boutique. The rings had once been worn by a Minoan princess, and had been dug from the soil of Crete by Sir Arthur Evans, and given to the vicar of Youlbury, who had sold them to an antique dealer in St Aldate's, who had sold them to another dealer in Kidlington, whence, after a circuitous route, including an unsuccessful and miserly bid by the Victoria and Albert Museum, they had eventually arrived at Stygia's. Rosalynn said the price of the antique bronze rings would be put on his battels, by Perkins.

Ben screamed, as Iphigenia pierced his nipples with a hot wire, heated in a charcoal brazier, but the pain was not lasting, and, when he had his bronze nipple rings inserted, he knelt, and kissed her feet.

'Thank you, Mistress Iphigenia, for my nipple rings,' he said. 'Thank you, Mistress Cybele, for my flogging.'

Dr Demande threw him a pair of her soiled pink silk knickers. They were stained red and brown, and stank of her body fluids, and Ben pressed his nostrils and lips to them, sucked the fouled gusset, then donned them, drawing them tight round his testes, and sporting an enormous erection.

'Make your own way back to College, Ben,' she drawled. 'Perkins will understand.'

Perkins did understand, while reminding Ben that his battels would be quite large this term, in view of his purchase of the Minoan bronze rings.

'They're quite in demand, these days, sir,' he said. 'Young gentleman like to imitate the Grecian style, I believe.'

The next day, Ben attended Lucy Parvis in her rooms at St Hilda's. With a wicked gleam in her eye, Lucy ordered him to take off his shirt, and Ben obeyed.

'Oh! Nipple rings!' cried Lucy. 'They are so pretty! May I kiss them? I wish I had a pair like that. Real bronze! And antique! But I suppose they are only for boys.'

She knelt, and kissed Ben's nipple rings, licking his breasts at the same time.

'Mm,' she said, 'you have been working out. Such lovely big teats.'

'Thank you.'

'Well, you know why you're here, and there's a lecture on Jean du Bellay I don't want to be late for, so let's be naked and wank off, shall we, Ben? And you don't mind if Abigail and Felicity watch? Abigail is third-year, heading to be a postgrad, and Felicity is postgrad, doing a thesis on Petronius Maximus, one of the last Western Roman emperors, who reigned for just two and a half months, a completely worthless man, who conspired with the eunuch Hercalius to murder his predecessor. Proclaimed emperor the day after the emperor Valentinian the Third was murdered, Maximus immediately forced Valentinian's widow, Eudoxia, to marry him. At the same time, a Vandal fleet, perhaps invited by Eudoxia, was approaching Rome; Maximus tried to escape but was caught by the enraged Roman populace and torn limb from limb in 455 AD. At the same time, the Anglo-Saxons were invading Britain. Imagine tearing a fellow limb from limb! Those were fascinating times.'

'My subject,' said Felicity, 'is the poet Anacreon, after Archilochus, the most important writer of personal lyric poetry in the Ionic dialect. Only fragments of his verse have survived. Isn't that so sweet and tempting? Like your bottom, Ben. A good obscure poet is really like a boy's gorgeous bottom: a girl just itches to get to know it better. Anacreon spent most of his life at the court of Polycrates of Samos, and later he lived at Athens, writing under the patronage of the tyrant Hipparchus. His poems were chiefly in praise of love, wine and revelry. He also wrote in praise of masturbation, if we are to believe his commentators. Only a few fragments remain, but they tend to confirm this. He liked to stand nude at the crossroads, and masturbate with naked male and female athletes, the bodybuilders of their day. Greek scholars in Alexandria had an edition of his work consisting of five books of verse, of which various fragments are still extant.

'Hellenistic and Byzantine writers tended to exaggerate the strain of drunken eroticism and frivolity in his work. So there arose the Anacreontea, a collection of about sixty short poems composed by postclassical Greek writers at various dates and first published by Henri Estienne as the work of Anacreon in 1554. These had a great influence on Renaissance French poetry, as Lucy will agree. The word "Anacreontics" was first used in England in 1656 by Abraham Cowley to denote a verse measure supposedly used by the ancient Greek poet and consisting of seven or eight syllables with three or four main stresses. Anacreon himself composed verse in a variety of Greek lyric measures. I'm looking into the wine-women-and-song aspects of his work. And, most importantly, masturbation, to which he often alludes.'

Felicity lit a cigarette, and poured herself a glass of Barolo.

'But the main thing is,' Lucy said, 'this isn't a tutorial. We girls here at the Hymen Club are all virgins, and we wank. My friends might even want to wank off with us.'

'Of course I don't mind,' Ben replied.

'It's what we do, you see, at the Hymen Club. We are virgins and proud, and we celebrate our virginity by masturbating. Boys *excuse* or compensate for their virginity by masturbating, which we think is silly, for girls *celebrate* their virginity by masturbating.'

Ben stripped off his dark-grey woollen trousers, revealing his lemon nylon thong panties and stockings. The girls cooed.

'How beautiful!'

As he took off his thong, he was already erect. The girls raised their skirts, and lowered their own panties, Felicity's pink, Abigail's blue and Lucy's white. Then they squatted in a circle, with thighs parted, and quims glistening pink and moist. Their fingers were on their already engorged clitos.

'Show us the way, Ben,' said Lucy. 'We wank, to celebrate our virginity, and I think you can manage to do that too. But your poor bottom is awfully bruised. Go on, skin your prepuce, and show us your glans. That's awfully exciting to a girl.'

Ben pulled back his foreskin, exposing his swollen glans, started to rub the helmet of his phallus, and grinned sheepishly. The girls gasped and cooed, and rubbed their clitos.

'The Spartan ladies, the Lacedaemonian Society, they are very tough, you know,' he said, as he stroked his bell end, showing the girls his glistening peehole, and as his foreskin moved up and down over the glans. 'I had a whipping in Christ Church Meadow, just before I had my nipples pierced, and these rings inserted.'

'What a lovely phallus,' panted Abigail, as she frigged. 'Did those girls wank you off, when they whipped and pierced you?'

'No. They hung me naked, upside down from a tree, in Christ Church Meadow, quite near the Isis. Masturbation seems to be forbidden, at least I think so. But rules are made to be broken, aren't they?'

'Not the rule of virginity,' said Lucy, harshly. 'Now, let's do some serious wanking. You can lick our toes, if you want. That's permitted.'

'Do you want me to?'

'I'd rather like it,' said Lucy, blushing deep red.

Ben crouched, bare bottom up. His nipple rings jangled, as he licked the girls' toes, taking their naked feet fully into his mouth.

'That's awfully nice,' said Felicity, her fingers reaming her clito.

'Yes, he has a lovely tongue,' said Lucy, her fingers squelching in her wet pink pouch.

'A boy who knows how to suck a girl's toes is a precious boy,' said Abigail, rubbing her stiff brown nipples.

'A lovely mouth, a treasure,' said Felicity, wanking her extruded clito quite vigorously, as Ben had her foot in his mouth.

Abigail put each big toe into his nipple rings, and pulled gently.

'Does that hurt?' she said.

'Yes, a bit,' Ben answered.

'That's good, then, isn't it?'

'If you say so, miss, yes.'

The girls of the Hymen Club masturbated to orgasm, and permitted Ben to do so, too, at this time, even though they were unsure whether a mere male could become a full member of the club – males being notoriously undisciplined, and prone to lose their virginity on a whim. When Ben came to climax, it was Lucy who removed his fingertips from his glans, swooped her head to his stiff phallus, cupped his tight balls in her palm, took his cock shaft to the back of her throat and, somewhat greedily, as with her appetite for tea, swallowed his spurted cream.

'Oh, Lucy,' he gasped, as he spurted in her throat, while her masturbating friends looked on, 'I do like you so much.'

Skirts up, and panties down, Felicity and Abigail brought themselves to spasm, then each girl kissed Lucy on the lips, tonguing her, to suck Ben's seed from her open mouth.

'Darling! Mwah!'

'Mwah!'

'Mm,' said Lucy, as she licked her lips of the glistening remnants of his sperm, and the spittle of her virgin friends.

'As long as it's no more than *like*, Ben,' she said, after she had swallowed every drop of his sperm. 'We don't want any soppy boys' talk about *love*, for we are all devoted to remaining virgins, aren't we?'

7

Strong Tea

Like most young men, Ben had longed to lose his virginity
as soon as possible, to put his phallus into a girl's hot wet
quim – the magic and the smell of girls, the scent of their
hair, the thrust of their breasts and the sway of their legs
and bottoms, and that pink lustrous girlflesh inside their
pouches! – and spurt his sperm into her womb, and,
masturbating, he had dreamt of that, dreamt of Louella
and others, until the exquisite and almost supernatural
feeling of his orgasm, as his sperm jetted. And, like most
young men, he had masturbated copiously over nude
photos in magazines, or images gleaned from the Internet.
His experience with Louella – for real, a piping-hot,
fragrant girl! – had indeed been magical, though frustrat-
ing, and, in fact, though he had not admitted it to Elena
Ramsey, he had spermed in his underpants, while Louella
was tonguing his mouth, and he was feeling the springy-
firm bare globes of her bottom under her beautifully moist,
smelly and well-soiled panties, which he knew were well
soiled, from sniffing his fingers, scented with her fluids.

That orgasm had, however, been hurried, a surprise, less
than exquisite, and it was only as he blossomed under Dr
Demande's tutelage that he learnt the experience of
orgasm, the ejaculation of the male *sperma*, was generally
more intense, hence more spiritually satisfying, not to say
socially wholesome, when accomplished in the full mastur-
batory act, preferably with a girl's soiled panties curled
around his nose and lips, so that he could taste, smell and

worship the divine fragrance of her exudations, as he spurted. To masturbate on the instructions of a woman, and perform the act before a woman's eyes, was a spiritual as well as physical pleasure. In fact, it was not his pleasure that counted, but the pleasure of a mistress, lustfully watching his *sperma* jet from his phallus, as he rubbed his glans.

Now, in Oxford, he was beginning to relish his status as a virgin. Lucy said to him that she and her friends were nudists, that they spent their summer vacs on Greek islands, where you could bathe nude and virgin in the same turquoise sea as Theseus and Ariadne had bathed in. Being nude in the azure ocean enhanced and enriched a girl's virginity, as if she were giving her young bare body to the caress of the water, rather than that of some brute male. Being naked, among other naked people, freed you from the curse of sexual desire. You were all equal, nude, under the sun and sky, and with the water to bathe in.

Ben said that there wasn't a lot of water in Hereford, apart from the River Wye, and not a lot of sun, either, but, enchanted by Lucy's earnest words, resolved that he would *not* put his phallus into a girl's quim, unless, of course, ordered to do so by one of his mistresses, at which point he would do it by delicious obedience to a female, not by brutal lust. In the Bear Inn, where he took luncheon of his pint of ale and meat pie with brown sauce, he would hear, with some distaste, swaggering blowhards boasting of the girls they had fucked, and Ben would think of Lucy, of her and his virginity, and was proud that he had never fucked a girl, that a legion of stern mistresses such as Lefthera – and he felt a little guilty about lustfully thinking of her, too – would flog his bare arse severely if he even thought of such a thing, and that, unlike those beery oafs, he wore a mistress's nipple rings, and that he was still pure. His nipple rings felt good, under his grey woollen shirt, for they reminded him of his obedience to girls, those sublime, cruel, smirking, giggling and incomprehensible creatures. That he was a slave of Spartan women.

* * *

And soon, he was summoned once more to the Iffley Road. Perkins, at the porter's lodge, handed him the slip of light-blue paper. After his luncheon in the Bear, he made his way, on a bright but chilly afternoon, to the house of the Spartan women, and was admitted by the naked Lefthera, who simply pointed with her finger to the chamber where his treatment was to take place. Cybele, her nude body gleaming with olive oil, awaited him, and, her nipples stiff, carried a long cane, cut from a willow tree on the marshes, by the Isis. The other boys were there, naked, and Ben doffed his clothing, down to bra and panties, but had to doff those, too, on Cybele's barked instructions, until he was nude, like the others. His nipple rings remained. She showed him to his oaken flogging block, which, she said, came from Eton College, in the reign of Queen Elizabeth I, and, obediently, he bent over it, beside the others.

'Now, you smutty helots have probably been naughty, and polluting yourselves,' she said. 'Boys are dirty creatures. So you'll have to own up. You'll get two strokes of this wand for every wank you've had. You! How many wanks have you had since you were last here at the Iffley Road?'

The fellow from Trinity groaned. All the naked young men were bent over their flogging blocks, with their buttocks spread for the cane they knew would come down on their naked skin.

'Not that many, mistress, honestly,' he said.

Cybele made her cane whistle in the air.

'How many is not that many?' she said calmly.

'Well . . . I suppose not more than ten wanks. Perhaps only nine.'

'We'll call it ten, and that gets you twenty cuts of my cane. And you?'

That was addressed to the student from Wadham.

'No more than five wanks, mistress.'

'We'll call it six, then, so that gets you a dozen cuts.'

The Corpus man confessed to three self-pollutions, the Univ man to 'about six'.

66

'You boys don't seem to understand that my cane hurts,' Cybele said. 'And you, Ben, how many self-pollution crimes have you committed?'

'None at all, mistress,' Ben said proudly.

'You think that your pretty nipple rings excuse you from telling the truth? You are not telling the truth, and that is a helot's worst crime,' spat the nude dominatrix. 'Prepare your buttocks for punishment, boys, and you, Ben, for lying, may expect a good two dozen cuts. Any crying or sobbing or moaning, by any one of you, and *all* of you are forthwith expelled from the Lacedaemonian Society.'

'But I haven't wanked! I swear!' Ben protested.

'Silence, worm. Whether you have, or haven't, scarcely matters. You wanted to.'

'I can't deny that,' Ben said.

'Then that is all that counts.'

'Bit stiff, old man,' said the fellow from Trinity, as the boys tensed their naked bodies to take their beatings. 'But we'll have to take the thing quietly. Otherwise we all get expelled from Sparta. That wouldn't do.'

'She's right, I suppose,' Ben said. 'Firm, but fair.'

'Nipple rings, eh?' said the Corpus lawyer. 'Rather fetching, if you like that sort of thing.'

'I do,' said Ben. 'More important, the girls do.'

'Silence, snails!' snarled Cybele.

Vip! Her long willow wand descended in a vicious cane cut on Ben's naked buttocks, and he gasped at the searing pain. He clutched the flogging stool, his nipple rings jangling against the wood, and clenched his fesses, in a vain attempt to dissipate the agony of the willow wand on his bare. *Vip!* He gasped repeatedly, as Cybele's cane lashed him, his nipple rings clashed, and tears sprang to his eyes. To his embarrassment, his phallus stood erect as the naked girl whipped him. The fellow from Trinity looked on, sympathetically.

'Got a bit of a stiffy, eh?' he said. 'That's quite normal when a fellow gets whopped by a girl.'

'Your turn next,' gasped Ben, as his flogged bare buttocks clenched under the girl's lash.

'Yes, I know.'

'Silence, you vile worms and gastropods!' shrieked Cybele again, her bare breasts, with stiffened crimson nipples, heaving in rage, and her own nipple rings jangling.

She took Ben to the promised two dozen agonising cuts of the cane, and then he had to watch, weeping, and his naked arse smarting, as the other college men took their floggings on the bare. All of them became erect at the cuts of the nude Cybele's cane. Lefthera, also nude, looked on, sneering, with a cigarette dangling at her lips, and her fingers playing at her erect clito, with come dripping down her pulsing bare thighs, as she watched the naked boys flogged. When the college men had been caned, their balls were tightly ribboned in pink or yellow by Iphigenia, they were permitted to don their girls' panties, and were dismissed, with notice that they must not be late for their next summons. Ben looked at Lefthera's insolent nude beauty, her legs glistening with oozed vaginal fluid, and was erect, wanting her, as he donned his panties, stockings and corset. But, he thought, and felt guilty for it, he wanted Lucy too, with her hard tan thighs. He wasn't sure how he wanted her, for he respected the Hymen Club, and his own private vows of virginity, but he wanted her somehow.

When Ben had been dismissed by the Lacedaemonians, he walked stiffly back into town, up the High, and telephoned Lucy on her mobile, inviting her to breakfast the next day at White's Café. She accepted with an enthusiasm in her voice that made Ben's phallus rise, despite his smarting fesses. On a chilly morning, they met, exchanged chaste kisses – mwah! – tucked into bacon and eggs, black pudding and beans, with pints of sweet tea, until eventually Lucy wiped her lips with the back of her hand.

'Would you . . . um, I don't really know how to say this.'

'I'm listening,' Ben said.

'Would like to go to bed with me?' she said shyly. 'I mean chastely. We would sleep nude together, but of course we would not pollute ourselves. Like Gandhi. He used to sleep with young nude girls, to test his chastity. I think you are strong enough to sleep with a naked girl, without pollution. Perhaps a test for us both. Of friendship.'

'Yes. That would be wonderful.'

'I have to tell you something.'

'Go on.'

'I'm thinking of having the hood of my clito pierced. Stygia can do it, she does that sort of thing. It gives a girl a sort of permanent orgasmic feeling.'

'Girls are lucky that way.'

'Yes. I know. Poor boys! You can only spurt once in a while.'

'But why tell me? It's your clito.'

Lucy blushed.

'Well . . . I thought . . . you know, you might not like it, or approve.'

He took her hand, and stroked it tenderly.

'Lucy, anything you do, I would like. It's I who worry that you might not like me. Yesterday, I took a caning of two dozen strokes on the bare, from Cybele. I dread to think what my bottom would look like to you.'

Lucy ordered fresh mugs of strong brown tea, borrowed Ben's Swan Vestas matches, and lit Player's untipped cigarettes for both of them, before passing one to Ben, with a mischievous smile.

'Obviously, I'm eager to see,' she said.

She touched his bottom, under his grey woollen trousers.

'Does that hurt?'

'Yes, a bit.'

'It's rather exciting. A boy caned on the bare! I must see the works, Ben. Your naked buttocks, all bruised black and blue, and everything. You don't know how exciting that is for a girl! To see a boy whipped, see him squirm, or his bruises, the evidence of his squirming. You know, when naval cadets were flogged naked, strapped to the gun, in the nineteenth century – it was called "kissing the gunner's daughter" – all the officers' wives would bring their daughters, dressed in their best finery, to watch, as the boys' bare buttocks writhed and bruised and wept under birch strokes. It was a fine spectacle for the women. Girls are very cruel, really. So let's sleep naked together tonight. And you may come with me to Stygia's this afternoon – actually, I've made an appointment, so I suppose that's a bit naughty of me, without telling you – and you can hold my hand, while you watch me being pierced.'

'Well, you know, Lucy, naughtiness deserves spanking,' said Ben, trying to sound frivolous, despite his erection.

'I'm not sure I wasn't hoping you'd say that,' said Lucy, draining her mug of tea, then extinguishing her cigarette in the dregs. 'Isn't that dreadfully Socratic?'

Stygia was dressed in a white blouse and short tartan skirt, which showed off her long nyloned legs to advantage. The flesh-colour nylons blended perfectly with the brown Scots tartan. They went to Aunt Alice's Café for tea and Alice's homemade steak-and-kidney pies, with lots of Bicester brown sauce and Alice's pie gravy, which was rich in onions, and had just a hint of basil, oregano and garlic, while Stygia explained the nature of piercings to the rather nervous Lucy. The red-headed Boltonian's tartan skirt rode up, for comfort – 'a girl must be at her ease, love' – and she did not bother to conceal her frilly stocking tops and brown garter straps, nor her hint of bare, white, succulent thigh, from any inquisitive tea drinker.

'This Bicester sauce is the best brown sauce there is,' said Stygia. 'It's made by a family who've been making brown sauce since the reign of King Charles the Second. Lord Rochester, the debauched poet, used to journey up from London, and sup it. Rochester was an Oxfordshire man, and lived at Woodstock, when not in town. Long before King Charles died, Rochester wrote his proposed epitaph:

Here lies our sovereign lord the king
Whose word no man relied on.
He never said a foolish thing
Nor ever did a wise one.

70

'Rochester brought the king's mistress Nell Gwyn a cask of Bicester brown sauce to her house in Teddington, near the Thames. I imagine he got a fuck in return. I'm not sure I wouldn't open my legs to get a bottle of Bicester brown sauce. Mind you, Rochester was always in search of girls, and sometimes boys. He had his buttocks pierced, with gold rings that he had stolen from the ears of a Dutch admiral in the wars on the North Sea. Some say he had an albert in his cock, before it was actually called an albert. In those days they called it a "French ring", I think – anything obscene or outrageous was always called "French".

'Anyway, brown sauce apart, female genital piercings cover a wide range, although there are only four or five core piercings that are commonly done. Many people call all female genital piercings "clito piercings" but that's not strictly true. Piercings of the clitoral hood include the vertical hood piercing and the horizontal hood piercing. Slightly related are the Helen of Troy piercing and the Clytemnestra piercing, as well as the deep hood piercing and the triangle piercing. Piercing was quite commonly done in the ancient Mediterranean, especially in Crete and Sparta, which is something most people don't know.'

'I didn't know,' Ben said, holding Lucy's hand.

Stygia laughed. 'And you a classical scholar! Then perhaps there's your doctoral thesis, Ben,' she said. 'Body piercing in the ancient Mediterranean! You'd make Rosalynn jealous, as I'm sure she is already, at all the things you know. Actually, I've thought of getting Iphigenia to give me my own nipple rings, and I must say I envy you yours, but my titties are so darned big, it would be hard to fit anything more inside my bra. Anyway, I think nipple rings look better on a boy. For girls, it's the clito.'

'I'm a bit scared,' said Lucy. 'I know I do want a piercing, but, you know, the first time . . .'

'Don't be scared, dear. Ben's had his nipples pierced, hasn't he? And how pretty they are! Those lovely bronze rings, you can see them through his shirt. Now, don't be embarrassed, Ben! You are a lovely young man, and it's a

71

pleasure to spank that delicious bottom of yours, although it won't be so easy when you get rings *there*. But I leave that sort of work to Iphigenia. Let's talk of clitos. Now, above the hood, girls get a common surface piercing usually known as a Leda piercing. There are outer lip piercings and inner lip piercings, with the piercing through the very back of the inner lips, which is called a fork. Lucrezia Borgia piercings – Lucrezia, who had a child by her own father, Pope Alexander the Sixth, she was pierced – pass through the urethra, as does the Catherine de Medici piercing, which is like a transurethral frenum for women. Catherine was pierced by her uncle, Pope Clement the Seventh, before he took her virginity, then married her in 1533 to Henri, Duc d'Orléans, who duly inherited the French crown. Clitoral piercings are of course possible if the clitoris is large enough. How large is your clito, Lucy? Of course, I'll find out when I examine you.'

Lucy blushed.

'I think it's pretty large,' she said. 'You see, I wank off a lot, with my friends at the Hymen Club. Wanking off increases clitoral growth, doesn't it?'

'It certainly does, just as a boy's wanking off increases the size of his tool. Well now, there are also hymen piercings and other unusual variations.'

'I don't think I want my hymen pierced, just yet,' said Lucy nervously. 'I mean to stay a virgin. That's why I joined the Hymen Club.'

Stygia helped herself to more onion gravy from the sauce boat.

'Hymen piercing is a rather arcane way of saying precisely that,' she said. 'In fact, all piercings are, in a strange way, a method of saying, Don't touch me, except on my own terms, because the metal is already touching me. The ancients knew that. Anyway, there's the Helen of Troy piercing, which combines the benefits of a hood piercing with the visual appeal of a Leda piercing. The piercing is of course named after Helen of Troy, renowned for her beauty and treachery. According to myth, and I'm sure it is only myth, her first lover, before Menelaus, I think it was Prince Antipater, after he'd fucked her, she actually cut his balls off, in the night, with a silver dagger, while he slept, because he'd not rewarded the sacrifice of her hymen, that is, her virginity, with sufficient gold. Then Antipater screamed and wept, while Helen actually ate his balls before his very eyes. I suppose that would upset a man. Afterwards, he was sold as a slave, and became an important eunuch at the court of Persia.

'But that is by the bye. Let us get to more practical matters. The lower half of this piercing should be treated as a vertical hood piercing, while the top should be treated as a surface piercing. Jewellery is usually a flexible bar such as nylon, although silver, bronze or copper could be used.

'That's considered much safer than the similar but deeper placement, the Clytemnestra piercing. As outer-lips piercing is to inner-lips piercing, Leda is to vertical hood piercing. The Leda piercing is a surface piercing, travelling from the very top of the hood through the small ridge where the outer lips meet, and exiting through the surface of the pubic mound. Naturally, this piercing is anatomy dependent and prone to rejection in women with a particularly smooth pubic region.

'Now, the Clytemnestra piercing. This extremely deep clitoral shaft piercing starts below the clitoris and just above the urethra, and then goes up through the clitoral shaft and exits at the top of the hood. Because this piercing intersects the shaft of the clito, some piercers maintain it has the risk of nerve damage. Either way, it is an extremely rare piercing.

'There is triangle piercing. The triangle is a piercing passing underneath the clitoral shaft. The piercing is so named because the tissue at the point where the inner lips and hood meet feels like a triangle when pinched. The piercing does not actually pass underneath the clitoral depth-wise, but in terms of being closer to the vagina – below the shaft would be a deep hood, which some women not suited anatomically for a triangle get. Many women hold the triangle to be the ultimate in female piercings. It is a ring, or sometimes barbell, passing underneath the clitoral shaft, in theory offering stimulation not possible either manually or with other piercings. Some women have experienced desensitisation over time, but this is rare. This piercing is anatomy dependent and requires an experienced piercer, like me – accidentally intersecting the clitoral shaft when piercing is at a minimum very painful, and could do damage to nerve structures in the area!

'Note that triangles tend to heal well. Women with a narrow pubic area or large outer lips or whose thighs compress the pubic area may find this piercing uncomfortable because the ring will have a tendency to twist. In this case, a symmetrical teardrop-shaped ring is often more appropriate than a round ring. The tapered shape of the ring prevents it from getting caught between the outer lips and painfully twisted and pulled, which can cause the piercing to migrate or tear during healing. Wearing a thicker gauge will also reduce the risk of migration or tearing caused by twisting of the jewellery. Now, the vertical hood piercing passes vertically, generally through a single central hole, through the clito hood – it is one of the most common female genital piercings.

'Many people erroneously refer to it as a clito ring but it doesn't pierce the clito itself, only the hood. The ring or, usually curved, barbell is meant both to decorate and to rub on the clitoris. So a girl always feels a bit fruity. While most people enjoy this a great deal, some people find its constant nature a bit much. Again, this is your choice, Lucy. The piercing heals very quickly and tends to be trouble-free, assuming the girl's anatomy allows it. Some girls with excessively tight hoods may not be able to take this piercing, but, as a general rule, if a matchstick fits under the hood, you can get it. So, Lucy, the choice is yours.'

Stygia called for fresh mugs of tea.

'I . . . I suppose . . . Have you a matchstick, Ben?' asked Lucy, gulping her hot sweet tea.

8

Pierced

Ben watched, holding Lucy's hand, as the girl received her deft surgical piercing – a vertical hood piercing – from Stygia, who inserted a pear-shaped, silver two-centimetre ring into the hood of Lucy's clito. The ring was thought to be three thousand years old, and came from a selection found in princesses' graves in Mílos in 1926 by the Oxford archaeologist Anthony Dunton-Smythe – a Balliol man and son of Professor Dunton-Smythe – the rings still attached to the clitos of the women's mummified remains, and had been offered to, but rejected by, the Ashmolean Museum, as 'frivolous', or even 'distasteful', and which had come into Stygia's possession. Lucy grimaced, and choked back a sob, at the sudden pain of the piercing, but her pain did not last long, and soon she was able to get up and enjoy a cup of strong sweet tea. She was still naked, and looked at her pierced clito hood and silver ring in the glass with increasing delight. She held her quim lips open for several moments, then rubbed her bare breasts, and clapped her hands.

'Oh, Stygia, it's marvellous!' she cried. 'It hurts, but it feels so good.'

That night, Ben went to bed with Lucy. It was the first time he had ever been naked in bed with a girl, and, in fact, the first time he had ever been in bed with a girl at all. Lucy's body, he thought, was a miracle, the legs long, the buttocks perfect ovals, the dainty young breasts full and jutting, with the big plum nipples slightly upturned. His phallus was stiff, but he respectfully kept to the other side of the bed from Lucy, until she summoned him for a cuddle. She caressed his flogged buttocks, while taking his nipple rings into her mouth, then twisted her nude body, to kiss the wealed fesses, rubbing her fingernails up and down the deep coruscated welts of his whipping, which were now turning to hard ridges, like cardboard.

'Those bruises! So lovely! You are so brave, Ben, to take that punishment from girls. We girls can be so vicious. You don't mind my kissing your lovely wounded bottom? This clito ring makes me awfully fruity. I think I'll get nipple rings, too, like yours. That would make me even fruitier. You must feel fruity, too. You're so big and stiff.'

'But, Lucy, you must keep your virginity. We both must. Like Felicity and Abigail.'

'Those jealous cows! Wanking's the way, and perhaps spanking also. I say, you can spank me on my bare bum, can't you? You more or less promised to. And I can, you know, suck you off, without offending your vows of chastity. Swallow the *sperma* that is longing to leave those lovely tight balls. That beautiful stiff phallus, just aching for relief! Gosh, it must be so hard to be a boy. I mean, wanting relief all the time.'

'I'm not supposed to masturbate, according to the Lacedaemonian rules.'

'You are so prissy! Sucking you off isn't masturbating.'

'I suppose not.'

'But before I do that . . .'

Lucy crouched on the Winnie-the-Pooh bedspread, with her pert young breasts brushing the pillow that showed Eeyore, and thrust her naked bottom up.

'Spank me, Ben,' she commanded. 'Spank me on the bare. As hard as you can. I want it. I'm jealous of your bruised bum. I've been spanked, of course, on my panties, but I've never been *properly* spanked before. That is, on the bare.'

'Are you sure you want to play with fire, Lucy? I warn you, it'll hurt.'

'Do it!' she murmured.

Ben's arm rose, and his palm cracked on Lucy's naked rump. Smack!

'Uhh!' she gasped.

Smack!

'Oh!'

Smack!

'Ah!'

As Ben spanked Lucy's bare, his naked phallus was rock hard. Lucy's bare buttocks clenched at each of his smacks, for he spanked quite firmly, and she pressed her thighs together, causing her hood piercing to press against her clito. Soon, shortly after Ben's thirtieth spank, juice was glistening on Lucy's inner thighs.

'Uhh ... harder ... harder ...' she moaned.

'I can scarcely do it harder,' Ben panted.

'The belt, then. The strap. Don't be a wimp, Ben. Find something. Give me a proper hiding. I'm giddy with pain, and the pleasure of submitting to it. Weal me, weal my naked bottom. *Please.*'

Ben took the leather belt from his trousers, and bent it double. *Vap!* He began to thrash Lucy's quivering bare buttocks. The strap left pink welts, whenever he struck. *Vap!*

'Oh! That's better.'

Vap! He set up a rhythm of flogging, seeing Lucy's clenching naked bottom as his own, so cruelly mistreated by Cybele, and understood that she needed to feel the lash on the bare, as much as he did. *Vap!*

'Turn the whip over Ben. Give me it buckle side.'

He obeyed, and thrashed her with the silver belt buckle as the tip of his whip. Livid violet scorch marks appeared on her naked flesh. *Vap! Vap!* He took her beyond thirty strokes, until her bottom was almost as bruised as his own. *Vap!*

'Oh, yes! Zeus, it stings!'

Vap!

'Ahh!'

Vap!

'Ooh! Oh! Yes! A whip on naked bumflesh is so cruel, so exciting. Can you see how you make my buttocks squirm? It's so shameful, to squirm under a cruel man, but I can't help loving it, honestly.'

Vap! Vap!

'Ah! *Oh!* Yes! *Harder!* Do me! I'm going to come!'

Vap!

'*Ahh* . . . it hurts so!'

Vap!

'Yes! I'm nearly there. Harder. Flog my arse, Ben! Make my bare bum wriggle. I mean, make me wriggle *more*.'

Vap! Her naked buttocks squirmed in a dance of pain, while her fingers were on her clito, rubbing vigorously on the swollen pink nubbin. Juice flowed from her squelching quim lips.

'Ohh! Yes!'

Vap!

'Yes, yes, yes! Oh, I'm coming! Oh! *Ahh! Ahh!*'

Ben put down this lash, and kissed her flogged bottom, his lips tracing the pattern of her welts on each trembling bare cheek. Juice flowed from her pulsing quim, and glistened on her thighs.

'Oh, I've never come so hard before,' Lucy panted. 'That's the best wank I've ever had. I mean, it wasn't really a wank, though: it was a punishment. For being such a naughty girl. Oh, thank you, Ben.'

As she gasped, in the aftermath of her orgasm, Lucy grasped Ben's rigid phallus with her lips, and plunged her throat to his balls, beginning a fierce sucking. Her agile tongue licking his glans, and flicking on his peephole, it did not take her long to bring him to sperm. When she sensed that his orgasm was imminent, she deep-throated him, so that his sperm spurted to the back of her throat, against her uvula. He clutched her head, as she fellated him, her lovely mane of golden hair dancing, as her lips moved on his phallus.

'Oh! Zeus! Yes!' he groaned.

Her throat quivered, as she swallowed his *sperma*. As his cream descended to her stomach, she moaned with satisfaction at the hot drink. Afterwards, grinning coyly, they smoked cigarettes, then snuggled under the bed sheets, where they lay naked, cuddling together, with hands gentle and loving on each other's bare buttocks, Lucy playing with Ben's nipple rings, and his softened phallus. She tickled his balls, and waggled his phallus round, like a soft toy.

'Is this what boys do to each other, when they're younger? Play phallus games? Wank each other?'

'Well, yes. It's just a phase. It's quite normal.'

'I know. You gave me quite a tasty seeing-to,' Lucy said. 'Thank you. But we're still chaste. You have a gorgeous phallus, so big and smooth. Your balls and hillock are so nice shaven. A boy is so lovely with a smooth body. Hair is so yucky, unless it's on your head. As for beards and moustaches, well, ugh! Who do they think they are? And – I feel a bit coy – you have such lovely *sperma*. So much of it! It tastes so nice, like a creamy pudding, with a touch of lemon. I ... I have to say, I've been groped and wanked off by other boys before, and had French kissing and everything, and I've tasted their seed, because that's the way to stay virgin, by despunking a boy, with your hand or your mouth, to calm him down, but yours is the nicest I've ever had.'

'Well, I have to thank *you*.'

He took each of her stiff nipples into his mouth, and kissed them.

'Oh! Thank you.'

'We must stop saying thank you.'

'Yes. We must.'

'You'd look nice with nipple rings, Lucy.'

'I'm sure I would. But this clito ring is already so exciting. I don't want to be too excited. I have an idea, though. You know how hard it is to survive on student loans and things these days? I mean, we can always do with a bit more money. There is a ducky little cottage for rent just past Magdalen Bridge, as you go up Headington Hill. It's too noisy to live in, because of the traffic, but it would be perfect for a business.'

'Yes?'

79

'I have this idea. A beauty salon for men. Not for girls – there are any number of beauty salons for girls. But for boys only. We would call it a barber's shop, and it would look very proper, with a striped pole outside. The staff would be girls, of course, well, me and Abigail and Felicity, I suppose, and we'd have sexy uniforms, and we would offer foot massage and breast massage, even bottom massage, the sort of things that boys are usually too embarrassed to ask for. Complete depilation, total body shaving, waxing and so forth. And we'd sell them girly thongs and petticoats and bras and things. Rather in competition with Stygia, only a more central location. But Stygia might come on board, and do piercings. We could call it Kit for Cats.'

'Or, Frillies for Fellows.'

'Or just the Greek Barber. Awfully postmodern!'

'And would you wank the fellows off?'

'Yes, of course, as part of the massage. We could suck them off, or do them by hand. It wouldn't be cheap, mind.'

'They might want spanking, you know,' he said.

'Yes, that could be arranged.'

'Some of them – I know there are chaps like this – they might want more than a spanking or whipping. They might want bumming up the arse, with one of those strap-on dildo things.'

'That can be arranged too,' Lucy said. 'I wouldn't mind. I'm sure Abigail wouldn't. She's half American. Her mother is from Wyoming. In fact, I wouldn't mind doing it to you, Ben.'

'Would you? Bum me up the arse?'

'Yes, I would. You've such a lovely arse, Ben. The Spartan girls in the Iffley Road haven't bummed you?'

'No. Not yet, at any rate.'

'I'm surprised. Those fesses are so tempting.'

'As are yours.'

'Thank you.'

'The Spartan girls like to whip fellows, and more.'

Ben wriggled down, and pressed his lips to her cunt, in a friendly kiss, and murmured that Lucy had a beautiful sex, as beautiful as her arse and back and breasts, and all of her delicious young body, and, should he ever wish to lose his virginity, it would be in just such a pink fleshy grotto as her perfect quim.

'Thank you,' Lucy gasped. 'I suppose you say the same thing to Lefthera, though.'

'No I don't, you goose. And we must stop saying thank you.'

Embracing chastely, and laughing at the prospect of their new venture, Ben and Lucy fell into a contented slumber.

At his next summons to the Iffley Road, Ben was greeted by the nude, frowning Lefthera, flexing a fearsome yellow willow wand, at least a metre in length, with which, she announced, she proposed to cane him twelve cuts on the bare. He lifted his skirtlet and bent over, on her instructions, touching his toes; she ripped down his lemon thong panties, exposing his naked rump.

'There's more for you today,' she said, her cigarette drooping from her full, beautiful purple lips.

'What, mistress?'

'Don't ask questions, you snail! You'll find out in due course. Now, take your caning in silence, like a man.'

Vip! The cane took him right across the mid-fesse. The pain of the cut was excruciating, but not as bad as the second, which followed almost immediately, taking him on the top buttock. A third lashed him on the underfesse, just above his thighs, and brought tears springing to his eyes. Lefthera paused.

'That's only three of a dozen,' she drawled, 'and already you're blubbing.'

'It hurts, mistress,' he gasped.

'Hold position, worm. You've been polluting yourself. Sleeping with that Lucy Parvis.'

'We are both virgins, mistress,' he said. 'Sleeping is all we do.'

'Liar. Do you want your dozen to start again from scratch? You pollute each other. Stygia tells me Lucy has had an antique clito ring fixed, so that she is constantly fruity. Have you been polluted, Ben?'

'I admit, she has sucked my phallus.'

'And swallowed your *sperma*, I imagine. Have you kissed her quim? Sucked her juice?'

'Well, yes, a bit. But that's not the same as polluting, surely!'

'I'll be the judge of that.'

Vip! Ben gasped, his bare arse squirming, as her cruel cane lashed him. Lefthera took him to the full dozen, then, as tears streamed from his eyes, and his arse smarted horribly, made him crouch over the bed, as if in prayer. She ordered him to turn his eyes towards her, so that he would know what was to happen. The nude Lefthera held a giant artificial phallus of black rubber, a dildo, held on a thong, which she was strapping around her muscled brown belly. Ben looked aghast, through his tears, from his stinging bare nates.

'Crouch, snail,' ordered Lefthera. 'Bend and spread those cheeks.'

Ben moaned in frightened anguish.

'Silence, you worthless gastropod!'

Lefthera thrust her willow wand into Ben's nipple rings, and pulled, stretching his breasts, and causing him to groan. She had a tube of jelly with which she lubricated the artificial phallus. Ben gasped, as he felt the tip of the monstrous wet thing touch his cringing anal pucker. Lefthera brutally pulled his wealed cheeks apart.

'I said spread them, snail!'

'I'm trying, mistress,' he blurted, 'but it's so frightening . . .'

'Silence!'

Ben spread his buttocks as far apart as he could. Lefthera thrust her hips, and the huge rubber tube penetrated his anus. The pain was intense.

'Ahh!'

'I said, silence, snail!'

She continued to push, as Ben groaned, and he felt the tube enter and fill his rectum, which suddenly gave way, to admit the whole colossal monster, until his whole body seemed filled with Lefthera. She began to fuck his arse, most savagely, with brutal and powerful thrusts, the dildo slamming his colon. In his ecstatic pain, Ben's phallus rose to rigidity, as the girl buggered him, her head twisting, her dark glossy ringlets swaying, and her teeth bared in a fierce white grimace of lupine cruelty.

'This is the way it is fitting for a virgin helot to come,' Lefthera panted. 'Your prostate – just beneath your bladder – an interesting little gland, capable of giving pain or pleasure . . .'

'Oh! It hurts!'

'You'll come, slave. I'll make sure you come. But like this, you remain virgin. You haven't put your filthy snail's tool into a lady's sacred crevice.'

As his buggery continued, with Lefthera's lithe young nude body tireless and ineffably cruel, in her disdainful and contemptuous thrusts into Ben's rectum, he felt his seed well up. His breasts heaved, as his nipple rings were wrenched against the willow wand, thrust through them. He *was* going to come! To come, while being buggered, was such shame! But it was too late. He panted as he orgasmed under the Greek girl's pumping loins, with her dildo filling his arse, and his *sperma* flooded from him.

9

Full Lipped

'I gather you've been buggered, Ben,' said Dr Rosalynn Demande, as she poured them both a glass of fino sherry.

Ben blushed deeply.

'Yes, I . . . well . . . Lefthera . . .'

'Don't burble. Lefthera flogged you, then buggered you with a strap-on. Lefthera is an Aegean she-lion, you know. It's healthy. It's a good thing for a young man to be buggered by a girl. Gives him an innocent pleasure, and, more important, teaches him his place.'

'She certainly taught me *that*. May I ask if *you've* ever been –'

'No, you may not. You've been sleeping with Lucy. Chastely, I hope.'

'Oh, yes. Well, you know.'

'I don't know.'

'We're both virgins, but she sucks my phallus and swallows my sperm. She's had a clito ring fixed, you see, by Stygia –'

'Yes, I'm aware.'

'– and it keeps her feeling fruity all the time.'

Rosalynn sighed.

'I was rather afraid of that. But I suppose it's all right, as long as you don't let it go any further. If you wank each other off, and she sucks you, then that's fine and normal, and within the Spartan guidelines. Have you spanked her?'

'Yes. She asked me to.'

'Good. You could bugger her, you know, Ben, and she'd still be a virgin, like you. Now you've experienced it, you know that anal sex is demanding, but in many ways more satisfying and pleasurable than the breeder variety. Girls like anal sex, just as boys would, if there wasn't the slur of perversion. But that's up to the pair of you, and I wouldn't want to pry. However, you do realise that, as a junior member of College, you are forbidden all sorts of things, including having a car, or a motorcycle, or any sort of business dealings. We want to keep you pure, undistracted, your mind unsullied by sordid commerce, and indeed the sleazy modern world. So, if you wish to start the Greek Barber, you'll have to get someone else to be the director. Lefthera, for instance. Her family is so rich, and owns half of Mílos, as well as a fleet of ships, she can do what she wants. Now, your essay. Piercings of genitals and nipples in Minoan civilisation? I like the sound of it. I like that green Minoan skirt you're wearing, and your nylons are well chosen – bronze goes quite well with green – and those nipple rings are truly divine. You *are* muscular! Quite the superb helot! We'll have to get you to Greece, of course. Get you naked and bronzed, on the beach on Mílos. The summer vac should do. Of course, you'll have work, and learn to wrestle and box, in the nude, for ladies' pleasure, and serve ladies with whatever they want, but Lefthera and Iphigenia will no doubt see to that. Lefthera's nipple rings are quite nice, too. Now read on.'

Ben's thesis was that a great deal of classical knowledge went unregarded, simply because it was misunderstood, or in some way disapproved. Items in the Ashmolean Museum classified as 'miscellaneous jewellery' were in fact nipple hoops, clito rings, buttock rings, even anus rings. The art of body piercing, like the art of flogging boys and girls on the bare buttocks, had been very prominent in the ancient Mediterranean. Rosalynn, once more the cashmeresuited doctor of letters, nodded her approval of his essay, although she said it was pleasingly controversial, and said she thought Ben possibly had the makings of a scholar.

85

She suggested he also look into the importance of nudism in ancient Greece, although, of course, in those days, it wasn't called nudism, for people simply went unconcernedly naked. And he might investigate the coincidence between male and female clothing in those days. Men wore skirts, and women wore skirts. Nobody wore underthings, and certainly not – with a grin, she put her hand on Ben's knee – nylon stockings. Men went barebreasted, and so did girls, if not downright nude. Young men and girls ritually masturbated naked at the crossroads. When they dressed, in a skirtlet or a peplos, there was simply not that much difference between male and female clothing. Kings, of course, had beards, and gowns, the emblem of their kingship. But, from the ancient vases, one saw that naked young athletes, male or female, were devoid of pubic hair, or any body hair at all, and the young males were clean shaven. Rosalynn suggested that Ben wear a peephole bra, available from Stygia, to accommodate his nipple rings.

'Razors and body shaving in the ancient Mediterranean,' she mused, sipping her sherry. 'Now that would be an interesting doctoral thesis. I wonder what Sarah would think of it. You know, Ben, you might look at some of those so-called miscellaneous artefacts in the Ashmolean, and determine if, apart from clitoral, anal or breast adornments, there are also, in fact, razors for body shaving. They must have had razors, mustn't they? Otherwise, how could they have had clean bodies?

'There's so much history that has simply been neglected by the greybeards! In the bright light of the ancient Mediterranean, a fresher, truer time than our own, there wasn't that much difference between males and females! Males went out and fought battles, of course, and grew beards, when they aged, but, apart from that, boys and girls were just naked gymnasts under the sun, and it was the women who ruled. The gods such as Zeus and Apollo were feared, but the goddesses were worshipped, Aphrodite and Demeter and Selene and in fact Helen of Troy – or I should say Helen of Sparta? – are still worshipped today.

'Look at the guards of the Greek army, around the presidential palace in Athens – splendid in pleated white skirts, and tights, and jewelled shoes. The most virile of men, dressed as girls! And you see, Ben, until the blighted nineteenth century, people didn't wear any underthings at all. There's a wonderful painting by Fragonard, in the Wallace Collection in London, *The Swing* – it's a pretty girl on a swing, as the name suggests, with her skirts floating up, and a fellow underneath leering at her, and the whole point of the swing is that girls on swings were naked under their skirts, so you got to see their bare vaginas, if you were lucky. Nudity was such a normal and important thing before the Victorian era. And even during it. There is a book I have, a rather secret book, published in Paris by a Victorian English gentleman who was a great lover of women. It's quite instructive. Would you like me to read you a favourite passage?'

'Yes, please,' said Ben.

'It's not pornography,' said Rosalynn, 'it's just realistic. I adore reading it. Do pour us another sherry.'

She went to her bookcase, and took down a thick volume.

'This man was, I suppose, a sex maniac. He was devoted to females. Most important, he knew that all women are naked beneath their skirts. I'll read you what he says about the vagina, which he worshipped. There is some unseemly language, but I hope you can excuse that.'

She began to read.

'In my travels in various parts of the globe, I have never failed to have the women of the various countries passed through, as well as many of the women of the provinces, countries and nationalities, which in some cases make together what is called an Empire. Thus women of Croatia, Styria and Dalmatia, and those of Vienna and Pech, although all belonging to the Austrian empire, are of absolutely different physical types. A Dalcarlian and a woman of Gothenburg differ greatly, yet both are of the Swedish kingdom. In Great Britain, the English, Irish, Scotch and Welsh are of different types, and there is even

87

a great difference in face and form between a Yorkshire and Devonshire woman – both English.

'I have tasted the sexual treasures of all these fair creatures in their capital cities, and many of their large towns; not only in Europe, but in lands and countries away over many oceans. I have sought abroad variety in races and breeds at the best brothels, where they keep women of different nationalities to suit the tastes and languages of travellers. Thus I have had women of all parts of the world, and from parts in which I have not set foot. They may differ in face, form and colour, but all fuck much in the same manner. Their endearments, tricks and vices are nearly the same, yet I found great charm in the variety, and always voluptuous delight in offering the homage of my priapus to a woman of a type or nationality unknown to me.

'Looking through diaries and memoranda, I find that I have had women of twenty-seven different empires, kingdoms or countries, and eighty or more different nationalities, including every one in Europe except a Laplander. I have stroked Negress, Mulatto, Creole, Indian half-breeds, Greek, Armenian, Turk, Egyptian, Hindu, and other, hairless-cunted ones, and squaws of the wild American and Canadian races. I am not old, but the variety I have had astonishes me. May I live to have further selection, and increase the variety of my charmers.

'I have probably fucked now – and I have tried carefully to ascertain it – something like twelve hundred women, and have felt the cunts of certainly three hundred others of whom I have seen a hundred and sixty naked. My acquaintance with the others mostly is the streets, with the delicate operation of what is called stink-fingering. My sense of the beautiful in all things, which makes me now more than ever look to form in a woman more than to face, has shown to me distinct beauty in some cunts compared with others.

'For many years, though perhaps it did not absolutely determine my selection of the woman at first, I still must have been conscious of it. It must in a degree have determined afterwards whether I had the woman a second night or not. Although the reasons why I selected the lady for the second night's amusement are mixed and difficult to analyse, my recollection dwells pleasantly on those women whose cunts pleased me by their look, while the externals of those whose slits lacked attraction and looked ugly to me, I think of even now with some dislike. For years past this perception of the physiognomy of cunts has been ripening by experience and reflection, and now, when I lift a woman's chemise, my first impulse is to see if her cunt is pretty or not.

'I have in fact become a connoisseur in cunts, though probably my taste in that female article is not that of other men. There are perhaps many who would call those cunts ugly which I call handsome, and vice versa; just as they might differ from me about what is beautiful in form, face or colour of a woman; and even about her style of fucking, her manners, language, or other particulars.

'Not only is beauty, or want of beauty, to be seen in the externals of a cunt, but it is to be noticed when the fringed covers are opened. Many a woman looks well enough as she lies on a bed with thighs nearly closed, and the triangle of hair, be its colour what it may, shadowing the top of the rift which forms her sex at the bottom of her belly, but whose vulva looks plain enough, seen when the outworks are opened wide, and large nymphae growing from a clito protrude, and the opening to the avenue of love looks large and ragged. Other cunts with small delicate inner lips, which merge into the general surface before they reach the small-looking opening at the lower end, are pretty, and invite the entry of the prick beneath the little nubbly red clito. The charm of colour also enters into the effect. The delicate pink coral tint of a very youthful virgin is much more pleasing than the deep bluish carmine, the colour of many matured, well-fucked or well-frigged quims, or of those which have let through them several infants.

'The saying that every woman is the same in the dark is the saying of ignorance. It implies that every cunt gives equal pleasure, an error which I think I have exposed before, and combated with several men. The pleasures which cunts give men in coition vary greatly. Scores of women I never seem to have properly entered or enjoyed. In some my prick seemed lost, in others felt an obstruction. In some it seemed to move irregularly, meeting obstacles here and there, as if the cunt resisted its probing, or when a snug place was found for the tip – wherein lies all male pleasure – at the next thrust it was lost and difficult to find again. Up others my prick has struck their end before half its length was sheathed in it.

'Sometimes a pretty-looking little orifice leads to a capacious tube inside, and is wanting in gentle pressure on the prick when within its folds. I have had some women, up whose cunts I have thrust a finger by the side of my pego when within it, though it was swollen to full size, and seemed large enough to fill any cunt, and yet the vagina seemed a cavern to it.'

Rosalynn looked up from the book. 'Pego was a Victorian euphemism for phallus,' she said. 'And I think he is misguided in saying that all male pleasure lies at a girl's womb neck. As you have undoubtedly found in reading Plato, the supreme pleasure is philosophy. However. *Je continue.*'

She looked back down at the page, and resumed her reading. 'There are cunts which fit me to perfection, in which my prick revels in voluptuous delight, from the moment it enters till it leaves it; in which it cannot go wrong, whether lying quiescently within its warm lubricious folds, whether the thrusts be long or short, quick or slow. Such cunts make me feel that I have an angel in my embraces. Others do their work of coition uncomfortably, making me almost glad when the orgasm is over, and leaving me indifferent to the woman when my prick leaves her. What my experience is must be that of others.

'I have either fucked, felt or seen the cunts of females of all ages, have seen them of all sizes and developments, and in colour from pale coral to mulberry crimson – I have seen those bare of hair, those with but hairy stubble, those with bushes six inches long, and covering them from bum

90

bone to navel. It might have been expected that I was satiated, that all curiosity, all chain in this female attribute had gone from me.

'Nevertheless the sight of this sexual organ pleases me as much as ever, sometimes I think more. Little intrinsic beauty as it may have, little as it may add artistically considered, to the beauty of the female form in those parts wherein it is set. Nay, although at times I may have thought it ugly in a beautiful woman, it has still a charm, which makes me desire to see the cunt of every young female I meet. This is the reflex in the brain of the joy that the penetration of the cunt has given me, of the intense mental and physical pleasure of fucking, pleasure which for the time makes the plainest woman adorable, and her cunt a gem which the mines of Golconda cannot match.'

Rosalynn once more looked up. 'Golconda is in India,' she said. 'It was famous to the Bactrian Greeks, who, under Alexander the Great, colonised what is now Afghanistan, and later the Romans, for its diamond mines. An interesting analogy, that a woman's quim is a diamond mine. I'll continue to read.'

And she did. 'There is no more exquisite, voluptuously thrilling sight, than that of a well-formed woman sitting or lying down naked, with legs closed, her cunt hidden by the thighs, and only indicated by the shade from the curls of her motte, which thicken near to the top of the Temple of Venus as if to hide it. Then as her thighs gently open and the gap in the bottom of her belly opens slightly with them, the swell of the lips show the delicate clitoris, and nymphae are disclosed, the enticing red tint of the whole surface is seen, and all is fringed with crisp, soft, curly, shiny hair, while around all is the smooth ivory flesh of belly and thighs, making it look like a jewel in a case. Man's eyes can never rest on a sweeter picture.

'Then, as the thighs widen for man's embrace, and the cunt shows itself in all its length and breadth, red and glistening with moisture and lust, all seen but the lower end where lies the entrance for the prick, which is partly closed by the ivory buttocks, and seems of a darker red, by the shade in which it lies, telling of the secrecy and profundity of the tube which the prick is to fathom, and in which it enters, stiffens, throbs, emits, and shrinks out while its owner almost faints with the pleasure it receives and gives, is there aught in this wide world which is comparable to a cunt? How can any man cease to have curiosity, desire and a charm in it?

'At such moments my brain whirls with visions of beauty and of pleasure, past, present and to come. My eyes embrace the whole region from anus to navel, the cunt seems invested with seraphic beauty and its possessor to be an angel. Thus even now I can gaze on cunts with all the joy of my youth, and even though I have seen fourteen hundred, long to see fourteen hundred more.

'Of the physiognomy of cunts, and of their pleasure-giving capabilities, perhaps I know as much as most men. Physiognomically, I classify them as follows: clean-cut cunts, clean-cut with stripes, lipped with flappers, skinny-lipped and full lipped.

'Clean-cut cunts are those resembling a cut through an orange; the flesh on each side is full, thick, swelling up, turning inwards slightly, and forming a fattish pad rather than lips, although a tendency to the form of lips may be seen. Neither clitoris nor nymphae are seen in some, though in all the flesh seems reddening as the sides turn inwards and meet; showing the slightest coral stripe, a mere hint of the red surface inside. The pads of flesh are firm yet elastic, and that of the motte, which is full, is equally so. This class of cunt generally alters by age, but I have seen it in one thirty-five years old. There is usually ample space between the thighs where there are these cunts in full-grown women, so that a man's hand can lie comfortably between them, and grasp a whole handful of vulva. Perhaps the bones of the thighs are set widely apart in the pelvis, but I have seen and felt this width of cunt in short women.

'Straight-cut cunts with stripes are much like the former, but the nymphae are slightly more developed, as well as the clitoris, not largely, but sufficiently to give a visible red stripe between and seeming to open the outer lips. Sometimes the red shows largely only when the thighs are apart; in others it shows even when the thighs are closed. In some the little clitoris (not an ugly big one) just protrudes itself under the dark hair, which thickens just about the split, and an inch below it the nymphae are lost to view unless the thighs be wide apart. I have seen this cunt in women up to thirty, and it is to me certainly the most delicate, most refined, handsomest and most exciting cunt. I have nearly always found it in the finest modelled, plump and loveliest woman. It is indeed the only class of cunt which can be said to be handsome. A cunt is perhaps not a really handsome object at all, though sexual instincts make its contemplation exciting and charming to a man.

'Lapped cunts with flappers have the lips usually fully formed, the clitoris sticks out and the nymphae hang out from it nearly the whole length of the split down towards the vagina. Women towards forty have mostly this cunt and, if they have fucked or frigged themselves much, the colour is of a very dark pink or carmine. I have seen it in women of nearly a mulberry red. The nymphae I have also seen hanging out of or projecting beyond the lips, from three-quarters to an inch and a half in depth; it was so detestable to me, that it quite spoilt my liking for a really well-made pretty woman of thirty-five whom I once knew. Many French gay women in the bawdy houses get this sort of cunt, I expect through excessive venery. They grow thus oftentimes in women if they have children.'

Rosalynn looked up again, and said, 'And here there is a footnote, for this is a second edition, and it reads, "Years after writing this I had a girl with nymphae hanging an inch and a half outside the lips and a quite large clitoris. The nympha on one side was much larger than the other, and her vagina would have engulfed the prick of a giant. I saw and fucked her a second time, out of sheer curiosity."'

Rosalynn continued with her reading. 'Skinny-lipped cunts may be either with or without the nymphae showing. Poor, slim, youngish, half-starved women with thin thighs and miserable rabbit backsides have this form of cunt. It is not ugly, actually, unless the nymphae are too obtrusive, which they frequently are. Women with this class of cunt usually sham modestly, put their hands over their gaps, say they don't like it looked at, and giggle in an affected manner. I suppose they are conscious of the want of beauty in those parts.

'Full-lipped cunts are usually mature. They puff out like the half of a sausage, then die away into ample flesh on each side under a fat, fully haired mons veneris or motte. Women fleshy and well fed have them, and they look well and handsome between the large white thighs and the big round buttocks below, between which they are enclosed and lie. They were the cunts which I loved most in my youth and long after. I expect they are most attractive to quite young men, for they realise the cunts which all boys, as I very well recollect, figure to themselves before they have seen the sex of a woman. The general effect of the cunt is that it is capacious. Women with this class of cunt usually allow them to be looked at and fingered freely, and smile voluptuously at the man while the inspection is going on, as if proud of their notches, and they like the men to look at and to appreciate them.

'All classes of beauty may be found with one or other of the defects, for the variety in combination of outer lips, clitoris, nymphae, motte and hair in quantity, size and shape is infinite. No two cunts are exactly the same in look, hence the charm of variety, and the ever-recurrent desire for fresh women by the male. There is always a charm in novelty; it is born with us.'

Rosalynn, during this reading, had lifted her skirt, and revealed that she was wearing fetching brown nylon split-crotch panties, and she had been fondling her naked cooze lips through the hole in her panties. Ben saw that her quim was quite wet and glistening.

'So you see, Ben,' said Rosalynn, 'the job of a male in this life is to worship a female, or many females. Stink-fingering! Well, that's always a thrill. Reading this man always excites me. Though he was a prosperous Victorian businessman, he was, in some ways, an ancient Greek. He took women where he found them, on the street, or in the railway train, wherever. *And women want to be taken.* But there must always be worship. And, in fair play, there must always, and I mean always, be punishment of the male in return, for his insolence, in daring to worship us. He suffered agonies of frustration and jealousy, as much as he enjoyed girls' quims.'

'He doesn't say much about girls' bottoms, though.'

'No, he doesn't. He was a quim man, not a bottom man. Which do you think you are, Ben?'

'I'd have to say a bottom man. If that man worshipped girls' quims, I'd admit that I worship their bottoms. A girl's buttocks are so gorgeous, so tempting, so mysterious. So pure and wholesome. Whenever I've wanked off, you know, looking at naughty pictures in magazines, it has always been over girls' naked bottoms.'

'But do you find my split-crotch panties attractive?'

'You must know I do. My skirt and petticoat are bulging, Dr Demande.'

'And do you find my bottom attractive?'

'Yes, of course,'

'There is never any "of course". Check your Plato's *Republic.* What sort of cunt do you think I have?'

'A full-lipped cunt, Dr Demande. Shaven, and swollen. The most beautiful nude cunt imaginable.'

'Well said. I think you may get down on your knees, Ben. Right now. You are due for a little bottom worship. In my way, I shall worship your bare fesses.'

10

Netherworld

'The thing is, Ben,' Rosalynn drawled, as she rolled up her skirt, smoothed her flesh-coloured nylons, garter straps and suspender belt, and slowly, casually, slid down her chocolate-brown split-crotch panties over her rippling nyloned thighs, 'the essays you have read me have the effect of making me horny. It's like reading a poem by Catullus, or looking at a painting by Titian. I think you have to be punished for that. Furthermore, you've been with Lucy, you've been with Lefthera and Stygia, but I am your tutor, so I think it's reasonable that I should want you, or most of you, for myself. In particular, that lovely arse, those beautiful breasts, those big tight balls and that magnificent phallus. Tight balls and a big phallus in a young man turn me on.'

'Oh, I see.'

'Stop saying you see. You're just a boy, a beautiful boy, and you don't see. I'm going to flog you until you do. Then you're going to worship me properly.'

Rosalynn still wore her skirt, and her stockings and suspender apparatus, but without her panties underneath.

'I'm not a clean girl, Ben,' she said, with something of a smirk. 'It's one of my modest thrills. I like having soiled, smelly panties, because I know they attract boys. You see, Ben, I like young men. Like Lefthera, I like to have them in my thrall.'

She put her panties to his nose, and made him sniff, then wadded them in his mouth, as a gag. Ben's phallus became rigid, as he savoured the acrid taste of his tutor's genitals and anus. Meanwhile, Rosalynn, still garbed as the stern English tutor, went to her glass-covered bookcase, slid back the glass and removed a scaly wooden model of a snake, about a metre long. She whipped the air with the wooden snake, and Ben blanched, in the knowledge of what was to come.

'This is from Mílos, actually,' Rosalynn said. 'They make these things as amusements for the tourists, for they have snakes in Mílos, just grass snakes, and not poisonous, but I suspect the tourists buy the wooden souvenirs, knowing they are for a specific purpose, which you are just about to find out. I'm going to whip you with this. Mílos was one of only two Spartan island colonies, while the other Greek city-states had colonies in Sicily, Italy, Africa, and even Marseille started as a Greek colony. But the Spartans stayed close to home. That's by the bye. Be warned that the wooden snake hurts.'

Without more ado, Rosalynn lashed Ben's naked buttocks with the snake. *Vap!* His buttocks clenched tight, for the pain was electrifying.

'Oh!' he gasped, through the fragrant gag of his tutor's split-crotch panties, drenched in the aroma of her genital and anal juices.

'Silence is golden, Ben,' she hissed, 'so keep silent.'

Vap!

'Uhh!'

'I said, silent. I'm going to give you a dozen, and I don't expect a real man like you to whimper like some girly.'

Ben clenched his teeth, and, despite the tears that filled his eyes, took his tutor's whipping in silence, save for massive gasps, as the wooden whip seared his squirming bare bottom. Twelve strokes landed on his naked flesh and, twelve times, his bare buttocks clenched tight, he squirmed and writhed, but knew there was no way he could escape his punishment, for Rosalynn was in command. His whipping over, and Rosalynn laying down her whip, he felt her tongue licking his bruised arse, then the tip of her tongue licking his balls, and the lower shaft of his cock, and then he groaned, as he felt her penetrate his anus, with the full depth of her tongue.

'That tickles!' he mumbled, through his panties gag.

'It's supposed to tickle, fool,' she said, after she had tongue-reamed his rectum for over two minutes, and then extracted her tongue from his anus, with a little squelching sound.

When she let him rise, he felt his buttocks, and they were bruised with hard ridges, like corrugated cardboard. Rosalynn lifted her skirt, cleared some books from her rosewood desk and bent over it, her hands clutching the rim of the desk. She was clad in cashmere and silk and nylon stockings, every bit of her stern body that of a strict tutor, but her bottom and cunt basin were deliciously, tantalisingly bare. Her muscled naked buttocks, tan from the sun, were, Ben thought, twin golden melons of delight. She permitted him to remove his panties gag, and said he could wear the split-crotch garment himself, for she thought it would fit. His phallus could poke amusingly through the aperture.

'Now, you may suck my quim and put your tongue in my bum, until I tell you to stop, then bugger my arse with that nice hard phallus,' she ordered calmly. 'I want your *sperma* to bathe my colon. Don't worry, you'll still be a virgin, technically speaking.'

Ben knelt, and applied his mouth to his tutor's buttocks, licking and kissing them, while she said, 'Yes . . . yes . . . good technique . . .' His phallus was rock hard, as he smelt the fruity, acrid skin round her anus, ran his tongue up and down the hard, muscled arse cleft, then penetrated the anal pucker with his tongue, giving her a reaming just like that she had given him.

'Do you like my moons?' Rosalynn said.

'Can't you tell? You know I adore them. They're nicer than Lucy's, or Lefthera's, or anyone's. And your bumhole tastes so strange, so delicious.'

'Flattery! Why, thank you. That was prettily put, even though I don't entirely believe you. I suspect my bumhole tastes pretty grotty. But that's what a good boy likes, to smell and taste a woman's netherworld, while her buttocks enfold his nose and mouth. You may continue.'

Ben got his tongue inside Rosalynn's tight quim, which was already wet and streaming when he entered it, and began to lick her swollen clito. She gasped, trembling slightly, as she gripped her desk.

'Always the boy underneath, you see,' she moaned, in a faraway voice. 'The boy is there to serve. Now, drink my juices.'

Ben swallowed the copious come gushing from Rosalynn's quim, while her fingertips alternately gripped and tapped the tabletop. He sniffed her quivering stockinged thighs.

'Yes, you do have a good technique, Ben,' she gasped. 'When I come, and I know I will, don't stop, keep tonguing my clito. Then, when you sense it's time, put your fingers to my quim, and oil your phallus with my cunt juice, and get your cock into my bumhole, and give me a good hard rogering up the arse. You see, Ben – oh, yes, *that's* good – unlike you, or Lucy, I'm not a virgin. But I prefer it the Greek way, the phallus in the rectum, the male's cream spurting at my colon, and myself groaning in submission. It makes me feel like a boy. Oh, Zeus, yes, that's good! What a lovely tongue you have! Yes, this is the moment, give it to me, Ben. *Now*.'

'I've never done this before,' Ben stammered

'Well, do it now. Strip back your foreskin, before you penetrate my anus. I like the feel of a boy's naked glans.'

He rose, licking his lips of his tutor's come, with his phallus rigid, and slopped his fingers in Rosalynn's dripping cunt, to oil his shaft. He obeyed her instruction, and, with his helmet nude and swollen, placed his peehole at Rosalynn's pulsing anal pucker.

'You must thrust hard, it may seem difficult, but after a few shoves it will slide in, right up into my belly, and then you can fuck me hard in the arse, pound me with utmost vigour, imagine that you're having revenge for your own buggery by Lefthera, and then I'll come. Don't worry, I know. The Greeks know.'

He parted her cheeks as far as he could – with her willing help – and his glans entered her anus. It was very tight, and he obeyed her orders to thrust hard, and soon the anal elastic gave way, and admitted his stiff phallus to her rectum, which seemed a welcoming, warm and wet space, full of delight. Her soft rectal tissue clenched his phallus like a clinging glove.

'*Yes!*' groaned Rosalynn. 'Do you like it, Ben?'

'Oh, I do,' he moaned, beginning to thrust with his hips, as Rosalynn used her sphincter muscle to clamp his phallus.

'Now, fuck me, Ben. Fuck me as hard as you can. Do me in the bum, boy! I want your cream up my hole, and when I feel you start to spurt, and bathe my colon in your *sperma*, then I'll come.'

Ben's back and thighs rippled, as he began to slam his phallus into the groaning girl's tight, clinging rectum, and he experienced a strange feeling of power, as she writhed and groaned and wriggled. His nipple rings jangled, and his stockings slithered together. He was a Greek boy or perhaps girl, buggering another Greek girl! The girl's arse – and he could not help thinking that Rosalynn, for all her grandeur and grace, was just a girl – was a very tight fit, tighter than the most earnest masturbating hand, yet he did not feel an urgency to spurt his seed. He enjoyed having his tutor squirming on his phallus, as he had squirmed under Lefthera's buggery of his own arse. So he took his time.

'More! Harder!' Rosalynn panted.

'I think you should be naked,' Ben said.

'What? Just bugger me, boy!'

'No, I think I want your blouse off,' he said, still buggering her rectum, but unfastening the buttons of the garment, until he had stripped it from her.

'Now, I think I want your bra,' he said, as Rosalynn gasped and writhed on his powerful phallus.

'You Spartan swine!' she gasped, but could not resist, as he unhooked her bra, and cupped his hands around her naked breasts, squeezing them, then pinching the nipples quite brutally between his fingernails.

'Oh! Oh! You bastard! Fuck me! Fuck me!'

'I want your skirt, too,' he said. 'I want to dress as you. I want to be you.'

'Oh! Yes! Anything! Just keep fucking me with that filthy, horrible big cock!'

When Rosalynn was nude, but for her suspenders and stockings, and he had folded her clothes neatly, on top of her smelly split-crotch panties, Ben resumed a rather lazy, though vigorous thrusting in her rectum, with his strokes spaced at twenty or thirty seconds.

'You fucking bastard!' cried Rosalynn. 'Do me! Fuck me! Harder! Faster! Come in me! Give me your fucking spunk!'

'I'm a virgin, Dr Demande,' Ben drawled. 'You know I'm not used to this.'

'Hurry! I want to come.'

'Ah, yes.'

With deft fingers, he started to roll down her stockings.

'You virgin bastard,' she moaned. 'Oh, do whatever you want with me. Just make me climax.'

He ripped the stockings from her quivering legs, and placed them in the neat pile of her clothing. Rosalynn's muscled nude body writhed, helpless, impaled on Ben's phallus, lodged at the depths of her rectum.

'I want to keep your clothes.'

'They are expensive!'

'That's partly why I want to keep them. They are precious to you, so they will remind me of you, when I wear them, or just sniff them, to breathe your aroma. Otherwise I shan't bugger you.'

'Damn you! Anything! Just bring me off.'

'Very well.'

He increased the vigour of his strokes, buggering the girl vigorously, feeling the sperm welling up in his balls, and told his tutor that, with her permission, he was going to sperm in her anus.

'Yes! Oh, be quick!' she panted.

Suddenly, Ben withdrew his cock from her anus, and she wailed, 'Oh, no . . . oh, you fucking bastard!'

He put his hand between her quim lips, and cupped a copious amount of come, with which he smeared her bare buttocks.

'What are you doing?' she moaned. 'I want your phallus inside my arse.'

'Your arse needs a seeing-to. A spanking. Girls need spanking, just as boys do. Wet bum always hurts more, and now you're covered in your own naughty oily juices.'

'Oh, no, please . . .'

Ben began to spank Rosalynn's naked buttocks, glistening with her own come. *Smack! Smack!*

'Oh, no!'

Smack! Smack! He kept up the hard slaps for fifty or more spanks. Her cooze gushed come over her quivering thighs. *Smack! Smack!*

'Yes!' she gasped. 'Do it to me! Do anything to me!'

Holding her head down, he spanked the backs of her thighs, and she moaned, in pain and pleasure. He lifted her feet, and sucked her toes, before applying the wooden snake to her soles, which made her scream in agony. *Whap! Whap!* The wooden snake lashed her soles, and her lovely bare feet wriggled, before he covered them in kisses, and took the toes once more into his mouth, for a tender sucking, which made Rosalynn writhe in pleasure.

'Oh . . . yes . . . more . . .'

He continued to worship her naked feet for several minutes, then lifted the snake and lashed her a dozen on the naked buttocks, before brutally plunging into her rectum once more.

'Yes! Yes! That's what I want! Fuck my arse! Oh, Zeus, don't stop!'

Nipple rings clanging, he spent several minutes at vigorous buggery, with Rosalynn urging him to come inside her arse, before he let the swirling pleasure in his balls overtake him, and spurted his cream at her root.

'Ahh!' she shrieked. 'Oh! Yes! Your *sperma*! I'm coming! Oh, you filthy sweet slave, you dirty virgin bastard. Oh! Oh! *Yes!*'

Afterwards, Rosalynn donned a peplos, and summoned Mrs Lord for tea and cakes.

'You said I could keep your clothing,' Ben said.

'I suppose I did, and I must keep my word. You *are* a bastard.'

'I want to dress and look like you. I want to feel like you. To *be* you.'

'Ah, Empedocles, the transmigration of souls. Then you'd better have a few pairs of my soiled knickers – they're just thongs – so that you'll feel more like me.'

Rosalynn opened her armoire, and found three thongs, yellow, red and purple.

'They're not washed.'

He sniffed each pair of her knickers.

'That's what I like, mistress.'

He crouched, and kissed her toes.

'By Zeus! You know, that was good. I've never had a swiving like it!' Dr Rosalynn Demande declared. 'You're a real bugger, Ben, and that's meant as a high compliment. Now, I hope you are going to put in some good serious work on your next essay. But if you want to wear my clothes, and I've promised them to you – that blouse cost me a fortune at Dickins and Jones! – well, why don't you?'

Ben rolled up Dr Demande's stockings, put on her bra, over his nipple rings, which was slightly uncomfortable, then zipped up her skirt, and buttoned her blouse. He was fully dressed in silk and cashmere, when Mrs Lord arrived with their tea, crumpets dripping with butter, Battenberg and Eccles cakes. Mrs Lord, whose sight was not of the best, placed the tray on the table in front of Ben.

'There you are, Dr Demande,' she said.

They both laughed at that.

Then, in serious voice, Dr Demande, biting into a crumpet, with the butter drooling down her chin, said to Ben that sex, to which he was still technically virgin, was not about orgasms, but was all about power.

'We are all a slave of something. My nineteenth-century memoirist was a slave of women's cunts. But it's not about putting your widdler for a brief moment into a winky-wanky place. That's the beauty of anal intercourse. It hurts, it's an expression of power, and it's gorgeous because it hurts. The question is, Ben,' she said thoughtfully, 'who is in whose power? You in mine, or I in yours? Or both of us in Lefthera's?'

She put her hand on his thigh.

'You see, I have to confess that Lefthera, with that monstrous toy of hers – well, Lefthera has buggered me, too.'

11

Lefthera

Lefthera scrutinised her nude body in the looking glass. Although she loved the beaches of Mîlos, and to swim in the turquoise sea, where gods and goddesses once bathed, she did not need to lie nude for hours, like the northern visitors, to get a sun bronze, for she did not need a sun bronze. Her gleaming, slightly oily tan skin was already perfect. Her long coltish legs with their ripe-muscled thighs were perfect, too, like her long lustrous hair, and her jutting breasts, with their big grape nipples, adorned by golden rings, and her flat belly, and her pert, full buttocks, hard and firm and smooth as a green olive skin.

Having stroked her thighs, of which she was particularly proud, she began to stroke her ringed nipples, making them stand to attention, prior to her daily act of self-worship. Then her finger strayed to her clito, which she brushed very softly, gasping at each touch. She was young, she was rich, for her father owned land, and a fleet of ships, and she herself had a trust fund, since her father adored her, and she was the most beautiful maiden in the world, and could, she insisted, trace her ancestry back to King Menelaus of Sparta, and, who knew, possibly to Helen of Troy – why should such a princess not worship herself? She wondered if she should not have golden hair, like Helen, or the slut Lucy Parvis, but golden hair could be arranged.

When her nipples were erect, and her quim moist, Lefthera selected two cylinders from her collection of dildos and vibrators, not the ones she used on boys, or other girls, like Rosalynn or Iphigenia, but those she kept for herself. All were of course thoroughly cleansed and disinfected, after each hygienic operation – as Lefthera thought of enculement – but the prettiest ones were reserved for her own cunt, and, more importantly, her own anus. Like Rosalynn and Lucy, Lefthera knew a lot about masturbation. When she masturbated, she thought about the joys that had made her the young woman she was. There was Spiro, there was Timothy Dunton-Smythe, both virile young men with big cocks, who liked to fill her rectum with their *sperma*, as she squirmed, gasping, in the Mílos sand dunes. Spiro was the first mate of one of her father's ships, while Timothy was the great-grandson of Professor Dunton-Smythe, the archaeologist. It was Timothy who had suggested that, after finishing school in Lausanne, where she had, by the bye, learnt to spank eager Swiss boys on their bares, she should go to Oxford.

Early in her life, as a young teenager, Lefthera had – technically – taken her own virginity, by masturbating with a piece of sea-polished driftwood, on a beach on Mílos, and orgasming, as she stood with legs apart, under the sun, worshipping herself, as she worshipped the ocean. She had grown up swimming nude, with her sister Zenobia, supervised by her nanny, in the azure waters of the Aegean, where there were many foreign nudists, with whom she made friends, and played beach games. Her family saw no harm in this, although her nanny would sometimes whip her or Zenobia's bare bottom with an olive branch, for trivial things, such as letting breadcrumbs fall from her lips, or dripping olive oil, at table: it was bad manners, oil and bread were precious, the two staffs of life, and must not be disrespected. Lefthera never cried when she was whipped on the naked bottom, or, most shamefully, on her superb thighs, in front of all the family, but Zenobia always did.

Understanding the dictates of her Greek family, she had by decision remained a flesh virgin, like the girls of the Hymen Club, for no man had ever penetrated her quim.

Zenobia was also virgin, as far as Lefthera knew, although the girls did not exchange many secrets. They had learnt to wrestle naked together, and with other girls of the village, in the Spartan tradition, before an approving audience of aunts and uncles, the aunts eating sweets, and the uncles sipping retsina wine. The village boys would also wrestle naked.

The wrestling, for boys or girls, was freestyle, as in ancient Sparta, with no rules, save for a prohibition on eye-gouging and kicking of the testicles, in the case of the boys, although girls were allowed to kick or bite each other in the vagina, and a player who was down in the dust could be beaten, or spanked, until he or she submitted. All biting, clawing and kicking, whether of ears, face, buttocks or breasts, were otherwise permitted. Girl wrestling was particularly savage, less artistic than that of the boys, and particularly appreciated by the audience, with knee pummelling vagina, and teeth gnawing the opponent's nipples, or biting her thighs and quim, being the favoured methods of gaining a submission.

There would be prizes of sweets and sherbet for the winners, while the weeping losers would receive a light, purely ceremonial, whipping of a few rather jesting strokes with an olive rod on the bare buttocks, quite unlike the savage floggings of ancient Sparta. Lefthera had excelled so much at wrestling that she was permitted to pit herself naked against the boys, in their arena, and often won, relishing the punishment – albeit a mere ritual – of the vanquished boys' bottoms, after she had sat with her buttocks crushing their faces, and forced them to submit. Zenobia, too, was a champion girl wrestler, and was permitted to wrestle with boys, but the boys generally won, and Zenobia did not seem to mind. In fact, she seemed to let them win, relishing her own submission, crushed under a hard, young, male body.

The sisters would share their father's fortune, and his ships, when he passed on, and divide his ample lands on Mílos between them. Virginity was both a spiritual and material asset. A virgin would marry well, or automatically go to heaven. As a reward for her virginity, Lefthera already had title to a large estate on Mílos, where the Lacedaemonian Society had their summer headquarters, for the cooling summer breeze in the Aegean made the islands freezing in winter, and so most of the population, like Lefthera's family, migrated to Athens or Paris or Miami for the winter season. It was in summer that the Lacedaemonian girls trained and brutalised their volunteer troop of helots, or naked boyslaves.

In the Spartan tradition, and Mílos was an ancient colony of Sparta, anal sex did not count as non-virginity; indeed, it scarcely counted as sex at all, just healthy play. Lefthera suspected that the handsome and lustful Timothy Dunton-Smythe had buggered Zenobia, too, in the dunes, but this caused her no ill will. In youthful days, she and Zenobia had masturbated together, standing naked at a crossroad of goat tracks in the deserted hills, and so they were firm, if perhaps distant, friends.

Her preference, and, she assumed, Zenobia's, was for anal submission to a powerful phallus, attached to a lithe, muscled male body. Then, when it was time, Lefthera would make a hapless male squirm in submission to her own strap-on dildo, as she fucked him, Greek-style, in the arse. She had fucked both Spiro and Timothy that way, and liked it as much as being arse-fucked herself. She liked to make males squirm, as they made her squirm. Spiro had only reluctantly accepted a whipping with a driftwood branch, but Timothy – being English, she thought – had willingly offered his bare arse for a severe flogging of two dozen cane strokes. That was one of the reasons why Lefthera had chosen to come to Oxford. An Englishman knew his place, either behind a lady's bottom, crushing his face, or with his own bottom beneath her lash.

Above all, Lefthera liked to masturbate before the looking glass, performing her daily ritual of worshipping her own virgin beauty, as she was now about to do. She had a black rubber vibrating dildo for her cooze and a pink rubber dildo for her anus, which also vibrated, both devices being battery-driven. The pink anal dildo was a little larger than the cooze dildo; Lefthera scorned girls who said that an anal dildo must be small. Raising her left thigh, and placing her bare foot on the table, so that she could clearly observe her spread genitalia in the glass, she turned the vibrators on, listened to them buzz for a few seconds, then lubricated them with water-based jelly (for her preferred olive oil, which she rubbed all over her nude body, and her driftwood dildos, to masturbate on the beach on Mílos, used on a modern rubber dildo, would destroy the rubber), and introduced the black rubber dildo into her quim.

It had a small attachment, which was a clito tickler, and, as she thrust the shaft deep into her pouch, she made sure that the buzzing little clito tickler was firmly in place. Her mind filled with thoughts of the lovely lithe body of the English boy, Ben Fraunce, even more muscular than Timothy's, as she masturbated. Gasping, she came almost at once. As she was still in the throes of her orgasm, she pushed the greased pink dildo into her anus, groaning a little, then gasping in relief, as it sank into her rectum, and began to fuck herself hard with both shafts.

The black dildo rammed her womb neck, with the clito tickler doing its infernal work on her stiff nubbin, while the pink dildo filled her rectum, and she pushed it against her sigmoid colon, still thinking of Ben, and how sweetly his arse had squirmed, while she buggered him, and she came again. Lefthera brought herself to a third orgasm with the vibrators, imagining both phalluses buggering her anus at once, Timothy's and Ben's cocks beside each other in her rectum. Would boys like to do that? Of course they would, the lustful creatures! Looking at herself all the time in the glass, she then squatted on the floor, the vibrators still working in her holes, and twisted her legs, so that she could climax a fourth time, while sucking her own immaculately manicured toes.

That was her most tumultuous orgasm, and, when it was done, she showered, whistling a Greek lullaby, washed and dried the dildos, then stored them neatly away. Her self-worship done, it was time for the day's business. The

Greek Barber sounded an interesting proposition. A beauty salon, to make boys completely, perfectly naked! It would be owned by the Lacedaemonian Society, of course – had to be. Lefthera's money could pay the rent and set-up costs. And Ben would be on her payroll. That golden-haired slut-doll Lucy, too. But she and her Hymen Club would have to be put in their place. In fact, the Hymen Club must come under the domain of the Lacedaemonians. Then Lefthera would have even more power. When that was up and running, next summer vac, she had to get Ben to Greece, and make a real slave of him, one of her helots. Weekly sessions in the Iffley Road, with kettle boiling for tea, and the buses rumbling past, were all very well, but a boy needed to be enslaved naked on the sun-baked Greek land, with no escape, to taste the true life of a helot. Dr Rosalynn Demande, who craved buggery with Lefthera's strap-ons, could help there.

The end of the Michaelmas term came, and with it, the Christmas Vac, and Ben returned to Hereford with a caseful of books, for a cold, sometimes snowy, Christmas, gnoming in his room, and writing on his computer what he hoped might become his doctoral thesis. It was taking shape, a sort of unified field theory, though still inchoate: a study of slavery, cross-dressing, masturbation and anal sex in ancient Greece. His family said how well he looked; he had removed his nipple rings, until he returned to Oxford, and he wore no women's clothing except Dr Demande's pastel thong panties, which he discreetly washed himself, after masturbating daily into the gusset, for he did not think Lefthera's prohibition of wanking applied to Hereford. It was outside her Spartan remit.

There were Christmas cards too and, to his joy, from all the newfound girls in his life, and family walks in the snow. He enjoyed pints of ale and hot Worcester meat pies, with lots of brown sauce and Gloucestershire mustard. He met an old girlfriend named Pam, on whom he had once been sweet, and learnt, not without relief, that she was engaged to be married to a boy named Gavin. He looked up Louella Potts, thinking he might taste her tongue, smell her hair, and get a feel of her breasts and bottom, but Louella was skiing in Austria with some other boy, and presumably tasting *his* tongue, while *he* felt her bottom. Again, Ben felt a slight relief that he didn't have to bother. Wasn't it Dr Jowett who had said that we all admit to a feeling of relief when we get to a museum and find it closed?

Hereford Hellenic was shuttered for Christmas, when he went there in search of Elena Ramsey. So he contented himself with his pleasure of masturbation in front of the looking glass, with his nipple rings in, and Dr Demande's panties, and wanking off directly into the panties, still fragrant with her odour. He enjoyed a lavish family Christmas dinner, a lazy Boxing Day, and a rather drunken New Year's Eve, where there was a Scots piper – in fact a neighbour, from Glasgow, who was an accountant in a firm in Shrewsbury – piping in the haggis, which tasted remarkably good, with mashed turnips, although he eschewed the proffered toasts of whisky, in favour of a pint of ale. Pleading pressure of work, he was glad to escape back to Oxford, earlier than the start of term, shortly after the beginning of January.

'Cold for the time of year, sir,' said Perkins.

'It is, isn't it?'

'There's a message for you, sir, that came yesterday.'

Perkins handed him a flimsy blue envelope. It was a summons from Lefthera. Still in his overcoat and grey wool suit, he hurried to the Iffley Road.

Lefthera greeted him, nude, as was her custom, with the heating full on, for it was one of those delicious cold Oxford winter days, the earth bright with snow, and the cloudless sky azure.

'While you've been pigging out on your Christmas pud,' she said, playing with her nipple rings, 'I've been busy with our barbershop. I suppose you've been polluting yourself. Pulling your pud.'

Ben blushed.

111

'Don't deny it – I can see it in your face. And were there any girls, any disgusting gropings and fumblings and bottom rubbings and deep kisses?'

'No, mistress, there were not,' Ben said, not blushing now, for he was telling the truth.

'Not for want of trying, I suppose. Get your kit off, I'm going to thrash you for being absent, and for all the things you've done – wanking off – and all the things you probably tried to do, or dreamt of doing.'

Eagerly, though apprehensively, and gratefully, Ben obeyed. He stripped down to a pair of Dr Demande's red thong knickers, which Lefthera eyed quizzically.

'I know those panties,' she said. 'They are Rosalynn's.'

Ben admitted it was true.

'What have you been up to, you dirty little beast?'

Ben told her the whole story of his tryst with Rosalynn, before the Christmas vac, and how he had spanked her.

'You animal! I was going to whip you a dozen, but now I think I'll cane you two dozen, with my springiest wand. Bend over, no need to lower your panties, your moons are bare enough. I'll shred those panties, you dirty beast.'

'Yes, mistress,' Ben said, trembling in fear.

He listened to her hum a Greek lullaby, as she selected a cane from her rack, a willow wand, a full metre long, and about a centimetre thick, and swished the air with it, making a terrifying whistle.

'Of whom did you think, while you were masturbating, Ben?' she murmured. 'Of what naked girl?'

'Of . . . of you, mistress,' he blurted, not entirely without truth, though he had thought of imperious naked Rosalynn, and sweet flaxen-haired Lucy Parvis, too.

'And what was I doing, in your fantasy?'

'Whipping me. Buggering me. Sitting on my face, with your buttocks crushing me, and my nose in your anus. Then, making me wear your clothes, your smelly underthings, your stockings and dresses. Parading me round, for shame, dressed as a girl. And sometimes, making me wank off in public, with my arse bare, in my caning bloomers, showing my stripes from your whip.'

112

'What would you really, really like, Ben?' she drawled. 'What would make you a total man?'

'To be naked, stretched out, under the sun, and under a girl's whip. To be whipped by a girl for ever. To be dressed like her, and buggered by her. By you, mistress.'

'A good answer. There's hope for you yet, you snail.'

Vip! Her cane lashed Ben's bare buttocks. It seared his naked flesh with agonising pain, and he stifled a scream.

'That's one,' intoned Lefthera, lighting a Dunhill. 'Twenty-three to go.'

12

Winner Take All

Vip!

'Ahh!'

Ben squirmed, sobbed and shivered, as he took the two dozen from Lefthera's cane. It was one of the hardest, most painful canings he had ever taken, at Oxford or elsewhere. His naked arse was seared by unbearable white-hot lances of agony. And the witch – the sibyl, the priestess – took her time! Cruelly, she left a pause of eight or nine seconds between cuts, just time enough to allow the pain to sink in fully, then ebb a little, before a new stroke took him to further heights of suffering. Yet his phallus stood, rock hard. True to her promise, Lefthera placed her cuts so that Rosalynn's thong was lashed to shreds, the elastic waistband easily snapped, and at the thirteenth stroke of the cane, its tatters fell from his squirming bottom, leaving him helplessly naked. *Vip!*

'Uhh . . .'

'Silence, worm!' Lefthera hissed.

Vip! Ben's bare buttocks writhed in agony, under the nude Greek girl's fearful cane strokes. Lefthera wore nothing but a snakeskin belt, with a jewelled dagger poised in a loop, and a necklace of tiny seashells, which clinked delicately, as her body whirled, and her breasts bounced, with every lash to the boy's arse. Lefthera was panting slightly, as she put down her cane, after marking Ben's naked bottom so severely.

'There's work for you to do, Ben,' she said.

114

'Yes, mistress,' Ben said, choking back his sobs, for his flogged bare bottom was on fire from his beating, and the smarting seemed unbearable.

She smiled sympathetically, while rubbing her naked breasts against her ribcage, and massaging her stiff nipples.

'It never gets any better, does it, Ben? The thrashing, I mean.'

'No, mistress. It seems more and more painful, each time I'm flogged.'

Lefthera lit another cigarette, and threw the extinguished match to land on Ben's balls. He winced, but made no sound, as the hot phosphorus cinder sizzled on his skin.

'That's good,' she drawled blowing smoke over his bruised bottom. 'That's the way things should be. And now here's your task, helot. You'll work naked, of course, and under whip. The premises for the Greek Barber at Headington Hill are secured, and you and the other slaves will install the fixtures and fittings.'

She withdrew the long, springy jewelled dagger from her belt.

'Your bum's well blackened from my cane,' she said, 'but I think we want an overlay of tasty crimson. We must be colour-coordinated at all times.'

Ben bent over once more, and felt the flat of the dagger blade spanking his bare. After the agony of the cane, the blade was no more than a tickling, yet, after a hundred whops, he was sobbing with a different kind of pain, almost welcome: a crimson, not a black, pain. He was still erect, and Lefthera commented caustically on his phallic stimulation.

'Your bum's a pleasant colour,' she said, 'but you *are* a beastly worm. After a whipping, that horrible big phallus, still stiff! At least your balls and hillock are well shaven. I detest a hairy man. But now there's only one thing to do. I order you to masturbate, over my bare body. That will soften your phallus. In fact, just at the moment, I want to feel your come spurt all over my belly and teats.'

She parked a lit cigarette at the corner of her mouth, then lay down, parting her legs, rubbing her nipples, and showing him her glistening cunt lips.

'Isn't this what you like, Ben?' she said, pluming blue smoke. 'To wank off over a naked girl? Only I'm not a picture in a magazine. Begin the operation, slave, skin your helmet, and start rubbing. Remember, you must never touch me. Only your creamy hot spunk shall bathe me. It is an order. You are permitted to pollute yourself, on the order of a priestess.'

Ben knelt before Lefthera's open cooze, and began to masturbate.

'Let me see you work. Tickle the peehole, caress the neck of the glans, the corona and the frenulum. No hard rubbing. A delicate treatment.'

'Yes, mistress,' he panted, as he wanked off, gently rubbing himself.

At that moment, the doorbell rang.

'Rats!' said Lefthera, although not angrily, rather in amusement. 'It'll be the fellow from Trinity, I expect, or some other wretched snail.'

She got up, with a sly smile – for she could see how excited Ben was – draped herself in a white robe, and went to open the door, leaving Ben with his phallus in his hand, and a melting desire in his balls to achieve orgasm, and spurt his sperm over Lefthera's nude body. He wondered whether, in the Spartan cosmogony, there was some platonic difference between worms, snails and gastropods. To his astonishment, he heard Lucy's voice.

'Do come in, Lucy,' drawled Lefthera.

'We have some things to talk about,' said Lucy, angrily. 'The Greek Barber, I mean.'

Lucy was introduced into the chamber of punishment, where Ben stood naked and erect, his flogged bottom glowing with stripes.

'Oh!' she cried, putting her fingers to her lips.

Lefthera let her robe drop, and stood nude between Ben and Lucy.

'Yes, Lucy?' she said. 'I've just had to thrash Ben and, as you see, he has been wanking off. On my orders, naturally. He was just about to come all over my naked breasts.'

116

Lucy glowered.

'Oh! I'm sorry,' she blurted. 'But . . . look, Lefthera, the Greek Barber was my idea.'

'And it's my money,' Lefthera replied.

'Well, I want to be the managing director.'

'There's certainly a place for you in the Greek Barber,' said Lefthera, briefly caressing Lucy's golden tresses, and then her buttocks, a caress to which Lucy did not object. 'But I'm not sure if managing director is quite what I have in mind.'

'What do you have in mind?'

Lefthera stroked Lucy's bottom quite firmly.

'You would make an excellent service maid,' she said. 'At a good salary, plus tips.'

'A service maid!' Lucy gasped, her face darkening in anger.

'Yes! With a lovely frilly skirt, and bodice and everything, like a French maid.'

'You must be joking! Now come on, Lefthera . . .'

'I gather you've had your clito pierced,' drawled the Greek mistress. 'How brave of you! I have only had my nipples done, like sweet young Ben.'

Lucy coloured.

'And what of it? It's my clito.'

'Nothing, except it's perhaps a little odd for the virgins of the Hymen Club to have their clitos pierced. And that's another thing I want to tell you. I think it's time for the Hymen Club to merge with the Lacedaemonian Society. There are too many competing clubs in this city, and it confuses people.'

'Merge? How?'

'I mean, the Hymen Club becomes part of the Lacedaemonians. We take you over. You, Felicity, Abigail and the rest shall become Lacedaemonian virgins, under my direction, and that of High Sibyl Rosalynn Demande.'

'No way!' Lucy cried. 'I'd fight rather than give in. Why, if anything, it's the Hymen Club that should take over you beastly Spartans!'

Lefthera frowned.

'Then there may not be a job for you at the Greek Barber,' she said, with acid in her voice. 'And you need the money, Lucy, don't you?'

Lucy looked at Ben's erect phallus, then at his scarred bottom.

'Oh, Ben, what has she done to you?' she wailed.

'She's flogged me,' said Ben, rather sheepishly, 'and I've been ordered to wank off over her breasts. A man must obey his mistress, Lucy.'

'You said you'd fight, Lucy,' said Lefthera.

'Certainly! I would!'

'Then let's fight. Out in the garden. Take your clothes off, and we'll wrestle naked. Ben can be referee, to make sure neither of us fights unfairly.'

Lucy bit her lip, looking at Ben, who nodded his agreement.

'But it's all cold and muddy out there,' she said.

'Fighting will warm us up. Are you afraid?' sneered Lefthera, lighting a cigarette, and throwing the expended match to land on the exposed piss-stained glans of Ben's phallus.

'No!'

'Then get naked, and we'll fight. Mud enhances the contest. Makes things deliciously slippery. Winner take all.'

Lucy's eyes gleamed with fire.

'All right, Lefthera, you scheming bitch,' she said.

Lucy unzipped her short tartan skirt, and took it off, folded it decorously, and handed it to Ben; then took off her pink angora sweater, and unbuttoned her blouse, before removing it, to reveal her peach-coloured bra. When she was stripped to her peach nylon stockings, bra, suspenders and garter straps, she asked Lefthera if she was sure she wanted to wrestle completely nude.

'All proper wrestling is completely nude,' said Lefthera contemptuously. 'It's the Spartan way. Besides, you wouldn't want to muddy your skimpies, would you?'

'No, you're right. Very well, then. Let's do it. First to submit loses?'

'Agreed.'

Lucy unhooked her bra, letting her big bare breasts spring out, and handed the bra to Ben; then, took off her peach nylon petticoat, rolled down her peach nylon thong and stockings, undid her matching suspenders and garter straps, which made a popping noise as she unsnapped them, and, when she was in the full nude, handed all her underthings to Ben, asking him to take good care of them. As Ben stowed Lucy's clothing carefully, after sniffing and kissing her petticoat, and the gusset of her panties, Lucy followed the swaggering Lefthera into the walled garden, which was muddy and slippery. Lefthera took off her belt and dagger, and set them to one side.

'Well, Lefthera,' Lucy said, 'how shall we –'

She did not get time to finish her sentence, for Lefthera swung, and kicked her between the legs, right in her cunt, toppling Lucy, who cried out in agony. In an instant, Lefthera was on top of her, biting her nipples, and grinding her body into the mud. Lefthera's teeth were bared in a grimace of cruelty. Lucy wriggled, landing punches on Lefthera's face and breasts, but the Greek girl held her down, with her hand clamped between Lucy's legs, and cruelly masturbating her pierced clito. Ben looked on, helpless to intervene, and the morning cold did nothing to dampen his erection, as he gazed at the two nude girls, grappling in the mud, which came to cover their bodies. They were two naked primeval beasts, or Aphrodite and Demeter wrestling, in a sea of mud.

Lucy fought back bravely, and from time to time gained the upper hand, pummelling Lefthera in the crotch and breasts, pulling her muddied hair, and biting her nose and nipples and ears, until Lefthera screamed; yet the Greek girl was more vicious, and less merciful, less fair, than Lucy, and her kicks, gouges and bites were harder. Lucy's screams died down to long moans of agony, as Lefthera pushed her face into the mud, and began to spank her wet muddied buttocks. Buses rumbled outside, on the Iffley Road; it seemed strange to Ben that a heroic battle from ancient Greece should be taking place in this damp Oxford suburb. Lefthera ordered Ben to hand her the belt, and he

119

obeyed; Lefthera, her foot on Lucy's head, pressing her face to the mud, began a vicious flogging of her naked muddied bottom. Lucy wriggled and writhed under her whipping, but was helpless.

'Oh! Oh! I submit!' she wailed.

Lefthera ignored the submission. When she had given Lucy more than fifty strokes from the belt, she ordered Ben to hand her the dagger.

'No! No!' Lucy gurgled, under the mud, as Lefthera sliced off her golden tresses, right down to the scalp; Lucy was weeping. Lefthera carefully put her golden locks into an empty flowerpot.

'I accept your submission, Lucy. Cane her a dozen, Ben,' snapped Lefthera, rising, her nude body heaving, and dripping with the brown garden slime. 'From now on, Lucy, you call me mistress. Abigail and Felicity must do so too.'

Ben fetched the cane, took up a fencer's stance, and lashed Lucy's mud-slimed bare buttocks. *Vip!* Lucy howled in anguish. *Vip!* She began to squirm and wriggle, as Ben's muscular caning laced her naked fesses.

'Oh! Stop!' she begged.

'I'm sorry, Lucy,' Ben said. 'But an Oxford man must obey his mistress's orders. You are my friend, but Lefthera is my mistress.'

Vip! The cane lashed Lucy's squirming bare buttocks, with a muddy plopping sound, while she sobbed and howled. Lefthera returned, with an antique cutthroat razor, its handle of white pearl nacre, and, when Lucy had taken her dozen agonising cuts, ordered Ben to wash the cane of mud. As he did so, she shaved the remnants of Lucy's hair, until Lucy's skull gleamed completely bald. That done, Lefthera ordered Ben to complete his wank, over Lucy's shaven head. Lucy crouched in the mud, sobbing, while, after only a few strokes, Ben ejaculated his seed over her naked scalp.

'Ben, how could you?' Lucy sobbed.

'Orders,' Ben grunted, as he spunked over her. 'Oh! Oh! Yes! You are so beautiful, Lucy.'

Lefthera had the long green tube of a garden hose, and sluiced them both down, then took her own shower, until the three naked bodies, two female and one male, were glistening clean.

'Well,' she said. 'that's that, then. You've submitted, Lucy, so the Hymen Club is in my domain. You will inform Abigail, Felicity and the others, that they must come to make obeisance.'

'Yes, Lefthera, I mean, mistress,' sobbed Lucy. 'You've beaten me. Fair's fair.'

Lefthera ordered Ben to put the kettle on, and make them all a nice hot cup of tea, with plenty of sugar, then embraced her vanquished opponent, pressing their breasts together, and kissed her full on the lips, with her tongue in her throat.

'So you'll all be service maids at the Greek Barber,' she commanded.

'Yes,' Lucy said.

'And you'll obey.'

'I must. You have vanquished me, and I have submitted. My virgin friends must do the same. It is our lot.'

'You'll have lovely wigs, I promise. You'll look Greek. Like Helen of Sparta.'

'Thank you, mistress.'

Lefthera scooped Lucy's copious blonde tresses from the flowerpot, and held them to her breast.

'Tea's ready,' said Ben.

'May I have my clothes back, mistress?' said Lucy, as they returned to the house.

'But of course,' Lefthera replied gaily, as she secreted Lucy's blonde locks in her armoire, beside her canes. 'Unless . . . oh, I'm afraid . . . Ben . . . he is incorrigible . . .'

Ben served the two nude ladies their tea, with ginger-nut biscuits; he was already dressed in Lucy's peach-coloured underthings, her bra, petticoat and stockings, and his phallus was stiffening under the tiny gusset of her peach nylon thong.

'Well, you know, winner take all,' he said, blushing.

13

The Greek Barber

The Greek Barber was a success from the beginning. College men wanted to be shaved, smooth and clean, their nails manicured, their eyebrows plucked. Both Rosalynn and Sarah visited frequently, and approved. They amused themselves by donning a French maid's uniform and shaving a man's balls.

'So you built all this?' said the chap from Balliol to Ben.

'Most of it. We were under the whip, you know.'

Ben, and the fellows from Trinity, Univ, Wadham and Corpus, had laboured naked for a month, under the various lashes of Lefthera, Roxanna, Iphigenia and Cybele, to get the Greek Barber into shape. Coming from Hereford, Ben had certain skills in plastering, bricklaying, woodwork and plumbing, which he used to good account, although they did not save him from daily whippings on his bare buttocks or shoulders, as he worked as a helot, which they called him – or else worm, or snail, or gastropod – from the cruel Spartan girls.

'It's damn fine. Very sound place. It's good to find somewhere with a decent sauna, and where a totty gives you a manicure, and a pedicure, and shaves you clean. Body hair is such a no-no these days and a fellow can do his armpits and legs and whatnot, with a Bic razor, but it's impossible to shave your back, and so difficult to shave your own bollocks, ain't it? I mean, you have to peer down . . .'

'I know what you mean,' Ben said.

'Better have a totty do it for you. And more fun.'

'Yes.'

'I do like those peach-coloured thingies you're wearing. Girl's thingies, aren't they?'

'Yes, I suppose so,' said Ben, skirted and stockinged in the clothing he had claimed from Lucy, and wearing her bra, but without a blouse. 'But they're mine now.'

'You work here? You don't sound like a townie.'

'Not really. I'm reading Mods and Greats at the House. Here, I help out. I'm a member of the Lacedaemonians, you see. Sort of a slave. I have to do what the girls tell me.'

'Quite. Very sound.'

'Would you like another glass of champagne?'

'Sound move!'

Lucy, dressed in a French maid's uniform, with shiny black ten-denier nylon stockings – incongruous, perhaps, in the Greek Barber, but tasty nevertheless – was lathering the naked Balliol man's balls and phallus with scented foam, while she wielded a cutthroat razor, to rid him of unwanted hair; at the same time, Felicity was clipping his toenails, and Abigail shaved his chest and belly. Lucy's hair was now a short, thick blonde crop, *en brosse*, while Lefthera, prowling, as owner, wearing a white silk blouse, short black rubber skirt and sheer pink nylons of ten denier, sported a luxuriant blonde wig woven from Lucy's shorn tresses. Lucy pouted at Ben, wearing the peach frillies and stockings that had once been hers. She was not really angry, but quite proud that he wanted to look like her.

Several young Oxford men lolled nude, enjoying the same depilatory treatment, or else sweated in the sauna, or splashed in the cold pool, playfully slapping each other's bottom. There was a menu of treatments, at varying cost: manicure, pedicure, full-body shaving. Champagne and tea were on the menu, and the young gentlemen could enjoy a meat pie if they wished. There was standard treatment or deluxe, and most opted for the deluxe. There were extra 'private' treatments, too. Felicity, Abigail or Lucy would suck a man's phallus to orgasm, for quite a steep extra charge, and, if he wanted the girl to swallow all of his sperm, which most fellows did, there was an extra charge for that, too. Usually, that went on in the backroom.

'I'm doing my postgrad thesis on the poet Bion,' said the Balliol man.

'Ah, yes, Bion,' said Ben. 'I'm not sure if –'

'About 100 BC, born in Smyrna, Lydia, which is unfortunately no longer Greek, it's Izmir, in Turkey. There were a few ructions last century, and the remaining Greeks all got kicked out or murdered. I've been there. Heavens, it's shabby! Then Bion lived in Sicily. I have to sort all that out. There are only seventeen surviving fragments of Bion's Bucolica, mostly about love. He makes veiled references to the joys of wanking, too. Then he's been credited with the *Lament for Adonis*, a bit steamy, but there was a cult of Adonis, where Bion came from. He's described as a minor Greek bucolic poet. Isn't that a lovely thing to be? Wouldn't you like to be a Greek bucolic poet, and, furthermore, to be *born* a Greek bucolic poet, *always* to have been a Greek bucolic poet, and never to have been anything else?'

'Yes,' Ben said.

'Except a girl,' the Balliol man said. 'Sappho, for example. It would be sound to be a girl, just once in a while. Like Lefthera. I've known her, and her sister Zenobia, for quite a long time. I live most of the time in Greece, you see, on Mílos. The girls there are the most beautiful in the world. Olive skins, curly black hair, and they swim nude in the turquoise Aegean. No inhibitions, just as in the ancient days. I suppose we can only adulate, aim and hope. It would be so nice to be a girl, or at least to wear a girl's things. Where did you get that lovely outfit? In Greece, I often wear girls' clothes, you know, skirts and bras and blouses and petticoats and things, when I'm not simply naked. Either way, the Mílosians find it quite normal and healthy. I'm Timothy Dunton-Smythe, by the way.'

'Ben Fraunce.'

'*Enchanté.*'

124

'Stygia's boutique, in the Woodstock Road, is the place to get kitted out. It's not cheap, but Stygia's very understanding. She's sound. And –' Ben lowered his voice to a whisper '– she'll spank a fellow, on the bare, if he wants.'

'I say! Well sound! Sometimes a spanking is what a fellow needs. For the circulation, you see. I must check it!'

Lucy completed the task of shaving Timothy Dunton-Smythe's balls and hillock, and then shaved his legs, his breast and armpits. He was completely smooth, his tan bare body gleaming.

'That feels better,' he said, his phallus swaying half erect.

'Would you like a spanking?' Lucy said coyly. 'It's included in the deluxe price.'

'I say! I would, rather.'

Timothy turned to Ben.

'I suppose you've been spanked, old chap. Thing is, a spanking from a girl's hand, or even her whip, is sort of cleansing and invigorating, don't you find? Makes a new man of you.'

'Turn over, and present your buttocks,' Lucy ordered.

'What, here? In public?'

'Unless you want to pay for a private room. It's quite expensive.'

Timothy smirked.

'I'm man enough to take it in front of the other chaps. And I'm a bit short of ready cash at the moment, so I'll take it here, not in private.'

He turned over, and thrust up his naked arse. His muscular buttocks were tan and firm, and quivered slightly.

'Go on, then,' he said.

Lucy began to spank him on the bare. Her arm rose and fell, in a savage rhythm, as her palm cracked on Timothy's naked arse, and the other fellows chortled. Timothy's bare buttocks began to squirm under her spanking, and after fifty smacks, he was panting.

'Yes . . . that's good . . . but harder.'

'You can have the cane, if you like. Since you had the deluxe treatment, that's included in the price, too.'

'Oh! Yes, the cane.'

Lucy fetched a one-metre willow wand of bright-yellow wood, and the chortlers fell silent.

'This one?' she drawled, flexing it.

'Yes. Yes, I can take it.'

'You haven't much choice,' snapped Lucy. 'My hand is sore from spanking your bum, so I'm rather angry at you. Have another glass of champagne before I cane you, sir?'

'Yes, I rather think I need it.'

Ben served Timothy his champagne, and the naked boy gulped it quickly. Ben then made the rounds of the other customers, serving them champagne, which was sold by the glass, or else pint mugs of tea. Some of them ordered hot meat pies, heated in the microwave, with brown sauce, mustard and tomato ketchup. The Greek Barber made a tidy profit on selling champagne, tea and meat pies. When everyone was settled and served, Timothy's caning began. Lucy's willow wand flashed. *Vip!* It laid a dark crimson welt on Timothy's bottom, already pink from her hand spanking.

'Ahh . . .' he gasped.

Vip!

'Oh!'

Vip!

'Oh! Oh! Yes! Harder!'

Lucy's arm and thigh muscles rippled, as she caned the squirming naked boy two dozen savage stingers on his bare buttocks. Timothy's phallus was erect, throughout his flogging.

'Oh! Zeus, yes,' he moaned, as his buttocks clenched under Lucy's rod. 'Oh, that's good. Yes!'

Vip!

'Yes!'

Vip!

'Ahh! Good!'

Ben, in his peach frillies, shimmered among the watching naked college men, serving them champagne; they would receive their battels in due course, and were expected to pay cash. The Greek Barber did not take plastic cards. All

126

the boys – there was a chap from St John's, a chap from Univ, even chaps from St Cat's and Pot Hall – were erect, as they watched Timothy flogged. Cybele, Roxanna and Iphigenia moved discreetly among them, whispered about money, and put their lips around their stiff members. They began to deep-throat the shaven and manicured boys, taking their phalluses to their uvulas, after stroking and licking their hairless backs, balls and buttocks.

'Yes!

'Jolly good!'

'I say!'

'Oh!'

'It's almost better than wanking.'

'Spank me, won't you?

'You're on standard treatment, so that'll be extra.'

'You'll put it on my battels, won't you?'

All the naked and shaven college men wanted to be spanked. Lefthera said to Cybele that perhaps the back-room was a waste of space, for boys seemed to like being pleasured in public, in front of other boys. Exhibitionism was something in their makeup. The Spartans spanked the college men on the bare, and some of them – most enthusiastically, the St John's man – wanted the whip, too. The girls obliged, with a variety of hide whips, wooden canes or rubber quirts. Iphigenia, as cashier, kept track of things. Lucy inserted a black plastic phallus into Timothy's anus, motioned to Abigail, and Abigail began to bugger him with it, switching on the battery for its vibrating motion, as Lucy continued the flogging.

While the blonde-wigged Lefthera looked on, cigarette drooping at the corner of her mouth, Lucy took the strokes past thirty, with Abigail ramming the vibrating dildo into the boy's arse. At the fifty-third stroke, Timothy orgasmed, ejaculating a copious flood of white creamy sperm. Abigail removed the dildo from Timothy's rectum, and threw it to Ben, for cleaning. Lefthera looked on with approval, as the girls swallowed the college men's sperm, while masturbating themselves under their wet skirts and panties. There was no extra charge for that.

'How much would it be, for, you know, a bit of bumming?' said the Univ man, still erect, to Roxanna. 'I mean, er, putting my phallus up your lovely arse. You're a choice piece of shank, you know.'

'More than you can afford.'

'Try me.'

Roxanna whispered in his ear.

'Cripes.'

'But Cybele will do it for nothing. Provided there are two of you inside her at once.'

'Is that true, Miss Cybele?'

Cybele, lighting a cigarette, nodded yes. Her dark eyes were hooded with lust. There was a hurried conversation between the Univ man and the St John's man. Both had spunked, but both were newly erect, as Cybele raised her skirt, and lowered her green nylon string panties, to show her bare buttocks, which she parted. Her anus bud was wide, and her cigarette drooped from her lips. She took a last sip of her cup of tea.

'Take me, gentlemen,' she purred. 'My bumhole is yours.'

'Cripes.'

'All right, then.'

The St John's man was below Cybele, and the Univ man on top. First, the Univ man got his phallus deep in Cybele's arsehole, until she moaned in anguish.

'Sorry . . . I'm afraid I'm a bit big. I say, can you get in?'

'Yes, I think so.'

The St John's man pushed his phallus into Cybele's stretched bumhole, beside the erect phallus of the Univ man. Cybele groaned in agonised pleasure.

'Fuck me, both of you,' she hissed. 'Fuck my arse hard.'

'Tight fit.'

'Yes.'

'Can you manage?'

'I think so. I say, it doesn't feel bad.'

'No.'

Both cocks were tight, filling Cybele's rectum.

'Well, let's do the lady, as she desires. Regular strokes, like rowing on the Isis.'

'OK.'

Both males began to bumfuck Cybele, their cocks touching each other in Cybele's rectum, while Cybele, panties at her knees, masturbated her clito. Her face was knotted in a grimace of pain, as the twin phalluses filled her anal elastic to bursting. Roxanna watched, her skirt up, and blatantly masturbating herself on her white nylon panties gusset, which was staining with her quim moisture.

'All right?'

'Yes. Tight fit. How are you doing?'

'It's quite exciting, really. I say, you do have a knobbly cock.'

'And yours is no better.'

'Fuck me harder,' moaned Cybele. 'Oh, Zeus, I've never had my hole stretched so wide before. Yes! It's so good! Fuck me! Split me in two with your meat, you filthy helots.'

Her anus was stretched by the two stiff phalluses to the size of a grapefruit. Roxanna, masturbating, licked her lips, showing her pearl-white teeth. Her panties were soaking wet, as she rubbed her clito. The two males redoubled their efforts, fucking hard in Cybele's arse, and both came at the same time, filling Cybele's rectum with copious sperm, which bubbled, overflowing from her anal lips, while she brought herself off, with deft flicks to her clito. Roxanna, too, climaxed, her white panties darkly stained from her quim fluids. The St John's man and the Univ man withdrew their phalluses from Cybele's anus, with loud squelching plops.

'Two cocks in one arsehole!' said the St John's man. 'I've never done that before, not even at Harrow!'

'Nor I,' said the Univ man. 'But it wasn't bad, was it? We must do it again sometime.'

'That was a tight beating!' Timothy gasped. 'But it was so good!'

'Just like Mílos, eh?' drawled Lefthera.

'Not quite like Mílos, Lefthera, darling,' Timothy said. 'Nothing can be quite like Mílos. Those fellows had both their phalluses in one girl's bumhole. But that's nothing, in Greece. Mílos is different: it's antique, and a bit shivery.'

'We'll all be there this summer vac,' said Lefthera. 'And I'll make sure you shiver, helot. I'll never forget what you did to me before. Double buggery is the least you can expect.'

Ben was listening, with puzzlement on his face. Lefthera smiled cruelly.

'That goes for you, too, Ben, my lovely.'

As the spring came, and the flowers blossomed in Christ Church Meadow, the Greek Barber continued to do brisk trade. Men motored from London or Birmingham for their deluxe treatment; there were articles about it in the colour supplements, featuring photographs of the girls in their French maids' uniforms, and of Ben, in his peach-coloured skirt, nylons and bra. The establishment was decorously presented as a simple barber's shop, where girls wore sexy outfits, and boys wore girls' clothes, and the Sunday-newspaper readers thought it all a bit of a giggle, good wholesome English fun. But there was no mention of any sexual services, such as buggery or fellatio. Even so, Ben no longer minded what the people in Hereford would think. Oxford was liberation.

Rosalynn Demande, as High Sibyl of the Spartans, took to strutting in the nude – which, of course, pleased the naked boys – asserting her superior status over Lefthera and the other Spartan priestesses. Ben, a humble servant in his nylons, bra and panties, could see that this was irksome to Lefthera, and that the clash of wills would come to a head. Sure enough, one day, Rosalynn let fall a remark about Zenodotus of Ephesus, superintendent of the library at Alexandria, who produced the first critical edition of Homer, deleting doubtful lines, transposing others, making emendations, and dividing the *Iliad* and the *Odyssey* into 24 books each. Zenodotus's edition – knowledge of which is derived almost entirely from later scholia on Homer – was severely attacked for its subjectivity by later scholars, notably one of his successors at the library, Aristarchus of

Samothrace, who modified Zenodotus's work. Rosalynn was scornful of Aristarchus, and Lefthera flared up, saying that Aristarchus was a much better scholar than Zenodotus.

'Never!'

'You bitch!'

It was the work of a moment for the Furies, the sibyls of Sparta, to pinion their high priestess, and, since her body, rippling with muscle, was already (superbly and insolently) nude, to part her buttocks. Lefthera was already strapping on her monstrous black rubber dildo, while Iphigenia was administering a sound spanking to Rosalynn's naked buttocks. When Iphigenia's palm had tired, after well over six dozen spanks, Cybele took over with a short ashplant cane, and began to lash Rosalynn on the bare, cutting her naked arse flesh with deep crimson welts. Ben watched, as Rosalynn's whipped bare bottom squirmed, and her eyes were screwed tightly shut, in a grimace of agony, but, strangely, she did not cry out or protest at this treatment, as though she secretly wanted it. Rosalynn took three dozen cuts on her bare, from the little ashplant cane, but she only moaned, and then very slightly, in acceptance, not protest, when Lefthera's dildo brutally plunged into her anus, in one savage thrust.

'Ahh ... yes ...' Rosalynn gasped. 'Oh, you fucking bitch.'

Lefthera, cigarette drooping at the corner of her mouth, contemptuously thrust her hips, so that the strap-on dildo penetrated Rosalynn's rectum, filling her completely.

'Ahh ... more ... harder, you filthy slut ...'

As Lefthera buggered her, for over ten minutes, Rosalynn's hard-muscled bare buttocks pumped, and fingers were feverish at her clito, and she masturbated herself to two orgasms, before Lefthera withdrew the dildo from her anus. After that, Rosalynn knelt, and sucked Lefthera's sandal-clad toes.

'You luscious bitch,' she panted. 'I hate you so much.'

'I have money,' sneered Lefthera. 'That's why you hate me, and need me. You English worship money, because you don't have any. Money is the phallus, and the phallus is power.'

Her cigarette sizzled, as she stubbed it out in the sea of Rosalynn's sopping wet cunt, and Rosalynn groaned in delight.

14

Belles Fesses

It was the summer vac, and Ben was on his way to Greece, for the first time in his life. He had passed his prelims, then his Mods, with flying colours, and he had quite a lot of spending money, for he had made good tips in his girl's outfits, serving champagne and meat pies to the Oxford men at the Greek Barber. They thought him and his cross-dressing highly droll. They appreciated the chilled champagne, and the traditional homemade Bicester brown sauce. A touch of class, they said.

'Civilised people travel by train,' said Lefthera, at Charing Cross station. 'The *canaille*, the hordes of the unwashed, travel by air.'

'Yes, mistress,' Ben replied dutifully.

'And we've made so much money from the Greek Barber that we can afford to do it in style.'

Regal and haughty, her nose turned up at the *canaille*, Lefthera was in a business suit of white silk, with a pink blouse, high pink stilettos, from a fashionable designer, and pink nylon stockings of eight denier. She had a short pink petticoat which peeped cheekily from the hem of her white linen miniskirt. Carrying Lefthera's heavy suitcases, Ben wore a discreet blue outfit of linen skirt and nylon blouse, with powder-blue ten-denier nylon stockings, held by frilly suspenders and lacy garter straps, and sensible navy-blue court shoes. Lefthera said that was his helot's uniform – a slave's uniform. On this journey, and henceforth, he was her slave. He was not to address his mistress unless she addressed him first. If he offended his mistress, he would be soundly whipped, in addition to his daily, token caning of four strokes, which he was to take on his naked buttocks. That was to remind him of his enslaved status.

He loved the tightness of the suspender belt, and the slithery feel of the nylon on his thighs. It was July, and quite hot, as they boarded their first-class carriage at Charing Cross, on the train to Dover. There were a few raised eyebrows at Ben's transvestism, but they were appreciative and envious eyebrows. Dressing as a girl was something many of the grey-suited commuters secretly wished to do themselves. After crossing the Channel to Calais, they would take the TGV to Paris, first-class, of course; then the *Orient Express* to Venice; then, the slower train to Rome and Bari, still first-class; and the ferry *Lefthera*, owned by Lefthera's father, to Patras, and around the Peloponnese to Kithera and Mílos. On the ship, they would sojourn in a private cabin, away from the 'goatherds', as Lefthera put it.

At Dover Priory station, they took two taxis to the ferry port, one for Lefthera and one for Ben and all her trunks and suitcases. The sun was shining over the seafront and its tiny beach, with seagulls following their prey, the never-ending parade of giant ferries, like huge floating seabirds. The Seafrance ferry would be leaving in forty minutes; tickets obtained, and porters engaged, they went to the departure lounge, where there were not many foot passengers, as most of the traffic through Dover consisted of cars and trucks. In the tiny snack bar, Lefthera treated Ben to a plate of pea soup and a meat pie, with commercial brown sauce in little sachets. She had a glass of fruit juice, and a carton of yoghurt.

'I suppose this is quite an adventure for you, Ben,' she declared rather loudly.

'Yes, it is. I'm awfully excited. My first visit to Greece, mistress. I can't thank you enough.'

'You won't thank me, after you've been there a while. You're a helot, Ben. It will be tough. I'll give you four

134

strokes of my cane every morning, on your bare, just to remind you of your place. You'll be wearing a girl's thong, of course, so your bottom will be already bared, and thus you won't need to lower your panties. And you'll keep my canes and whips well oiled, as part of your slave's duty. Tell me, did you like it when I whipped and buggered you?'

Heads turned. There were Scotsmen, going over to buy cheap tobacco in Belgium.

'Yes . . . yes, I adored it, mistress, because it was from you.'

'Well, there will be more of the same where we are going. And worse. Remember, you are a slave.'

'Yes, mistress. I am proud to be your slave.'

'A lassie wi' a slave!'

Lefthera patted his nyloned thigh.

'Good boy,' she said, just before their ferry departure was called.

On deck, atop the churning ocean, Ben watched the white cliffs of Dover slide away, and, as they faded from view, almost at once there was the brown prominence of Cap Gris Nez. The summer day was pleasantly hot. Lefthera, smoking, joined him on deck.

'Put your fingers under my skirt and wank me off,' she coolly commanded. 'I always want a wank when I get close to France. Even if it's just northern France, which is a beery country, much the same as England. But it's connected to the wine and flowers of Provence.'

Ben felt his fingers oily from her warm wet cunt, as he massaged her clito, for over twenty minutes, and Lefthera lit cigarette after cigarette. She was wearing no panties, and, with his other hand, he stroked her bare bottom, his fingers running up and down her cleft, and brushing her anus bud. She stood with her buttocks slightly parted, to show that his caress, or adoration, was welcome. At last she came, gasping slightly, but not crying out in ecstasy, just as the ship nosed into the grey waters of the port of Calais, to a chorus of seagulls.

'Well! That was acceptable,' she said.

The high-speed TGV train from Sangatte whisked them to Paris in an hour, and they took taxis from the Gare du Nord, to claim their reserved room at the Meurice. Ben, as her slave, was to sleep with her, chastely (unless she chose to bugger him, which would in fact not infringe his chastity); he was servant and protector at once. His feminine attire raised no eyebrows, and in fact attracted haughty nods from Parisians wishing to show their extreme sophistication and tolerance. It was late in the afternoon, and Lefthera said they would have an early dinner, then visit the Club Acropolis in the Rue Vaugirard, which was owned by Christo, a friend of hers. She telephoned to confirm their reservations for the *Orient Express* to Venice the next day.

They both showered, with Ben ordered to soap and shave his mistress. He shaved her whole body, including her cunt hillock, although there was no more than a little down on her skin, for Lefthera kept herself perfectly shaved. She ordered him to get down on the floor, and give her forty press-ups, which he obediently performed, while Lefthera, a bare foot on his straining buttocks, played with her clito; then, she commanded him to wank her off once more, using his tongue. Panting, he knelt, in the hot hissing spray of the shower, and did so, bringing her off quite rapidly.

'Paris always does that to me,' she said distractedly.

He could not help becoming erect at the sight and touch of her nude body and the sweet taste of her quim juice, but he realised that her casual nudity now reflected his own slave status. He was no more than an animal – *her* animal – and she could be naked with him as she would with a pet dog. How he loved to be her pet dog, with his delicious sexual frustration, and his full balls, the measure of his happiness!

They dined at Chez Pol in the Boulevard St-Michel, which Lefthera said was overrated, but she couldn't be bothered to think of anywhere else. Pol came from Concarneau in Brittany, and specialised in Breton seafood, so they gorged on mussels and lobster, washed down with a decent Muscadet. Ben was now in a fresh blue slave's costume, a miniskirt, blue stockings, bra and blouse, but a very dark navy blue, while Lefthera had changed into a brown blouse, black jacket, black nylons and brown rubber miniskirt, so short that her stocking tops and garter straps were visible, as was, fleetingly, her naked minge, for she still wore no panties. Ben wore his nipple rings under a peephole bra; he had to sit beside Lefthera on a banquette, for she would not let a slave dine facing her.

Nor could he order his own food. Lefthera ordered several dishes, and fed Ben with scraps from her plate, to the amusement of the other diners. After their meal, they strolled along the Seine, opposite Notre Dame cathedral, with Lefthera's hand idly cupping Ben's buttocks, as though to prevent him from escaping. Ben supposed they must look like two lesbians, but Paris did not seem to be short of those. They stopped in various crowded cafés, and Lefthera drank champagne, with Ben allowed an occasional sip from her glass, until it was time to taxi to the Club Acropolis.

The club was quite full and smoky when they arrived, but Christo, a tall bearded Greek man, naked to the waist, but for gold neck chain and nipple rings, and wearing skin-tight black leather trousers, welcomed Lefthera with a kiss, and long-lost greetings in Greek. He said to Ben, in French, that he looked very pretty. The club was decorated like a Doric temple, but in black velvet, rubber and leather, and with various apparatuses positioned both around the walls and on the tiny stage, which seemed quite sinister to Ben's eye. In fact, they looked like machines of torture, whipping frames, gibbets, racks, and devices for trussing the body and the like. There was a rack of whips and canes, all lovingly polished and gleaming. The customers were mostly young, although there were some white-haired gentlemen accompanied by girls of tender years, and most favoured dark clothing, black being predominant. Many dressed in leather or latex, and both men and women had painted their eyes dark with mascara. Christo

137

ushered them to a table near the stage. Lefthera ordered champagne, which arrived promptly, in a silver ice bucket, and she permitted Ben to have his own glass. Christo said the show was about to start.

A sinuous bouzouki music began to play, and a naked, full-breasted black girl, with cropped curly hair and golden nipple rings swinging from her pierced nipples, big and plump on very full, jutting breasts, sprang on to the stage, carrying a candelabra with eight lit candles, fat and red. Her navel was an outie, a hard, plump plum extruded from her flat belly, and that too was pierced, with a small golden ring dangling. She was followed by a naked blonde, also with nipple rings, and with very long, flat tresses that brushed the tops of her buttocks. Both girls had very full, voluptuous bottoms, and shaven hillocks. The black girl bared her teeth, and pulled the blonde by the hair, very hard, so that the blonde squealed, as she was forced to a crouching position. Still clutching the blonde's hair, to keep control of her, the black girl upended her candelabra, so that hot wax from the candles began to drip on to the blonde's naked breasts.

The blonde began to whimper, as her tormentress poured scalding wax all over her nude body, twisting her by her hair, so that she could aim at her buttocks, her belly, and then forcing her to part her thighs, so that she could pour the hot wax into her naked quim, which the blonde held open by the cunt lips. The black girl was masturbating her hugely extruded pink clito as she performed the torture, and the blonde was sobbing and crying; yet, she was masturbating, too, her own clito stiff, under its sheath of wax. The lion's share of the wax went to her buttocks, coating her arse cleft and anus.

'*Non ... arrête ... ça fait mal ... ah non ... je t'en prie ...*' she whimpered, as she wanked off, with her quim and anus full of scalding red wax.

The black girl ignored her protests, and continued to drip the candles over the crying girl, until her body was encrusted in a carapace of solidifying red wax, her bottom like the flesh of a bright-red melon. Then she dragged the blonde girl to a whipping gibbet, and strung her by her wrists, so that her toes dangled just off the floor. The black girl gestured to the rack of flogging implements, and, still masturbating her own clito, invited the audience to help her choose one. She touched each of the whips and canes, until she received enthusiastic cheers, and took down the selected implement, a long hide horsewhip.

With that, her legs parted in athlete's stance, she began to flog the strung blonde girl, shredding the crusted red wax, with special attention to her waxed buttocks. The squirming blonde sobbed and screamed. The aim of this show was to cleanse the girl's body of its wax coating, and the black girl would whip her until her body was clean. Now, a third actor entered the stage: a naked young man, Greek-looking, with black curly hair on his head, but the rest of his sleek, muscled body completely hairless, and a massive erection of his huge shaven phallus. He positioned himself behind the black girl, wielding her whip, as the blonde shrieked and wriggled, and parted her muscled ebony fesses. The black girl grunted, as his phallus penetrated her anus – with a second thrust, she groaned, and his phallus sank into her, right to his balls – and he began vigorously to encule her, his balls slapping her ebony fesses.

'*Ah, oui . . .*' the black girl moaned, but keeping her whipping arm steady, as the young male enculed her. '*Oui, plus vite . . . oh, que tu es grand, oh, que c'est bon . . .*'

Her masturbating fingers acted faster and faster on her clito, her open cooze dripping with come.

'*Ah! Je jouis! Ah, oui!*' she cried, as she shuddered in orgasm.

The male, apparently, did not himself orgasm, but removed his phallus from the black girl's anus, and took the whip from her hands. He resumed the flogging of the well-striped blonde, while the black girl disappeared into the shadows, to emerge with an enormous pink rubber dildo strapped to her loins. Now it was the young man's turn to be enculed. Expertly, the black girl parted his buttocks, placed the dildo in his cleft, and penetrated his anus. She began to thrust savagely, plunging the dildo to its full length, right into his rectum. He groaned, gritting his teeth, but his phallus was hugely erect, and he continued to whip the sobbing, shrieking blonde, her body now almost free of wax, and with massive crimson welts all over her naked back and buttocks.

The audience was entranced, many couples openly and lustfully caressing each other. One young man dragged his girlfriend by her mousy-brown hair on to the stage, and ripped her white blouse and red rubber miniskirt from her. In lemon-yellow bra and panties, she was clamped face down in a medieval torture rack, and her body winched to the full, stretched limit of its endurance, while she groaned, sobbed and sometimes screamed. Then her boyfriend selected a cane, and began to flog her bottom, until her panties were shredded, and her bare buttocks cruelly wealed. Then, with his girlfriend still strapped and groaning in the rack, he enculed her. When he released her, she knelt, sobbing, to lick his phallus, taking his shaft to the back of her throat, and tonguing him to ejaculation, which she swallowed, while masturbating her clito to her own climax. This occurred while the black girl was still enculing the Greek boy.

Lefthera sipped her champagne, and ordered Ben to remove his blouse and bra, and display his nipples. As he was buggered by the black girl, the young Greek man's phallus shuddered, and spurted sperm over the blonde's whipped buttocks. He laid down the whip, and a young woman from the audience, bare-breasted, in a blue rubber micro-skirt, leapt on to the stage, knelt by the buttocks of the strung, sobbing blonde, and licked all the sperm from her squirming fesses. The blonde was released from her bonds, and promptly crouched before the male who had whipped her, to take his flaccid phallus into her mouth, and tongue him anew to full rigidity. Lefthera ordered Ben to go on stage, and kneel, with his skirt lifted and panties down, to present his buttocks to the black girl. Trembling, Ben obeyed, aware that he had a full erection under his skirt. He knelt, lifted his skirt and took down his thong, showing his erect phallus to the audience, and then his bared buttocks. The black girl pinioned him by pushing a cane through his nipple rings. Her own nipple rings jangled as she did so.

The applause from the audience was some consolation, as he winced, feeling her dildo penetrate his anus. The black girl took a cane from her rack, and dealt him twenty rapid, contemptuous strokes on the bare, bringing tears to his eyes. Then, she began to fuck him vigorously in his arse, with her dildo, while the blonde tongued the young Greek, and the bare-breasted girl licked the blonde's cooze as she did so. Others from the audience began to invade the stage: naked boys, and naked girls, all performing a dance of debauchery, as Ben groaned, under his arse fucking by the black girl. The air rang with the dry crack of canes and whips on naked buttocks, as the victims groaned in bondage, gagged and tied and clamped by nipples, cunts or foreskins. Christo discreetly circulated, a contented smile on his lips, as he served bottle after bottle of champagne.

Lefthera ordered Ben to masturbate, and his hands went to his phallus, to rub his shaft, drawing his foreskin fully back from his swollen crimson glans. In a short while, his hands were pushed aside, and a small dark-haired girl, in the nude, took his phallus into her mouth, as he was being enculed by the black girl. A naked boy had his phallus in her anus, as she sucked Ben. Suddenly, Lefthera was on the stage beside him, her rubber skirt lifted, and her pantiless bottom exposed. Ben watched, groaning under buggery, as Lefthera was mounted by a young stiff boy, and her cooze filled by his massive cock. He fucked her vigorously from behind and, when he had filled her womb with sperm, another boy took his place, this time to take her in the anus.

Lefthera masturbated, as she was fucked and spanked by a succession of naked boys, bringing herself to orgasm several times, when she was enculed, or was sucking and swallowing a full load of *sperma*. Yet, in her deliberate acceptance of degradation, she somehow radiated power and mastery. Ben could hold back no longer, and, under the black girl's buggery, he spurted his sperm into the dark-haired girl's mouth. Then, Lefthera was herself strung to the gibbet, and flogged by the black girl. After Lefthera had taken thirty strokes of the cane on her squirming bare buttocks, the black girl penetrated her rectum with the dildo that had fucked Ben's arse, and enculed her, while the dark-haired girl who had swallowed Ben's sperm tongued Lefthera's clito, until Ben's mistress howled in orgasm.

The evening continued thus, sated participants relaxing with champagne, while they watched fresh players. While Lefthera was being fucked onstage, the black girl came to join Ben at his table to quaff some champagne. Her name was Neobule, and she was from Guadeloupe. Ben's French was adequate, though less than perfect, but he felt he had to make the effort, with this stunning nude black girl, sitting unconcernedly beside him.

'You are very beautiful,' Ben stammered, 'and very cruel.'

'*Merci bien, monsieur*,' said Neobule. '*C'est un vrai cirque ici, n'est-ce pas?*'

Ben agreed that it was a circus.

'Did I hurt you?' Neobule asked.

Ben said that she had hurt him a lot.

'Good. It is healthy for a pretty boy to be hurt. Especially a boy with beautiful buttocks, *les belles fesses*.'

'I don't think anyone could have such beautiful fesses as yours,' he stammered.

'Why, thank you.'

Close up, with her naked, ringed breasts almost in his face, Neobule was devastating. Her black breasts pointed like big soft cannon shells, the nipples huge and pointed, big brown pillows of desire. Under his skirt, he was erect again. She said that she liked his nipple rings; hers were gold, and Ben explained, not without smugness, that his were antique Greek bronze.

'It is so nice to see a beautiful young man who has the courage to a wear a girl's clothing,' Neobule said. 'And properly shaven, a clean body.'

'I am a slave, you see. I have to do what my mistress orders.'

'Your mistress is enjoying herself,' said Neobule, nodding at Lefthera, who was crouching onstage, with two naked young men buggering her simultaneously, their cocks stretching her anus to the size of an orange. 'Two phalluses in her arse! That shows courage, too. Do you encule her?'

'Well, no. She encules me,' Ben said, and Neobule laughed.

'Not two cocks at once, I hope,' she said. 'Or would you like that? I do.'

Ben said he was used to the strap-on dildo. Coolly, Neobule slid her hand up his thigh, under his skirt, and pushed aside his thong panties, for her fingers to embrace his naked phallus. She smiled, her white teeth dazzling, as she began to masturbate him, with deft, practised strokes, her fingertips caressing his peehole and glans.

'Oh . . .' Ben moaned, and lowered his head, to kiss her nipples, taking each nipple ring into his mouth, and sucking the soft brown dome through which it was pierced.

Neobule's soft fingers sent ecstasy through the helmet of his phallus – they were so loving, so gentle, and it was hard to believe this girl was so expert with a whip – and it was not long before he spurted sperm into her welcoming palm. Neobule removed her hand, brimming with Ben's come, from beneath his skirt, and rubbed the cream into her dark bare breasts.

'That's better, isn't it?' she said. 'Now, what are your plans?'

He explained that they were to take the *Orient Express* to Venice, and then proceed to Greece, and Neobule said it sounded very romantic. She would love to visit Greece.

'Come with us, then,' Ben blurted. 'I'm sure my mistress won't mind.'

Neobule lit a Gauloise, and blew smoke, musing that she would think about it. At that point, the nude blonde girl, whom Neobule had flogged, shyly asked if she might join them. Ben said yes. He supposed his mistress wouldn't mind, and the girl, whom Neobule introduced as Niobe, sat down, grimacing as her whipped bottom touched the seat, for her whole body, including her breasts, was well striped with welts. She held hands with Neobule. Niobe was from Papeete, in French Polynesia. She thought France was rather cold, after the balmy Pacific, but she had a special friend in Neobule. Neobule wiped some of Ben's sperm from her breasts, and rubbed it into Niobe's nipples, and some on her bare arse, into her arse cleft and anus bud. Niobe cried that she would have a sticky bumhole.

'I love Niobe for her big white bottom,' the luscious ebony girl said teasingly. 'So round, so firm, so spankable.'

'You really laid it on hard tonight, Neobule,' the lovely whipped blonde said coyly.

'Well, that's what you like, isn't it?' said Neobule.

'You know I do,' said Niobe, blushing.

'How would you like to visit Greece?'

'I'd love it so!' she cried.

At last, Lefthera, who had taken a dozen men in her anus or cunt, had sucked off several more, and had several spankings and whippings of her naked bottom, said that it was time to go, for they had to catch the *Orient Express* the next day. She gave a big kiss to Christo, and thanked him for a lovely evening.

She and Ben taxied back to their hotel, and they showered together, with Ben rubbing unguents and liniments into Lefthera's bruises. Putting on a sheer black nylon nightie, she ordered Ben to lick her toes, while she masturbated, with her nightie up around her breasts. Ben obeyed. When Lefthera had brought herself to a satisfying climax, she rolled down her nightie, and told Ben he was to sleep naked on the carpet, while she occupied the double bed.

'Now, Ben,' she drawled, 'you're probably expecting me to order your silence on what you've seen and done tonight.'

Ben promised not to breathe a word.

'On the contrary. You are free to babble about what I've done, and, of course, what you've done doesn't matter, for you're a mere slave. But a true mistress has no shame in what she does. In fact, my acts tonight at the Club Acropolis were an expression of my power. Daddy knows what I do, and he knows I am still a virgin. I have the power of cunt virginity. *Paris vaut une messe,*' Lefthera said to Ben, as they went to sleep. 'It's the sacred city of light.'

15

Orient Express

Ben's drudge uniform of slavery – blue skirt, blouse and stockings – matched the livery on the *Orient Express*. It was very hot, and he sweated in the bustle of the Gare de Lyon, carrying his mistress's bags to their compartment. Lefthera had ordered him to wear his nipple rings at all times. The heaviest suitcases were those containing books for Ben to read during the summer vac, for, at Oxford, they expected you to study during the vac. Rosalynn had been most insistent on that. There were Lefthera's books, too, for her ongoing work on the poet Stesichorus. Another heavy suitcase contained whips, canes, a selection of wigs and strap-on dildos. There was also Lefthera's Bullworker isometric machine, for muscle building. Lefthera was concerned to keep her belly flat, her thighs, buttocks and breasts hard.

Before they left England, Lefthera had obliged Ben to shave her head clean, along with her pubis, and the rest of her body, and now she wore her blonde wig of Lucy's hair, sporting it like a battle trophy, and looked stunning, impeccably cool, in a translucent cream silk blouse, almost transparent, which showed her braless, gold-ringed breasts to good, aggressively teasing effect, and clung tantalisingly to her bare ringed nipples; shiny cream glassine eight-denier nylons, and a tiny skirt of pleated cream silk, itself almost transparent, with a frilly white gossamer petticoat, caressing her thighs, the hems of the garments scarcely lower than her pubis.

The skirtlet and petticoat allowed a blurred, tantalising vision of her suspender apparatus in vivid crimson, around her cream-pantied quim, in its tiny thong, which Ben had dutifully shaved, along with her head and armpits – longing to kiss those forbidden, tempting places – before their hotel breakfast. Her ensemble was completed by crimson designer shoes with high stiletto heels, and a crimson designer handbag, perfect matches for her glimpsed suspender belt. A dream in cream and crimson. Ben was made proud by the lustful glances his mistress attracted. He was glad to have sensible court shoes, not teetering stilettos like Lefthera's, otherwise he would be hard put to act as drudge.

He had not had his hair cut for a long time, and it had grown long, like a girl's. Lefthera had even pinned it back from his brow with a cheap blue plastic hair slide. It was clear who was mistress, and who was slave, and Ben was fiercely proud of that, too. He hoped Lefthera would encule him again soon, or at least give his bare arse a sound thrashing, not just the few token cane strokes he took before breakfast, almost as one of Lefthera's afterthoughts.

The *Orient Express* was designed for luxury, the best food and wines, and obsequious service to its rich passengers. Their compartment had a private shower, and twin bunk beds, made as luxurious as possible, given the cramped space. There were flowers in the room, and a complimentary bottle of champagne. At the last moment, she sent him to the station pharmacy to buy condoms. They had to be flavoured: strawberry, banana, raspberry, anything would do. And they must be the largest size, and lubricated. In his girl's kit, Ben performed his duty, getting a smirk from the lady pharmacist, who thought they were for him. Perhaps they were. He hoped so.

The train rolled out of the station, snaked through the grey eastern suburbs of Paris, and then was humming across the flat green plains of the Seine-et-Marne, now, in summer, blossoming with poppies, honeysuckle and hyacinth. Soon, Lefthera said, it would be time for luncheon.

She generously tipped the maître d', to assure herself the best table in the dining car, and explained that her servant would be eating with her, but must not sit facing her. In fact, Ben could sit at the table behind her, or even squat on the floor, and accept scraps from her plate. The official, ogling Lefthera's coolly exposed body, under her scanty raiment, pretended not to raise his eyebrows, and with Lefthera's hefty tip in his pocket, urbanely assured her that madame's wishes were paramount.

Lefthera made no secret of her strong, tautly muscled thighs, exposed almost fully by her crossing and uncrossing her legs. Her thighs were big and superbly formed, promising delights unimaginable, at their glimpsed apex. The official brought the luncheon menu to her apartment, and, when he had departed, bowing, and staring at Lefthera's thighs, she ordered Ben to uncork the champagne, while she studied the menu. He obeyed, pouring his mistress a flute of champagne, and lighting a cigarette for her.

'This looks good,' she drawled. 'Pressed duck à la mode de Caen! Salmon fillets en croûte! Catalan fish soup! Escargots en persillade! Yum! I think I've time to thrash you, Ben, before luncheon. The exercise will give me an appetite. Select a small cane from my case, then bare your bottom for it.'

Ben's heart beat fast at the knowledge that his mistress cared about him enough to thrash him. He selected a yellow willow wand, and presented it to her, glad of her approval, then crouched, with his skirt up and panties down to his knees. Lazily, Lefthera dealt him twelve agonising strokes, smoking and sipping champagne in the trembling ten-second intervals between cuts. *Vip! Vip!* Clickety-click! *Vip! Vip!* The rhythm of her flogging matched the rhythm of the rails. Ben's phallus was erect, and Lefthera laughed at him, saying he was incorrigibly lustful. His eyes blurred with tears, for her strokes were incredibly painful, and he could not stop his beaten naked bottom from squirming, but was glad that seemed to amuse her too.

As he took the twelfth cut, with tears streaming from his eyes, his bare bum clenching frantically, and his face wrinkled in pain – he was worried that a chance cut from Lefthera's cane might split the waistband of his frilly suspender belt – the restaurant man passed through the corridor, announcing that luncheon would now be served. After smoothing his skirt and hair, and making sure his suspender belt and garters were intact – they were – and that his pale-blue nylons had no ladders, and that he looked sufficiently pretty, with his long hair swept back by his plastic barrette, Ben followed his mistress to luncheon, as the train passed Nogent-sur-Seine.

Lefthera was seated by the fawning maître d', and allowed her skirt to ride up, almost to her garter belt, giving him another eyeful of her superb thighs. They were what the French called 'casse-noisettes' or nutcrackers. Ben ogled his mistress's long legs and powerful thighs, with an occasional glimpse at her cream thong nylon panties, and thought that a man could be trapped inside there, his phallus locked in one of her secret nether holes, without any hope of getting out, nor any wish to do so. Her olive skin, beneath the cream stockings, made the hose deliciously flesh-coloured. A woman's thighs, built to trap a man, and make him willing to be trapped. He longed to kiss those powerful nude brown thighs, lick them and suck them, as he did her feet, worship her in that way. And to press his lips to her cunt – *that* would be worship beyond worship, ecstasy beyond ecstasy!

Lefthera ate everything that had excited her on the luncheon menu: snails in garlic sauce, salmon in pastry, pressed duck in its own juice. She had a selection of good red wines. Of course, none of it was cheap, but, when waiters sense that a customer is prepared to spend money, and wants to eat well, rather than economise, they are the most servile creatures on earth. Ben, sitting behind her, was thrown scraps of salmon and duck, a few snails, doused in sauce, and was permitted to enjoy a glass of a rather good Médoc. He bristled when a handsome, muscled young boy, with long curly hair – Italian by the looks of him, and who, like Lefthera, had the sleek and arrogant beauty of the easily moneyed, though he was slim, a head smaller than Lefthera herself – begged Lefthera's permission, in French, to join her, and perhaps he could offer her coffee and liqueur. Lefthera readily assented, crossing her thighs, with a delicious slither of nylon stocking, and giving the boy the smile Ben had hoped to have for himself. The boy's rosebud lips returned her smile, and his body, especially his tight buttocks, swayed in perhaps unconscious delight, at the spectacle of her shimmering stocking. Ben saw the definite hint of an erection. But she drawled, in French that he did not look old enough to purchase a liqueur.

'I am eighteen, on my last birthday,' he said, blushing. 'Here, I show you my ID card.'

Lefthera inspected it.

'Well, well. Guido Frasconi, from Padua,' she said. 'Do I know you?'

'My father owns the Frasconi factory, in Mestre, not far away. That is why I am going to the Stazione Santa Lucia in Venice, across the lagoon. Padua is not far, but it is better for living. In Mestre, we make belts, buckles and buttons. Leather jackets, ladies' undergarments and other things. Um, intimate things. Things for sexual pleasure. Harnesses, straps, and rubber and leather *godemichés*. Dildos, you know.'

'I do know.'

'We sell a lot in Japan.'

'Yes, you would. If you are from Padua, you will be familiar with Giotto's marvellous frescos in the Scrovegni chapel. They are my favourites.'

'Naturally.'

'Well, then, you may indeed buy me a coffee and liqueur.'

Ben was astounded, for Guido looked just like a younger, slimmer version of himself. The boy was elfin, feminine. Guido cast him a look, with raised eyebrows and a quizzical smile.

'Is that a girl?' he said.

150

'Of course not,' said Lefthera, in Italian, which Ben could understand slightly, thanks to his Latin. 'Can't you tell? He is a boy, my slave. I dress him as a girl, to shame him. It is our Greek way.'

'I see,' said Guido. 'Of course . . . yes . . . it's just that he is very pretty, almost as pretty as you, *signora*.'

'*Mille grazie*,' said Lefthera, her lips curling in amusement.

Glasses of Strega with espresso coffee and little dishes of sweet biscuits arrived for both Guido and Lefthera. Ben expected, and got, nothing, except when Lefthera threw him a sugary biscuit, which he gnawed gratefully. It was not long before Guido was stroking Lefthera's hand, on the starched linen tablecloth.

'*Bella signora*,' he murmured, in a rather smarmy fashion. 'There is a long night ahead on this train. Why should we not make each other happy?'

'You are very young to be so forward,' drawled Lefthera. 'However, you do not displease me. I expect you to pay for champagne.'

'But of course!'

'Very well, then. We shall adjourn to my apartment, and drink some. Then we shall see if we are able to please each other, in some way. Ben! Order three bottles of champagne for me, and bring them on a tray. On Mr Frasconi's bill.'

Guido smirked as Ben went about the simple chore, and he followed Lefthera to her compartment, whither Ben shortly followed. When he entered, Guido had his hand up Lefthera's skirt, and was stroking her nylons, at her stocking tops or even nearer the string enclosing her quim, by the looks of things. Lefthera was smoking a cigarette, and did not seem to object, any more than she would object to the buzzing of a gnat. Guido, however, was obviously, frustratingly, erect. He watched with some irritation, as Ben took his time uncorking and pouring the champagne into crystal flute glasses. Lefthera and Guido clinked glasses; Lefthera swallowed her flute at one gulp, and signalled for another. When Ben had poured it, she said he could take one himself.

'Thank you, mistress,' Ben said, with a curtsy.

'Now sit somewhere, and don't interrupt,' Lefthera said vaguely.

Guido looked astonished.

'He is going to stay here?' he gasped.

'Of course,' said Lefthera frostily. 'It is his room, too. Surely you are not shy of a pretty boy in a girl's frock, Guido?'

'No ... no ... of course not ... it's just that ... I thought we could be alone.'

'We shall be alone, Guido. Ben is just a slave, and doesn't matter. He scarcely exists. Perhaps you are unfamiliar with the philosophy of Parmenides. There is only one being, and it is motionless. Motion, you see, is an illusion. We think we are moving across France on this train, but that is an absurdity, as proven by the paradoxes of Zeno. You don't get it? Well, no matter. Now, I suggest you take off your clothes. I would like to see you naked, to see what sort of being you are, before I decide whether to make love with you. I wish, in particular, to ascertain the dimension of your phallus, before removing my panties, to judge if it is worthy to fuck me in the anus. Ben! Take Mr Guido's clothing, and fold it neatly.'

Grinning sheepishly, but with a certain insolent pride, Guido stripped. To Ben's surprise, he too wore a girl's thong, a red nylon sliver. When it came off, and the boy was fully nude, his phallus was risen to monstrous rigidity. His pretty body, olive like Lefthera's, was hairless and sleek, and his pubis, legs and arms were perfectly shaven. Lefthera tapped the bell end of his phallus, pulled back his foreskin, right to the neck of the glans, and whistled, as she stroked his frenulum.

'That *is* impressive,' she said.

Ben's heart ached. He could see lust in his mistress's eyes, lust that he wanted to be kept for him! The events at the Club Acropolis had not mattered – they were just a game, played by an excited crowd, in the heat of the moment – but this was in the quiet space of their own room. He obeyed, though, without a word, when his

152

mistress ordered him to pour more champagne. He obeyed, too, hoping she could see the jealousy and sadness in his eyes, when she ordered him to unbutton her blouse, and unzip her skirt, then roll down her panties. Ben obeyed, heavy of heart, waiting for his beloved mistress to be fucked by another male. Lazily, Lefthera stepped out of her discarded clothing, leaving Ben to fold and stow it, and stood smoking a cigarette, in the nude, but for her nylons and suspender belt. Casually, she rubbed her nipples, until they were stiff. Moisture glistened at her shaven cooze flaps.

'Well, Ben, what are you waiting for?' she snapped. 'Strip off, you beastly slave girl.'

Ben's heart raced. He was going to play some mysterious part in this strange scene! Carefully, he unrolled his nylons, took off his skirt, peephole bra, through which his nipple rings poked, and his blouse, and was soon as naked as Guido, with his phallus just as rigid.

'Bend over, and touch your toes, Ben,' she said. 'You've been a sloppy servant today, and Guido is going to cane your bare bottom for it.'

Gasping in horror, Ben nonetheless obeyed promptly. To be caned by his mistress's new lover – by a boy, of whom he was already jealous – was shame indeed! Guido's white teeth were bared in a rictus of cruelty, as he lifted the cane over Ben's spread bare bottom. *Vip!* He brought down the rod, and lashed Ben squarely in mid-fesse, making his buttocks jerk in a frenzied clench. *Vip!* His nipple rings jangled.

'Ahh . . .' Ben grunted.

'Silence, worm,' snapped Lefthera.

Her hands were on her stiff pink clito, exposed between the spread lips of her naked cunt, and Ben saw she was masturbating. *Vip!* Ben suppressed his gasp of agony, as the cuts rained on his naked buttocks. Through the blur of his tears, he saw that the elfin Guido was still massively erect, as though he took some obscene or youthful pleasure in this barbaric ritual. Yet Ben himself was erect; the thrill of the pain searing his bare flesh, and his desire to expose himself to the nude haughty Lefthera, had the effect of exciting him sexually. *Vip!* Guido took the savage caning to fifteen cuts, until Lefthera drawled that it was enough.

'I suppose you had *both* better fuck me, now,' she said, sipping champagne. 'Two of you in my bumhole. You, Ben, on top, and Guido underneath. Both of you look awfully alike. You could be twins. I suppose that's what makes it fun. Guido will wear a strawberry condom.'

She instructed Guido to lie down on his back, and rolled a strawberry condom over his erect penis, then straddled his phallus with her buttocks thrusting the shaft deep inside her anus, while at the same time spreading her naked buttocks, beneath her suspender belt, to reveal her anus pucker to Ben. Guido began to sigh with pleasure and excitement, as he jerked his loins, fucking Lefthera, while she wanked off her clito.

'You, too, Ben. Bum me,' she commanded.

'Bum you, mistress? With him inside you too?' he blurted, as she writhed, with Guido's cock in her rectum.

'Are you deaf, slave? Yes, I want a two-phallus bumming. Now, bum me. Get that filthy phallus into my rectum, beside Guido's. A beating hasn't softened it, so only spurting your spunk at my colon will do the trick. And put on – I think – a banana-flavoured condom. I'm in a banana mood.'

'Yes, mistress. Right away,' Ben blurted, delirious with joy and wonder, as he opened the packet, and rolled the rubber over his stiff cock.

'What you don't understand yet, Ben, is that most girls spend their lives being confused. They don't know what to wear, or eat, or who to sleep with. Being a Spartan means you know what you want. Being Spartan means not being confused. Now bum me!'

He pressed his rubbered peehole to the brown wrinkle of Lefthera's anal pucker, already filled by Guido's massive cock, then, on impulse, before attempting to penetrate her, he pressed his lips to the anus bud, and began to shower it with kisses, while putting his tongue a little way inside her anal elastic, and licking her proud muscled thighs; all this, holding her magnificent bare arse cheeks apart, while Lefthera was writhing on Guido's huge phallus, which seemed grotesquely oversized, for such a slender boy. Lefthera gasped that Ben's tongue felt very nice, and, emboldened, he replaced it with his rigid phallus, thrust into her anus, and in an instant was filling her rectum with his stiff cockmeat, alongside Guido's thrusting bare phallus.

'Ah . . .' groaned Lefthera. 'That's good.'

Ben began to fuck hard, as the two cocks pumped Lefthera's anal elastic, slithering beside each other. He felt a competitive need to fuck harder than the Italian boy. Lefthera masturbated vigorously, as she was double-fucked. Ben shuddered, in some anxiety, at the feel of another man's naked phallus, beside his own, and yet there was a tremendously naughty thrill, that he was helping to stretch the cruel Lefthera's anus to the size of an orange, or at least a lemon. She squatted, until both cocks were embedded right to her colon, and only the boys' balls were visible at her anal lips.

'Now, come on, bumfuck me hard, both of you,' she gasped. 'As hard as you can.'

Ben bucked her from the top, and Guido from underneath. Both thrust their hips as hard as they could, until Lefthera was gasping, and writhing in unfeigned agony.

'Yes! Oh, yes! More . . .' she panted, through gritted teeth. 'Harder, you bastards . . . fuck me raw, split my arse in two . . . do it! Fuck for a long time! I'm your mistress! Zeus, I'm coming!'

Lefthera groaned and gasped, in her first climax. This excited Guido, and he was the first to spurt his sperm. Ben felt it trickle down his own pumping phallus, but he knew better than to displease his mistress, so he willed himself to keep his sperm inside, until he had fucked Lefthera to her required tally of orgasms. Guido groaned; his cock softened, and plopped from Lefthera's anus, leaving only Ben's phallus in place.

'Yes . . . more . . . harder . . .' she gasped, as he enculed her with all his might, and she feverishly masturbated her clito, while squirming atop the exhausted body of Guido.

Lefthera brought herself off several times, as Ben continued to encule her, until she at last ordered Ben to sperm at her colon. He felt his sperm rise; the sweet, delicious onset of orgasm; the vinegar stroke; the ecstasy, as Lefthera's sphincter muscle artfully squeezed his phallus, to milk his balls of spunk. Then, he too was limp, and the trio of sweating nude bodies disengaged. Lefthera took their condoms, and sucked the ejaculated sperm. Then she threw Ben a cane.

'This worm let me down,' she snarled, putting her foot on Guido's face. 'I wanted a two-cock fuck! No, he's a snail! Cane him two dozen, Ben, will you, please?'

She flipped the whimpering Guido on to his belly, and exposed his naked buttocks to Ben's cane.

'I obey, mistress,' Ben said.

'Of course you obey,' she snorted, lighting a cigarette. 'You are a slave.'

Vip! With Lefthera's foot on the Italian boy's back, holding him down, Ben lashed Guido's bare arse with the whippy little cane, and the boy groaned, his naked buttocks clenching. Ben flogged him as hard as he could, his nipple rings dancing, as his torso swayed in flogger's stance. The boy's bare arse squirmed and writhed, as crimson weals decorated the smooth brown flesh, and Guido wept.

'*Ah! No fustiga!*' he squealed, wriggling, as Ben whipped his naked buttocks. '*Per favore! No, signor!*'

Ben took him to the full two dozen, and, by the time of the last stroke, his phallus had risen to full height. While Guido wept and wriggled on the floor, Lefthera lazily took Ben's phallus between her toes, and began to wank him off with her foot. When she felt him trembling near orgasm, she removed her toes, and took his phallus between her lips, then to the back of her throat, and tongued him to another orgasm, swallowing all of his sperm. She masturbated as she fellated Ben, and brought herself off with her masturbating fingers, at the same time as she swallowed his sperm. Come flowed from her wanked quim, down her lusciously rippling bare thighs, and then – heaven of heaven! – Ben was ordered to lick her thighs dry of her vaginal fluid. He took as long as he could over the task, while worshipping her hard naked thighs with his mouth and tongue, and swallowing every drop of the cunt juice, which he licked from her satin-smooth thigh skin. Then she made him light her a cigarette, and pour her and Guido another flute of champagne. She kicked the sobbing, welted Guido, slapped his striped bottom and handed him his wine.

'Have some champagne and cheer up, Guido,' she said. 'We'll be in Lombardy by tomorrow, and I trust you can join us for breakfast in the dining car. They do a delicious English breakfast, I believe, bacon and eggs, black pudding, fried tomato, fried bread and baked beans. Quite an unusual refinement, for these Continentals. Frying a tomato is quite an art. Something you Italian snails have never learnt.'

16

Breakfast by the Po

Even in the air-conditioned train, as they swept across the plain of Lombardy, and the valley of the Po, towards Venice, it was quite warm, and Lefthera had, this morning, elected to go bare-legged and barefoot. Ben shaved her pubis, with a Bic razor, as was customary, in the tiny bathroom, then attended her while she excreted, before wiping her anus, then hosing it. After caning him his token four cuts on the bare, with a slender, yet very painful, yellow willow wand, she dressed in a simple pink miniskirt, with a pink nylon thong, very small of gusset, merely a token covering of her hillock, and a pink silk blouse, unbuttoned, to show her breasts, scarcely concealed by her tiny scalloped, pink satin bra.

Ben could not help his erection, as he watched her bare brown legs, topped by those hard magnificent thighs, and her supple bare feet, with their long prehensile toes, swaying towards the restaurant car for their breakfast, where Guido joined Lefthera, sitting beside her on the banquette, with a clear view of her naked thighs. Lefthera placed her pink leather purse on the impeccable damask Irish linen cloth, and studied the breakfast menu. The fact that Lefthera was superbly bare-legged and barefoot attracted envious glances from the ladies, and her bare muscled thighs attracted lustful glances from the men. She ordered the full English breakfast, with Darjeeling tea, and cream.

The service was prompt. Ben sat behind them, while Lefthera wolfed her steaming hot English breakfast – she pronounced the black pudding and fried tomato first rate – but Guido contented himself with milky coffee and a roll. Ben was content, for Lefthera threw him an occasional scrap of black pudding, or fried bread, done properly in bacon fat. She rubbed her naked thighs together, in almost lascivious delight at her food. Her big ringed nipples pressed through the tiny bra, against her silk blouse, which was unbuttoned so far that it showed most of her brown breast flesh, almost, in fact, down to the nipple domes. The long-aproned French waiters obviously approved heartily, for they knew Lefthera was a generous tipper, and they hovered, constantly refilling her breakfast teacup, and bringing her unearthed English delicacies such as Worcestershire sauce, brown sauce, mustard and ketchup, with which she liberally doused her food, while letting them peek down her blouse, to her ringed breasts, or up her skirtlet, to her skimpily pantied cunt. Lefthera was enjoying her breakfast on the *Orient Express*.

Sitting docilely in his blue skirt and nylons, with a tight white nylon thong – one of Rosalynn's – cradling his balls, Ben had an opportunity to observe the others in the dining car, which was not crowded. There was a white-haired man across the aisle, making no secret of lustfully eyeing Lefthera's bared legs, although he was trying to conceal the fact that he was rubbing his phallus under his trousers. Another, younger, male was positively drooling, at the sight of Lefthera's naked thighs, as she artlessly crossed and uncrossed them, pausing to wipe a smear of bacon fat from the very top of her thigh, near her apex. The young man had his linen napkin over his lap, and Ben saw that he was masturbating, while looking at Lefthera's legs; he saw, too, that Lefthera knew it, and was enjoying her power, encouraging the masturbator, by hitching her pink skirt up very high, and rubbing her powerful bare thighs together.

Then he saw that Guido, beside her, was also furtively masturbating. A crop-haired girl, sitting on her own, was eyeing Lefthera's bare skin, and she, too, had her hand under her napkin, at her apex, which she was rubbing with unconcealed lustful joy. A lesbian, too, masturbating at the sight of Lefthera's exposed flesh! The eyes of everyone in the dining car were on Lefthera, who was gulping tea, and chewing on beans and toast and black pudding. Another young male began to caress himself in the loins, then another, and another. Ben's phallus was stiff, and his hand crept to his erection, which he began to rub. Lefthera was chewing on a succulent slice of black pudding, or *boudin noir*, as it was listed on the menu, when a spurt of fatty juice sluiced from her mouth, and landed on her blouse, just below her left nipple.

'Oh!' she cried. 'Oh, dear me.'

Feverishly, like some worried schoolgirl, she began to rub the stain, but that only made it worse.

'Oh, dear,' she wailed.

Lefthera unbuttoned her blouse, and took it off. Her scantily sheathed breasts swung tightly in their skimpy, pink satin scallops, which were transparent, and clearly showed her nipples. The maître d' rushed to her assistance, all solicitude.

'Oh! I'm sorry,' Lefthera wailed. 'But this blouse . . . it's from Hermès, in Paris, you know . . . I'm awfully afraid of spoiling it . . . could you . . . ?'

'It shall be cleaned at once, madame!' pronounced the flunkey, his own trousers bulging as he eyed her almost bare breasts. 'Nothing is too good for madame! And we cannot have the finest products of French *haute couture* spoilt!'

'More tea, madame?' said another waiter, his own trousers bulging in erection, under his apron. The masturbators – Guido, the lesbian woman, the white-haired man and the various lustful young men, joined by another apparent lesbian – were becoming more blatant in their self-pollution, now that Lefthera sat, with such apparent unconcern, torso bare, and with such a skimpy bra that she might well have been nude from the waistband up. Another pot of tea was brought, and, as she was handing a cup to Ben, who was rubbing his own phallus, faced with her rippling bare back, she spilt the liquid on her skirt.

Outside, the cypress trees and oak groves of the Po valley rushed past, beside the placid brown river.

'Oh, dear!' she cried.

'It was my fault, mistress!' Ben cried.

'No . . . no . . . Usually, things are your fault, Ben, but I don't know, I'm so oopsy today. Help unzip me, Ben. This is a Christian Lacroix skirt, and I don't want it ruined. Tea makes a terrible stain.'

Ben unfastened her skirt, and Lefthera stood, letting the skirt drop, for Ben to pick up. The waiters buzzed around like flies, while the maître d' tenderly, reverently, picked up her skirt, and assured madame that it would be cleaned at once, and would be good as new. More tea was poured for her, and she instructed the waiter where to put dabs of brown sauce and ketchup on her bacon and eggs and baked beans. Another waiter brought fresh toast, with butter and Dundee marmalade. He insisted on spreading the butter for her, ogling the nearly naked girl, clad now only in pink satin scalloped bra and pink thong, which left her buttocks and thighs almost entirely bared, and the tininess of the gusset making it plain that her cunt hillock was shaven smooth. Lefthera began to chew on a slice of hot buttered toast, as she speared her fried eggs, cooked American style.

'Oh, no! she cried, once more, as she stabbed her eggs, and golden yolk spurted over her bra. 'I'm so sorry. I think it must be the excitement of the journey to Venice. Ben – my bra – unhook, please.'

There was a rustle of excitement from the spectators of Lefthera's clothing drama, and all of them, men and women, were now discreetly, though obviously, masturbating as Lefthera's bra came off – the maître d' once more assuring that no service could be too much, and the bra would be cleaned at once.

'It's a Versace, you see,' Lefthera said, as, bare-breasted, and now wearing only her tiny thong, she continued to devour her breakfast.

Guido was wanking off quite openly beside her, but she pretended not to notice; Ben had his hand up his girly

161

skirt, on his naked phallus, rubbing intently, as he ogled his mistress's jutting naked breasts, with their golden nipple rings. The entire dining car was in a state of high excitement, with many masturbators calling for champagne, which pleased the maître d', himself blatantly stimulated by the naked Greek girl greedily and unconcernedly wolfing her English breakfast. Lefthera opened the silver dish of Dundee marmalade, and began to spoon it on to her toast, when another disaster occurred. A gobbet of marmalade slipped, and splattered right on the gusset of her panties.

'You'll think I'm awfully clumsy,' she said to the waiter. 'I don't know what's come over me today. I think I'm just too thrilled to be in Italy. But these are Hugo Boss panties. I simply can't have them spoilt. I'll have to . . .'

She rose, facing her goggling audience, and rolled her panties, very slowly, down her naked thighs.

'I'm awfully sorry,' she said. 'I'm Greek, you know. An English breakfast is such a complicated thing!'

When she was nude, she handed the panties to the maître d'.

'This shall be cleaned at once, madame. You shall have all your clothing back in half an hour.'

'Oh, thank you so much,' she said, opened her purse, and handed out generous tips of bright euro banknotes.

Completely nude, she sat down once more on her banquette, to continue eating breakfast. More tea and toast were brought to the naked Greek beauty. More napkins were brought, too, for she kept spilling things on to her nude body – tea, cream, butter, egg yolk, tomato, bacon fat (she went 'ooh!' when hot fat spilt on her nipples) and had to stand up to wipe herself off with a linen napkin. She took her time doing the wiping, standing with her thighs apart. Once, she managed to spill cream on both her nipples, which were now nicely erect, and she took a long time rubbing them clean. Then, she spilt ketchup on her freshly shaven cunt hillock, and had to wipe that off, standing up, with her legs wide apart, and her glistening pink pouch well on show.

Guido groaned, as he came in his underpants. Ben, too, rubbed himself to orgasm, spurting into Rosalynn's white thong, as he gazed, entranced, at Lefthera's naked pink cunt, her brown bottom and thighs. One by one, the masturbators in the dining car, quaffing champagne at this early hour, gave up their seed, or, in the case of the lesbians, made their bellies flutter in climax. The maître d' was masturbating his phallus under his apron, like the other waiters under theirs. Lefthera sipped her tea, and waited, until the car was full of the gasps of discreet orgasm, at the spectacle of her nude body. There was only one waiter, the youngest and prettiest, an Italian, who blushed, and looked away. She beckoned the maître d', who had just ejaculated into his apron.

'May I have another portion of black pudding, please?' she said sweetly. 'I'll try not to be so clumsy.'

'Of course, madame!' he gasped. 'Anything! It is a beautiful woman's privilege to be as clumsy as she pleases.'

When Lefthera had eaten all her breakfast, including her extra plate of black pudding, she snapped her fingers at Ben, who followed her as she walked back to their compartment in the nude. The waiters bowed obsequiously, and there was a smattering of applause at her daring and her beauty from the other diners who had pleasured themselves. They would be in the ancient city of Venice, *la Serenissima*, in an hour. Lefthera lolled nude on the couch, thighs apart, and absent-mindedly stroking her clito, while she smoked a cigarette. There was a knock on the door, and Ben admitted one of the Italian train staff, who brought Lefthera's clothing, freshly and immaculately laundered. It was the young waiter who had refrained from masturbating at the sight of Lefthera's nude body. She did not stop rubbing her clito, as the blushing young man was instructed to place her clothing on the bed, which he did. She ordered Ben to bring her purse, and, all the while with her muscled thighs parted, and openly masturbating herself, extracted a ten-euro note as his tip. She rubbed her cunt with the banknote, until it was moist with her juice. The boy's eyes widened.

'But there's a small service you must perform first,' she drawled, lighting another cigarette by striking a Swan Vestas match on the sole of her foot. 'My servant here has been very naughty. While I was eating breakfast, and I was unfortunately without my clothes, I know he was looking at my naked body, and masturbating. You know you were masturbating, you smutty young snail. Don't deny it, Ben.'

Ben blushed.

'I . . . I can't deny it,' he blurted.

'So this young man of mine needs a caning. To get your tip, you must cane him a dozen strokes on his naked bottom, in punishment. I am far too lazy to do it myself. Ben, select a cane, and give it to our visitor, then get down and bare your bum for chastisement. Take your panties off, and throw them away, because I know they are soiled with your sperm.'

Biting his lip, Ben took out a small ashplant, and Lefthera nodded, saying it would do, but that the boy would have to cane up close, for maximum impact. All the time, she was rubbing the ten-euro note in her quim, and actually rolled it up, and thrust it right into her pouch, until it came out sopping wet. The liveried waiter was plainly erect. Somewhat perplexed, he took the cane from Ben, and watched as Ben crouched, lifted his skirt, threw away his thong panties and presented his naked buttocks for his caning.

'There's just one other thing,' she said to the waiter. 'I want you to be naked when you cane my servant. One naked boy caning another is a spectacle that pleases me. If you cane him hard and well, and I am pleased with you, then, who knows, *perhaps* you may fuck my anus, the Italian way, afterwards, while Ben watches, gnawed with the green dragon of jealousy. As you see, I'm quite wet already, and excited at the prospect of my servant's bottom squirming.'

The waiter simpered, and lost no time in stripping off his uniform. He stood, hugely erect, his phallus rising from an immense pubic forest, and he flexed the cane, but Lefthera tut-tutted.

'That won't do!' she snapped. 'You hairy Italians! Ben, fetch a razor, and shave this fellow till he's clean. Pubis, legs and armpits.'

Ben rose, and led the naked boy into the bathroom.

'This won't take long,' he said, as he applied the razor to the boy's pubic hillock, 'but my mistress insists on a clean body.'

After ten minutes, the Italian waiter emerged from the bathroom, gleaming smooth. Ben, still skirted, but pantiless, and with his skirt tucked up over his blouse, reassumed his caning position, and the boy picked up the cane once more.

'Do him hard,' drawled Lefthera. 'A whole dozen. Space the strokes on ten seconds. Close quarters.'

Vip! Vip! The boy began to lash Ben's naked buttocks, the muscular strokes making him squirm right from the start of the flogging.

'Uhh . . .' Ben gasped, but forced himself not to cry out, as his bare bottom writhed in pain and shame.

Lefthera masturbated herself quite openly, using the rolled-up ten-euro note to tweak her clito, and with a cigarette dangling from the corner of her mouth. *Vip! Vip!*

'Oh! Ahh!'

'Silence, Ben,' Lefthera cautioned.

Vip! Vip! The beating continued, with Ben's face contorted in agony, and his bare bum squirming and clenching, as the whippy ashplant rod seared his skin. When he had taken twelve cuts, he had to wipe the tears of agony from his eyes; the caner was still erect, and Lefthera pronounced his work good. She lay back on the bed, and invited him to fuck her in her wet pouch.

'You must watch, Ben,' she added. 'No looking away.'

The boy needed no encouragement. He straddled Lefthera, and plunged his phallus into her anus, beginning to fuck vigorously, while she lazily smoked a cigarette. There were more tears in Ben's eyes, but these were tears of jealous rage and shame, as he saw the girl he adored fucked by a stranger.

'Oh, yes,' said Lefthera, pretending to gasp. 'Fuck me

hard! Take me, you brute! Split me in two! What a huge hard cock! Oh, yes, I'm going to come!'

Ben saw that she was indeed going to come, but only because she was masturbating her clito with the ten-euro note, as the boy fucked her bumhole. Ben watched his slim bare buttocks pumping up and down, while his own arse smarted dreadfully from his caning. And all the time she was leering at Ben.

'Isn't it nice, Ben, to watch your mistress pleasured?' she said.

'Yes, mistress,' said Ben bitterly.

It did not take the excitable boy long to ejaculate, and Lefthera brought herself to climax at the same time.

'Yes! Yes! Fuck me! Fuck me! Give me all your spunk!' she howled. 'I want your full load in my arse!'

After he had deposited his sperm in her, he withdrew his now flaccid phallus. She held the banknote a few centimetres from her open, dripping cooze, and he had to reach across her bare belly and quim to take it. Blushing, he bowed, and stammered his thanks, as he dressed, then, wet tip in hand, retreated. Lefthera laughed.

'You can pack away the clothes, Ben,' she said. 'These Italians are a funny lot, you know. They love money. And Venice is funny. They have the tradition of carnival, when men and women would be in disguise, and wear masks, so that they could fuck strangers, without actually knowing whom they were fucking. There are comic stories of wives who discovered to their dismay that they'd been fucked by their own husbands! But, you know, the best disguise is nudity. So I'm going to try a little experiment. I'm going to get off the train naked. I'm going to walk around naked, get into a gondola or a *vaporetto* boat naked. It will be so astounding to them, like the little scene I staged at breakfast, that they won't know what to do about it, so they'll do nothing about it. You, of course, must be impeccably dressed in your girl's costume, but I'm going to spend my time in Venice in the nude. And if I see a beautiful young man, and want to wank myself off in the Piazza San Marco, or the Rialto, or on the Bridge of Sighs, why, I'll just do it. You see, Ben, that's why you should stay a virgin. Sex isn't about getting your rocks off, a quick spurt, like that boy who just fucked my arse. It's about *power*. Look at the power I had at breakfast time, with all those people wanking off, as they looked at my flesh! Sex is about owning people, as I own you. And nudity is supreme power, for a naked girl owns herself.'

17

La Serenissima

Coolly, Lefthera descended from the train at Venice, and she was stark naked, but for her white straw panama hat (panama hats, she told Ben, are actually made in Ecuador) and crimson stiletto heels. Porters rushed to take charge of her cases, but she said she already had a porter – Ben, now dressed in his dark navy-blue skirtlet, bra and panties, but with white silk stockings, on loan from Lefthera. Those with cameras, including a newspaper photographer, began to snap photos of the nude arrival, but Lefthera paid them no attention, either favourable or hostile, allowing them to see every part of her nude body, and behaving as if they were not there, in fact, behaving as if no one else in the world existed, except herself. That was the doctrine of Pyrrhon of Elis, the father of scepticism. She sent Ben to fetch a gondola, to take them to the Hotel Neptune, near Harry's American Bar, just off the Piazza San Marco, and, when he had secured one, Ben shifted her cases into the gondola, while Lefthera strolled nude to the Rialto Bridge, smoking a cigarette. When they were installed in the gondola, and the gondolier was poling them up the Grand Canal, she explained.

Pyrrhon was a pupil of Anaxarchus of Abdera and in about 330 established himself as a teacher at Elis. Believing that equal arguments can be offered on both sides of any proposition, he dismissed the search for truth as a vain endeavour. While travelling with an expedition under Alexander the Great, Pyrrhon saw in the fakirs of India an example of happiness flowing from indifference to circumstances. He concluded that man must suspend judgement on the reliability of sense perceptions and simply live according to reality as it appears. Pyrrhonism permeated the Middle and New Academy of Athens and strongly influenced philosophical thought in seventeenth-century Europe with the republication of the sceptical works of Sextus Empiricus, who had codified Greek scepticism in the third century. Pyrrhon's teaching was preserved in the poems of Timon of Phlius, who studied with him.

'My nudity, like your girl's dresses, thus, is simply reality as it appears,' Lefthera said. 'Cybele wrote an interesting paper on Timon of Philus, and Iphigenia did one on Anaxarchus of Abdera. Abigail did a good paper on La Sale, the French writer chiefly remembered for his *Petit Jehan de Saintré*, a romance with a great gift for the observation of court manners and a keen sense of comic situation and dialogue. From 1400 to 1448 La Sale served the dukes of Anjou, Louis the Second, Louis the Third and René, as squire, soldier, administrator and, ultimately, governor of René's son and heir, Jean of Calabria.

'The Angevin claims to the kingdom of Sicily brought him repeatedly into Italy, and his didactic works contain several accounts of his unusual and picturesque experiences there. He was in Italy for Louis the Second's 1409–11 campaign against Ladislas of Durazzo. In 1415 he took part in a Portuguese expedition against the Moors of Ceuta.

'La Sale visited the Sibyl's mountain near Norcia, seat of the legend later transported to Germany and attached to the name of Tannhäuser; he relates the legend in great detail in his *Paradis de la reine Sibylle*. He became governor of the sons of Louis of Luxembourg, count of Saint-Pol in 1448. There, near Dunkirk, on the shores of the North Sea, he wrote *Le Petit Jehan de Saintré*. Jehan de Saintré is a pseudobiographical romance of a knight at the court of Anjou who, in real life, achieved great fame in the mid-fourteenth century.

'Modern criticism ascribes an important place to La Sale in the development of French prose fiction and also extols his grace, wit, sensibility and realism. His realism extended to emphasising the important role of bare-bottom spanking and masturbation, which he called "tickling the rose petals", in a female's moral education. He also extolled the virtues of nudity, saying that men and women should swim naked together in the icy waves of La Manche – the English Channel – and masturbate chastely, nude on the beach. In his system, women were permitted to use implements of driftwood to stimulate themselves, with they liked to do, for the driftwood was covered in barnacles, which stimulated the clito.

'Certain ecclesiasticals in the Middle Ages, notably Gervaise of Bordeaux, argued that barnacles were sacred, and must not be eaten, since they were miniature phalluses, the proof being that girls masturbated with them so much. Sometimes, the women would bugger the men with driftwood branches, while the men wanked off. La Sale too had a thing about barnacles, thinking that they contained tiny morsels of cosmic wisdom, and were perhaps cosmic testicles. The spectacle of nude men and women masturbating on a North Sea beach using barnacle-encrusted driftwood was not shocking, for everyone did it, and it was simply categorised as sea bathing.

'So you see, if you suspend judgement on the reliability of sense impressions, and take reality as it appears, my nudity is not really nudity at all. I am just reality as it appears. If you present people with reality, such as my nude body, they don't know what to do about it, so they do nothing. They think that, if a girl is walking around Venice in the nude, it must have some sort of higher approval, otherwise it wouldn't be happening. So they ignore it, or ogle me, and have a quiet wank, which gives me a thrill.

'If people see a girl in the nude, and are worried by it, it's *their* problem, not hers. You see, people are trapped by categories. If I was categorised as Lefthera, some cheap celebrity, which I would hate to be, then that would put me in a category, and they would say, "Aha, there's Lefthera in the nude!" and I'd be pursued by paparazzi photographers. But, since I'm not a celebrity, I'm just a nude girl. It's all very simple, Ben, really. And it helps when you shave your pubic hair, as most girls do these days. It makes you look innocent. Pubic hair is a sign of aggression. So is having a phallus. So *you* can't go round nude.'

Sure enough, the clerk at the Neptune Hotel did not bat an eyelid when he checked in a ravishing, broad-thighed, nude Greek girl and a transvestite boy dressed as a girl in slave's blue, with sheeny nylon stockings, and a prominent suspender belt bulging under his thin summer skirt, to their penthouse suite, overlooking the Piazza San Marco on one side, and the bustling boat traffic of the Grand Canal on the other. The liveried hotel staff, white-haired gentlemen of the old Latin school, could not have been more polite. A gentleman does not make adverse remarks, or indeed any remarks at all, on a lady's clothing, except to compliment her on her taste in shoes, or other accessories. If her clothing of choice is complete nudity, then a gentleman does not comment on that, either. One of the servants was bold enough to say that the signora had a beautiful leather purse.

'Thank you,' Lefthera said, waggling her bottom a little, as she preceded him up the stairs. 'It's a Prada, you know. Frightfully expensive.'

'Isn't everything, these days, signora?' sighed the white-haired servant. 'I must say, if you'll forgive me, that you are wise to forgo clothing. The price of a shirt, or pair of trousers, these days! Why, the other day, I was in the Rinascimento department store in Padua, looking for a skirt for my granddaughter, and –'

Gently, Lefthera tipped the fellow, and encouraged him to continue their conversation some other time. When she and Ben were in their penthouse suite, she threw open the French windows, and stepped out on to the balcony.

'Naked, and overlooking Venice!' she cried. 'There are few grander feelings.'

* * *

In the days that followed, Ben was amazed that Lefthera kept to her vow of nudity, and was untroubled by adverse comment: quite the opposite, in fact. People cheered her in the street. It was so hot that summer, and Venice was so thronged with tourists and backpackers and the like that everyone wore as little clothing as they could, so nudity seemed a logical and refreshing idea. Lefthera was totally nude, and barefoot. The local paper published some telephoto snaps of her, with the saucy headline LA SEREN-ISSIMA È LA NUDISSIMA! and Lefthera phoned to complain.

They didn't need to steal telephoto snaps, she said. She would rather a proper photographer accompanied her, and took close-up nude shots of her. This was done: the newspaper sent a long-legged, big-breasted girl photo-grapher called Nicola, with bronze hair cascading over her shoulders, who, brown legs bare, and wearing the shortest of skirts and the skimpiest of cotton blouses over her braless breasts, accompanied Lefthera and Ben on their cultural rambles around Venice, snapping all the time, and wiping her brow in the heat.

Ben's body was now rippled with muscle, his pectorals and thighs bulging, like Lefthera's, for, as well as putting him through punishing sets of press-ups and other callis-thenic exercises every morning, while she gave him his four strokes of the cane on the bare, she made him work out, using her Bullworker device, specially for his thighs and pectorals. Nicola said, only half joking, that Ben's breasts were almost as big, firm and beautiful as Lefthera's. At length, Lefthera suggested that Nicola join her in the nude, and become part of the scene herself. Ben could operate a camera, and, anyway, her camera had an automatic mode, did it not? It would sell papers. Nicola laughed, and said she would think about it. They were sitting with espressos in an outdoor café near the Church of San Sebastiano.

'Saint Sebastian,' said Lefthera. 'A most interesting character. According to his legend, he was born in Gaul, went to Rome, and in about 283 AD joined the army of the emperor Carinus, later becoming a captain under the emperor Diocletian. When it was discovered that he was a

Christian who had converted many soldiers, Sebastian was ordered to be killed by arrows. The archers left him for dead, but a Christian widow nursed him back to health. He then presented himself before Diocletian, who condemned him to death by whipping. His body, thrown into a sewer, was found by another pious woman, who dreamt that Sebastian told her to bury his remains near the catacombs. His relics are believed to be in the Basilica of San Sebastiano on the Appian Way, to which many pilgrims were attracted in the Middle Ages. Sebastian's martyrdom was a favourite subject of Renaissance artists, and the saint is usually shown as a handsome youth pierced by arrows.'

'A handsome youth pierced by arrows,' said Nicola, licking her lips. 'So many of our saints are very sexy.'

'But the arrows were a cover-up. In fact he was whipped to death. Imagine the anguish of that! Join me in the nude, Nicola,' said Lefthera. 'Saint Sebastian will understand.'

'Yes, why not? It's so hot. I think I will,' said Nicola, taking her fingers from her crotch, which she had been discreetly rubbing.

Coolly, she stood, and stripped off her skimpy clothing, which fitted easily in her camera bag, beside her array of lenses. Like Lefthera's and Ben's, her body was shaven, her ripe, brown cunt hillock gleaming under the summer sun. As she sat down again, nude, and sipped her espresso, she smiled, and touched Lefthera's hand.

'It's so simple and blissful to be nude,' she said. 'Thank you for showing me the way.'

'You have *una bella colinetta*,' said Lefthera, tenderly stroking the girl's cunt hillock, which made her smile.

After their coffee, they strolled naked around the city, with the nude Nicola, giggling with pleasure at her nudity, snapping Ben and Lefthera, and sometimes Ben operating the Nikon, to photograph the two nude girls giggling, as they embraced each other, against a background of cheering tourists, and bemused but smiling policemen. Sometimes, they parked the camera on a wall, set it to automatic, and the three of them, two nude girls and a miniskirted boy with nipple rings, filled a roll of film.

A flattering photo set of Lefthera, Ben and Nicola appeared in the Sunday edition of the paper under the headline VENEZIA, CITTA delle nudiste: Lefthera and Nicola feeding the pigeons in the Piazza san Marco, Lefthera and Nicola gazing into a fusty little masterpiece-laden church near the Palazzo Grassi, Lefthera, Ben and Nicola elbowing their way through hordes of sweating Australian backpackers on the Rialto. Photos of Ben showed him stripped down to his skimpy thong, and the editors were particularly fascinated by his and Lefthera's nipple rings.

Since it was so hot, Lefthera permitted him to accompany her bare-chested, wearing only a skirt, sandals and petticoat, and of course his bronze nipple rings. Sometimes, she led him around barefoot, wearing just a thong, so that he was almost as naked as she was, also barefoot, and his buttocks, bruised by his daily caning, glowed crimson with stripes in the fierce sunlight of the Venetian lagoon. Nicola moved into their hotel room in the Neptune and slept naked with Lefthera. Ben, sleeping on the floor, listened to their kisses and squelching embraces, his phallus stiff. He heard Lefthera tell Nicola that her slave needed daily whipping. At that, the girls' embraces grew more fervent.

'Oh, your cunt tastes so good!' Nicola cried.

But Ben, his erection straining, was forbidden to wank off, for relief, without his cruel mistress's order. One day, Nicola said that, since his balls were shaven, there was no reason not to photograph Ben completely nude, apart from his nipple rings, which were *sensazionale*. His big phallus, she coyly admitted, was *sensazionale* also, not least, because it always seemed to be erect. Girls, she explained, found the limp phallus ugly and dull, but the erect phallus unbelievably exciting.

Torso bare, Ben wore his skirt and nylons, but was nipple-ringed and bare-breasted, and, when they went to a little secluded canal near the Ca' Pesaro, he stripped raw, and Nicola shot three rolls of film of him naked. Having a nude girl photographing him was unbearably thrilling, and

174

Ben's phallus was erect for the whole shoot. When Nicola said that she had several rolls of film left, and invited him to masturbate for her camera, Ben looked to Lefthera for approval. Lefthera was leaning over the canal wall, her lovely brown bottom caressed by the breeze, and smoking a cigarette. She nodded her agreement. Ben began to rub his swollen glans, while Nicola's Nikon clicked.

'Pull the foreskin right down at every stroke,' she ordered, every bit the professional. 'Let me see that lovely crimson bulb. Caress your balls. Yes, that's right. Now kneel, and kiss your mistress's bottom, while you wank off.'

Ben obeyed, getting his tongue in Lefthera's cleft. Lefthera parted her big brown arse cheeks and thighs, to help him in his task, and seemed amused by the proceedings. His nose was in her anus, and he smelt her divine musky scent, while he masturbated.

'Wait! I know!' cried Nicola.

She plucked a branch from a tree.

'Lefthera, darling, will you flog the boy's bottom?'

'Of course,' drawled Lefthera.

Ben bent over the canal wall, while Lefthera dealt him ten stingers, and Nicola's camera clicked. He looked round, and saw that both girls were masturbating their exposed clitos, while his bare arse squirmed under the makeshift cane.

'This is heavenly!' cried Nicola.

When Ben's ten strokes had been delivered, and he was wiping the tears from his eyes, Nicola knelt, and began to suck Lefthera's cunt, while Ben continued to masturbate. Nicola set the camera to automatic, and parked it on the wall, to photograph Ben, as he spurted his wide arc of sperm into the canal. Meanwhile, Nicola herself was playing with her clito, as she sucked Lefthera off, and her tongue brought Lefthera to a gasping orgasm, simultaneous with her own. Ben put on his thong and skirt, and walked back to the Neptune, girl-dressed, arm in arm with the two nude girls.

'I think that was a good photoset!' bubbled Nicola.

* * *

175

Thereafter, Lefthera took to masturbating in public, whenever she felt like it. She would stand in the Piazza San Marco, or on the deck of a *vaporetto* boat, nude, of course, and blatantly frigging her clito to orgasm. Nicola assured her that according to an ancient and unrescinded law of Venice, dating to the early thirteenth century, it was not actually forbidden to be nude in public, and not forbidden to masturbate, either. The precedent was established by a curious court case in 1202, just before the Frankish barons of the Fourth Crusade sacked Constantinople, with the help of the elderly but valiant Enrico Dandolo, who was at that time Doge of Venice.

A teenage boy of noble family had been surprised, masturbating naked by moonlight, into the petticoat of a girl his own age, on the balcony of his family mansion, overlooking the Grand Canal. He was accused not of nudity or masturbating, but of theft of the petticoat. The matter was complicated by the fact that the girl was nude beside him, and she was masturbating too. Each accused the other of subornation and misuse of affection, and the case dragged on for months, until Doge Dandolo ordered them both to be strung naked by their wrists to a gibbet, and dealt fifty lashes each, with a man-high rhinoceroshide whip (imported from Ethiopia) by the public executioner.

When the sentence had been carried out, and an enthusiastic crowd had witnessed the two nude bodies wriggling and squirming under the dreadfully hard whip, the weeping girl was sent to be confined in the nunnery of Santa Ursula, while the boy, also weeping, was delivered to the Venetian navy, where he distinguished himself in the Siege of Constantinople, and rose to be a powerful landowner near Adrianopolis, under King Baldwin, keeping a harem of many girlslaves, mostly Armenians. He kept them bare-breasted, dressed only in petticoats over their bare nates and cunts, and would frequently, after a good dinner, lift a girl's petticoat, masturbate, and ejaculate into it, or else spurt his sperm into her hairy pubic bush, for, oddly enough, he liked very hairy girls, well tufted at both cooze and armpit, and thus he preferred the earthy and lustful Armenians. The girl distinguished herself by her piety as a nun, and rose to be the Abbess of a convent in Trento. From there, she became the Abbess of Santa Ursula's in Pisa, and from there she went to Rome, where she became Grand Abbess of all convents in the Papal States and the Kingdom of Naples.

There was a hint of scandal when Cardinal Sepulchro accused her of keeping her own harem of naked altar boys, used for her own depraved pleasures, the boys whipped savagely on their bare bottoms when they did not perform adequately between the Abbess's spread thighs, and in fact the case even got to a closed cardinals' court in Rome, but it was thrown out for lack of evidence, none of her alleged lovers being willing to testify against her. Benefiting from the seclusion offered by her Abbess's role, she allegedly gave birth to several sons, including one who eventually became Bishop of Padua, and then pope, and incestuously gave her a new son, whom he in due course appointed Bishop of Calabria, but that was hearsay, and the venerable Abbess died, much lamented, with all praising her saintliness.

The point of the Venetian case was that it was established that it was perfectly legal to expose yourself in the nude, and to masturbate while in that state, because Venetians were unshockable by mere sexual peccadilloes, but that theft was shocking, unless it was from the Turks. Lying, too, was a grave matter. It was illegal to steal a petticoat (the boy's offence) or to bear false witness (the girl's offence).

Lefthera said she had intended to stay in Venice only a couple of days, but something happened to change this plan. Lefthera and Nicola nude, and Ben skirted and nylon-stockinged, they visited an art gallery, the Moderna, near the Teatro la Fenice, and met Count Scazzo, a sculptor, photographer and painter, whose gallery it was, and who exhibited his work there. Nicola said he was very important. Most of his work depicted the nude form, either male or female. Some of the sculptures and paintings depicted nudes in elegant poses; some depicted naked boys wrestling with naked girls, or naked boys wrestling together, or naked girls wrestling together. In some of the paintings, winged naked boys, with charming little erections, were taking floggings on the naked bottom with whips, from cherubs, goddesses or angels.

Count Scazzo was a dignified and handsome man, with thick sensuous lips, and a mane of lustrous white hair. He approved Lefthera's bareness, and that of Nicola, and Ben's feminine dress, and invited them to model for him in the nude, for his most ambitious sculpture ever. It would take some time – did Lefthera have enough time to spend in Venice? The sculpture – first, the photographs, of course, then the paintings – would take weeks, if not months. She said yes.

The papers from Rome and Milan took over the theme of 'Venice, the nudist city', came to do photoshoots of nipple-ringed Lefthera and Nicola together, and Ben, bare-breasted, in skirtlet and nipple rings, and there were learned articles, about nudity as part of the green movement, and nude Italians rediscovering their pagan past; after a while, it became fashionable for Venetian girls to go out in the nude. The blonde Australian backpacker girls were first and foremost in this, and many of them went to tattoo parlours to have their nipples pierced like Ben's and Lefthera's, and rings fitted, then paraded the streets casually, or arrogantly, naked.

The elegant Venetian ladies of the upper class soon caught on. They began to travel around their city in the nude, except for the all important accessories, so that perhaps they were not really nude at all – the leather stiletto shoes, the designer purses, the gold chains and bracelets, garlands of fresh flowers around the bare belly, even, in an increasing number of cases, golden nipple rings.

It became normal for upper-class ladies to make their promenade in the nude, in the Piazza San Marco, on Sunday mornings, then stop for coffee and cakes in one of the fashionable outdoor cafés, and compare their newly acquired nipple rings, or even clito or buttock piercings. All, of course, had completely shaven bodies, the thighs and naked hillocks gleaming golden. Ben, with his smooth-shaven body and nipple rings, had started a trend.

18

Nude Models

'I am particularly interested in Father Serenus Cressy,' said Count Scazzo, in his perfect Oxford-accented English, as his teenage servant girl, Sylvestra, who was nude and barefoot, but for a white miniskirt of pleated cotton, served tea to Nicola, Lefthera and Ben.

Sylvestra was darkly beautiful, her wide pouting lips taciturn. Ben thought she was about his own age. He was powerfully erect, as he looked at her long, shiny, auburn hair, which caressed her perfectly conic bare breasts, their skin golden, and satin smooth, and big strawberry nipples. Her body was strongly muscled, like Rosalynn's; Sylvestra was obviously a bodybuilder. Ben thought he would like to be a lock of Sylvestra's hair, caressing those superb naked breasts, tickling the luscious ripe plums of her nipples.

'Doesn't Sylvestra remind you of Canova's statue, *Venus Italica*?' said Scazzo. 'Those superb breasts and thighs, the glory of a woman?'

Both Nicola and nipple-ringed Lefthera were nude, and Ben was bare-chested, wearing only his skirt, petticoat, thong, nipple rings and pink nylons, which made him sweaty in the scorching summer heat. Having been shown the count's gallery of nude paintings and photographs of teenage girls and boys, sometimes alone, sometimes together – he always used a Minolta, which he said made the best lenses, although Nicola spoke up for the Nikon – they sat under parasols among the flowers and shrubs, overlooking the Grand Canal, in the roof garden of the count's palazzo, beside the tiny swimming pool. The count himself was nude, his muscular brown body completely shaven.

Gesturing to the pool, he invited his guests to take a cooling dip, whenever they felt like it. Lefthera and Nicola promptly accepted, and splashed with each other in the pool, slapping each other's bottom and breasts, with Nicola hooking her fingers into Lefthera's nipple rings, and wrenching her breasts hard, making Lefthera squeal, to the count's great appreciation. He candidly admitted he was a lifelong nudist, and that the greatest artists, such as Picasso, Renoir and Rubens, did their work in the nude, which concentrated the mind wonderfully. After several minutes' splashing, the girls emerged, dripping and laughing, and the count continued.

'Serenus Cressy was one of the great European mystics. Born in Yorkshire, and died in 1674, in East Grinstead. Did you know that in Colombo, Sri Lanka, there is a convent called the School of the Blessed Margaret, Our Lady of East Grinstead? Perhaps not. Serenus was an English Benedictine monk, historian, apologist and spiritual writer noted for his editorship of writings by Counter-Reformation mystics. Educated at Merton College, Oxford, Serenus became chaplain to Sir Thomas Wentworth, later Earl of Strafford, who of course was executed, and then to Lord Falkland; he was also dean of Leighlin, County Carlow, and canon of Windsor. While in Rome, in 1646, he converted to Catholicism and became a monk of St Gregory's, Douai, in 1649. After the Restoration of Charles II in 1660, he was appointed chaplain to Queen Catherine of Braganza at Somerset House. His *Exomologesis*, an account of his conversion, appeared in Paris in 1647; he also wrote *Church-History of Brittany or England, from the Beginning of Christianity to the Norman Conquest*, but his chief significance is as editor of the mystics Walter Hilton, Blessed Julian of Norwich, and Maurice Chauncey. Do you know Chauncey?'

'Up to a point,' said Lefthera.

Count Scazzo rubbed his delicately manicured hands.

'Which is a polite English way of saying no. I *do* like mysticism,' he said. 'I wonder if I'm not a gnostic. A nudist mystic, perhaps. Chauncey would doff his monk's cloak, and pray in the nude. Serenus, too, was a nudist. The great Gandhi would sleep naked with young girls, in order to test his piety, by not touching them. Yet even without touching, the presence of a naked girl is spiritually enriching. The contemplation of nude bodies brings us closer to God, for what is God if not the nakedness of the Universe? Let's to business. Before I start, I shall present you with an autographed copy of my book, *Storia della Nudità*.'

He presented both Nicola and Lefthera with copies of his richly illustrated book, a veritable history of nudity and nudism, beginning with Adam and Eve, proceeding through ancient, medieval, Renaissance and modern art, and ending with a summary of the modern nudist movement, the clubs and free beaches, which increasingly proliferated throughout the world. There were reproductions of photographs by Count Wilhelm von Gloeden, who spent most of his life in Taormina, in Sicily, photographing naked young fishermen with large cocks, and peasant girls with generous pubic bushes, with technical excellence, thanks to his superior German camera. Sylvestra brought the count a quill pen and ink, and, with a flourish, he wrote dedications in the flyleaf of their books.

Many of the illustrations were of his own paintings and photographs, depicting a variety of nude young girls, prominent among them being his servant Sylvestra, who, oddly, had a very hairy and untrimmed pubic bush, which Ben found curiously exciting, since he had assumed that all girls had shaven pubes like his own. Some of the paintings were very explicit, with Sylvestra crouching, buttocks parted, to show her anus, or with her fingers holding open her quim flaps, to show her glistening pink pouch. In some of the pictures, she was tied up and gagged, and her naked buttocks were being caned. There were also photographs of her nude in the gym, lifting weights. He supposed that Sylvestra was more to Scazzo than just a servant, and wondered what it would be like to fuck her, or any girl, in the cunt, not the anus.

'It draws, I am not ashamed to admit, on Sir Kenneth Clark's *The Nude* of 1955. My thesis, going a little in advance of Sir Kenneth's, is that the history of European art, which, of course, is the only art that counts, is the history of nudism. Jesus is presented nude. Women are nude. Rubens, Ingres's *Grande Odalisque*, or his *Bain Turque*, Cézanne's *Les Grandes Baigneuses*, Gérard's *Cupid and Psyche*, the *Venus de Milo*, which was found on the Greek island of Mílos, Delacroix, *David* ... The divine Canova created colossal sculptures of Napoleon in the nude.

'And of course you must know the sumptuous paintings of Lord Leighton. You have visited his Egyptian house in Kensington? It is a temple to the beauty of the naked human body. Western art is the worship of the nude body. I am a nudist! I know the free beaches of Guadeloupe, Croatia, Australia, Florida. There are certain beaches here, too, where you may see naked Swedish and English and Australian girls – but I have my roof garden. Sometimes the Swedish or English or Australian girls are happy to visit, and sunbathe in the nude, while I paint them. I believe in the naked body as a sacrament. Girls and boys like to be naked! Nudity is the only freedom. It is only prudish society which tells them they shouldn't have it. Now, I think Ben can remove his clothing, and I'll take some photographs of him in various poses, to see how I'm going to paint him in oils, and sculpt you all, in the finest white Carrara marble.'

Rather coyly, Ben rolled down his nylons, and stepped out of his skirt. At the contemplation of the two nude girls, his phallus rose, until it was trembling and fully rigid. Sylvestra looked on impassively. Scazzo clapped his hands.

'But this is capital!' he cried. 'I knew it was the idea I was seeking. Such a splendid big phallus! When I was at Balliol, and used to spend the afternoons naked, at Parson's Pleasure, I never saw such a magnificent specimen! In my tableau, I shall have Ben erect. A stiff Cupid, wrestling with two naked Furies. Better still – I have it! Adonis. The beautiful youth, fought over by Aphrodite, the goddess of love, and Persephone, goddess of the underworld. Adonis, a youth of remarkable beauty, was the favourite of the goddess Aphrodite. He was the product of the incestuous love Smyrna entertained for her own father, the Syrian king Theias. Charmed by his beauty, Aphrodite put the newborn infant Adonis in a box and handed him over to the care of Persephone, the queen of the underworld, who afterwards refused to give him up. An appeal was made to Zeus, who decided that Adonis should spend a third of the year with Persephone and a third with Aphrodite, the remaining third being at his own disposal.

'Adonis became an enthusiastic hunter, and was killed by a wild boar during the chase. Aphrodite pleaded for his life with Zeus, who allowed Adonis to spend half of each year with her and half in the underworld. The central idea is that of the death and resurrection of Adonis, which represent the decay of nature every winter and its revival in spring. He is thus viewed as having originated as an ancient spirit of vegetation. Annual festivals called Adonia were held at Byblos and elsewhere to commemorate Adonis for the purpose of promoting the growth of vegetation and the falling of rain. The name Adonis is believed to be of Phoenician origin, from Adon, or lord, Adonis himself being identified with the Babylonian god Tammuz.

'Persephone herself is an interesting story. She was the daughter of Zeus and Demeter, the goddess of agriculture; she was the wife of Hades, king of the underworld. Persephone was gathering flowers when she was seized by Hades and removed to the underworld. Upon learning of the abduction, her mother, Demeter, in her misery, became unconcerned with the harvest or the fruitfulness of the earth, so that widespread famine ensued. Zeus therefore intervened, commanding Hades to release Persephone to her mother. Because Persephone had eaten a single pomegranate seed in the underworld, she could not be completely freed but had to remain one-third of the year with Hades, spending the other two-thirds with her mother.

'The story that Persephone spent four months of each year in the underworld was no doubt meant to account for the barren appearance of Greek fields in full summer, after harvest, before their revival in the autumn rains. Of course, we Romans borrowed, or interpreted, the Greek gods and goddesses. Persephone is our Proserpine, Demeter our Ceres, and Aphrodite our Venus, just as the Greek Zeus is our Jupiter. Now, Ben, can you hold your erection?'

'I . . . I think so,' Ben said, blushing. 'Being a god is very flattering, but I'm not sure I want to be a vegetable.'

'You will remain erect, slave,' snapped Lefthera. 'That is my command.'

'Yes, mistress. I obey.'

'Then you may pose for me, if you please,' said Scazzo. His own phallus was half erect, as he took up his Minolta camera, with a 100-millimetre lens. As he photographed Lefthera and Nicola, holding Ben down, wrestling with him, embracing him, then playfully sucking his stiff phallus, with frivolous, teasing little licks to his glans, and giving him a gleeful spanking on his bare nates, Scazzo's own phallus rose to full rigidity.

'I am erect,' he crowed, 'which is the best and most creative condition for art. But to retain my creative power, I must remain chaste, even in the presence of two naked goddesses! It is the fate of the artist.'

The posing session turned to a vicious fight, the two nude girls, representing Aphrodite and Persephone, as combatants, wrestling with each other, and with Ben, or Adonis, who got the worst of things, his face pinioned under Nicola's naked buttocks, his tongue in her fragrantly juicing quim, and his nose in her smelly unwashed anus, while Lefthera spanked him.

'Capital!' cried Scazzo. 'Excellent! You see, photography is about possession, about ownership. Painting, too, is about ownership. One captures the person in the image. Why are so many young girls and boys eager to be photographed, or painted, in the nude? Look at the photoshoots in magazines, look on the Internet. People wish to exhibit their own naked bodies! They wish to exhibit themselves, and be admired! But also, they wish to be owned. They wish their body to belong to others, through the image. And sculpture, immortalising the nude body in stone, is the most powerful ownership of all. Now, Sylvestra must be in the tableau. She can be a Nereid, Amphitrite the water nymph, attending Adonis.'

He gestured to Sylvestra, who obediently stepped out of her skirt, and rolled down her lemon-yellow thong. Ben marvelled at the thickness and lushness of her pubic bush, over her golden nude body, her big breasts, fruity nipples and buttocks, and powerful meaty thighs, redolent of all the ripeness and fertility of the earth. Scazzo ordered Sylvestra, as a water nymph, to make obeisance to the god Adonis. Silently, Sylvestra knelt, and kissed Ben's feet. Then she rose, and put her lips around the helmet of his erect phallus. She began to suck gently, her tongue licking his peehole, until suddenly her head swooped, her hair cascading around Ben's stiff balls, and took his whole shaft to the back of her throat. Ben felt her naked breasts brushing his thighs and his sperm welled up, longing and ready to spurt. But Scazzo ordered his servant to desist; that was enough obeisance, for Ben must not be drained of his sperm. He must remain erect, full of his manly essence and power.

'Now, of course, both Persephone and Aphrodite are jealous of Amphitrite, so the nymph must be whipped.'

He produced two studded leather belts, and handed one each to Nicola and Lefthera, while Sylvestra, without a word, crouched on the floor, with her naked buttocks up and spread, and her head cradled between her elbows. Nicola and Lefthera lifted their belts, and began to flog Sylvestra's bare bottom, while Count Scazzo's camera whirred. *Vap! Vap!* The leather lashing her bare buttock flesh, Sylvestra bared her teeth in a rictus of agony, and screwed her eyelids tightly shut. The girl's golden fesses rapidly turned pink, and, when she had taken two dozen lashes from each of the sweating girls, her flogged skin was crimson with stripes. Yet apart from heavy gasping, as her breasts heaved, and her lungs powerfully inhaled and exhaled, she did not make a sound. Ben's erection was so hard, it was almost painful, and when the girls had finished flogging Sylvestra, he asked Lefthera for permission to take a cooling dip in the pool. Her eyes flashed in anger.

'You have addressed me without being first addressed, slave,' she hissed. 'That has earned you a lashing. Go into the pool, then, and return, to present your wet buttocks for a beating with the belt.'

'Sylvestra has earned a dip,' too,' said Scazzo. 'She may join Ben in the pool, and afterwards administer his lashes.'

Fearful of what was to come, yet relishing the cool water, Ben dived underwater, and felt the water surge as Sylvestra submerged herself beside him. Her luscious golden body entwined with his, and he felt her lips around his erect phallus. She sucked deep and hard, and he grasped her breasts, tweaking and stroking the big nipples. This time, Ben could not restrain himself, nor did he wish to. Underwater, he spurted his sperm into her throat, and she swallowed every drop of his discharge. When they emerged from the pool, both dripping wet, Sylvestra, sombre of mien, and her lips curled in a pouting sneer, picked up one of the studded belts. Lefthera ordered Ben to touch his toes, the most humiliating stance for a naked beating. Ben obeyed.

'Give the whelp four dozen,' Lefthera ordered curtly.

Ben knew his mistress had seen him sucked, and was angry at him for it. He gritted his teeth, as he heard the belt whistle, from Sylvestra's muscled arm, and then gasped, as the studded leather stung his bare buttocks. Four dozen of these! By the tenth stroke, he was crying, trying not to let the girls, or Scazzo, see his tears, as pain flooded him. He heard Sylvestra panting, as her bodybuilder's muscles wielded the cruellest of whips. Even though it was only a belt, not even a cane, yet the harshness of his flogger communicated itself to his tortured buttocks. The cane might even have been preferable: his four morning strokes from Lefthera were very painful indeed, yet dry and businesslike, and quickly done. There was a casual contempt in flogging a fellow with a belt. Sylvestra had sucked his sperm casually, and now was flogging him casually.

Scazzo watched, his phallus stiff, as he took photographs, and that was even more humiliating than being belted by a servant girl. Ben tried to count the strokes, but lost count after the second dozen. *Vap! Vap!* The leather whistled in the sultry air, as the lusciously naked Sylvestra lashed him, and his phallus stirred again. By the end of his beating, he was once more fully erect. He wanted to fuck Sylvestra in her cunt, wanted to be no longer a virgin. Fucking her *in cunno* would be punishing her, and worshipping her at the same time. When Sylvestra laid down her whip, Ben prostrated himself at Lefthera's bare feet, and kissed them. It was really Sylvestra's dainty feet he wanted to kiss, wanted to plunge his nose in her hairy pubic bush, and lick her cunt lips wet, but he knew better than that. Any disrespect to Lefthera would earn him another savage beating.

'Thank you, mistress,' he sobbed, as he sucked Lefthera's toes.

Scazzo threw him the belt that had whipped him, still hot from his flogged buttocks.

'Your work isn't done yet, Adonis,' he said.

He bent over the sculpted marble guard rail, and looked down at the throngs of tourists.

'You took your four dozen well,' he said, 'but I can take five dozen. Beat me as hard as you can.'

'Whip *you*, sir?'

'Yes. On the bare. It's the Balliol way. Guy de Bailleul, in Normandy, built Barnard Castle in Durham, and was the first of his family to receive lands in Scotland. He fought against David of Scotland at Northallerton in 1138, and with King Stephen was captured by Matilda at Lincoln in 1141. His son Bernard was present at the capture of King William I of Scotland at Alnwick in 1174. A descendant, Hugh, supported King John against the baronial party in England in 1215–16. Hugh's son and successor John married, in 1233, Dervorguilla, daughter of Alan, the last Celtic lord of Galloway, and also an heiress of King William of Scotland. His descendants were therefore able to have royal pretensions.

'John served as guardian of the young Scottish king, Alexander the Third. His loyalty to King Henry the Third of England in the Barons' War against rebellious nobles led by Simon de Montfort, Earl of Leicester, cost him the temporary loss of his lands and a period of imprisonment after his capture in the Battle of Lewes. About that time he began to support several students at Oxford, apparently as penance for a quarrel with the Bishop of Durham, who liked to be whipped by his monks. Guy liked to be whipped on his naked bottom by his wife, and by his students.

'After his death, his widow completed his endowment of scholars, and their house was formally chartered as Balliol College in 1282. one of the conditions of entry was the ability to strip naked, and take a severe whipping on the bare buttocks, from the widow Bailleul herself, or from a scholar, who was naked, while the widow Bailleul watched, and masturbated as he whipped the victim. So whip me, the Balliol way.'

Ben lifted the belt, and looked at Scazzo's bare arse, proffered for punishment. He wanted revenge, on anyone! On Sylvestra, for sucking his sperm, on Lefthera, but Scazzo would do. He began to flog him, and Scazzo grunted in pleasure, as his arse twitched under Ben's strokes. Meanwhile, Nicola photographed the scene with her Nikon. Sylvestra had disappeared, back to her pantry, presumably. Sweat poured from Ben's eyes, under the hot sun, as he flogged the artist's squirming bare.

'I think, by the end of this session,' Scazzo gasped, 'I shall have enough photographic material to make my paintings and sculpture.'

'We must go to Greece,' Lefthera said, discreetly masturbating Nicola, with alternate strokes to her own clito, as she watched the naked man's arse flogged. 'On my return, I shall purchase the sculpture, and take it back to Oxford. Agreed?'

'Agreed,' gasped Scazzo, as Ben completed his whipping of five dozen, leaving his tan buttocks bruised and swollen with crimson weals.

Now Sylvestra reappeared, nude, but for an enormous strap-on plastic dildo, coloured with red, white and green stripes, like the Italian flag, worn at her waist.

'I fear my punishment is not over,' Scazzo said, holding his buttocks apart. 'This implement comes from the Frasconi factory, over in Mestre. I am afraid Sylvestra is an avid collector of these vicious toys. Ahh!'

He shrieked, as Sylvestra thrust the massive dildo into his anus. A couple of plunges, and the entire bulk of the dildo filled his rectum. She began to bugger him vigorously, her muscled brown buttocks thrusting hard, while Nicola and Lefthera masturbated each other.

'Ah! It hurts!' moaned Scazzo. 'Sylvestra is the wickedest servant I have ever employed! Oh! Don't stop! Encule me, Sylvestra, my lovely!'

Ben's phallus was massively stiff, and hurt him. As he looked at Sylvestra's gorgeous bare buttocks, pumping, as she fucked her master, he could not restrain himself. Lefthera and Nicola were busy fingering each other's cunt; Lefthera was chewing Nicola's nipples, while Nicola moaned softly. Ben oiled his phallus from a jar of olive oil, then approached the buggering girl, and parted Sylvestra's buttocks – she acknowledged this with a grunt, seemingly of pleasure, or, at any rate, acceptance – and Ben thrust his oiled phallus into her anus.

Her next grunt, as his shaft filled her rectum, was definitely of pleasure. As she enculed Scazzo, so did he encule her, until they were all moving in the same rhythm, like a railway train. Scazzo was erect, and moaning under his buggery, while Sylvestra panted under Ben's vigorous thrusts to her colon. At length, as Ben spurted his sperm into her rectum, she panted, and shuddered in a heavy orgasm. Nicola, still photographing, brought Lefthera off, and her Nikon trembled briefly, as Lefthera frigged her to a heaving spasm.

'Yes!' cried Scazzo, his arse writhing, impaled on Sylvestra's dildo. 'Yes!'

His sperm jetted out, falling in an arc of delicate globules, to splash, pitter-patter, like creamy white rain-drops, into the Grand Canal.

'At least my slave is still a virgin,' Lefthera drawled. 'Please sculpt us, then, Count Scazzo. I shall pay, of course, and in fact, I shall send you a block of the best black obsidian, from Mílos, so that you may sculpt us twice. But I insist that, while you are working on these sculptures, you retain your creative sperm. No fornication, masturbation, or ejaculation of any kind. On your honour.'

'On my honour,' said Count Scazzo, bowing.

19

Ferry to Greece

Lefthera remained nude throughout their first-class train journey to Rome, Naples and Bari. In Rome, she sauntered in the nude up the Via Veneto, where she was mobbed by an enthusiastic crowd, including numerous photographers from German and Italian magazines, despite a dull crew-cut fellow, with a braying Midwestern accent, who emerged from the American Embassy, to say that she risked being arrested for terrorism, and sent to a camp for enemy combatants, where she could be detained without trial, for insulting the United States of America, by appearing indecently in front of their embassy. The supportive applause of the Germans and Italians saved her from American democracy, and since she was already known from her days of nude rambling in Venice, via Italian TV and newspapers, thanks to Nicola, fashionable ladies were in fact already strolling their lapdogs and taking their coffee and cakes in the Via Veneto, in the nude, with, of course, the latest high-heeled shoes, gold waist chains and crimson calfskin handbags. Every lady had her pubis, armpits and legs shaved gleaming smooth: it was simply not done to be hairy, except for a luxuriant mane on the head, often dyed blonde, and cascading over succulent golden breasts. ROMA NUDISTA, enthused the newspapers and TV.

By this time, the entire European press had latched on to the 'nudista femmina' of Venice, or, in the case of the left-wing media, the 'femminismo della nudità', and the trend spread to Milan, Florence and Naples, to Lake Como, even to Lugano and Bellinzona, over the border in Switzerland. *Stern* magazine in Hamburg pronounced that *'Nackt ist Gesund.'* Girls in Berlin and Hamburg and Munich and Amsterdam unconcernedly threw off their clothes, and walked naked in the Grunewald, the Rotherbaum, the Englischer Garten, or the Vondelpark, at least in greater numbers, for those places had been pockets of tolerance and legal nudism ever since the 1960s. It was the Germans, after all, who, in the last century, had reinvented ancient nudism. Archaeological evidence indicated that nudism, in the form of sunbathing, was practised in antiquity by the Babylonians, Assyrians, Greeks, and Romans. In modern times the rise of nudism began with the publication of *Die Nacktheit* – 'Nudity' – by German intellectual Richard Ungewitter in 1906.

Most of the Dutch beaches, and the German Baltic beaches, had long been officially or unofficially nudist, while, in Sweden and Denmark, all beaches were, officially, legally nudist. In faraway Iceland, it had long been the custom for teenagers to roam naked through the streets of Reykjavík, and splash in the fountain, during summer evening drinking sessions. The German commentators even made a few jokes about staid Swiss ladies abandoning their clothes to be fashionable, and wearing a lot of showy jewellery in order to show that they had a lot of money. Nipple rings, too, came into fashion. The richest Swiss ladies would appear nude, for their coffee, in Berne, or Geneva, or even in the Bahnhofstrasse in Zurich, with the biggest, most expensive nipple rings they could purchase.

It was by now *de rigueur* for fashionable Italian ladies to go shopping, or coffee drinking, or walking their poodles, stark naked. Italian lady skiers in the Dolomites performed their downhill runs in the nude, and, after an initial shyness, northern European tourists joined in the trend, although they did not really need much persuading. English, Swedish and German girls especially relished the freedom that nudity gave them, to enjoy their sport, and chose to remain naked for the hearty, wine-fuelled suppers afterwards. Lefthera, despite her reserve, had become a celebrity, thanks largely to Nicola's photographs, and Ben, too, as her 'boy-dressed-as-a-girl'.

She remained nude on the train to Bari, and nude on the ferry *Lefthera* over to Patras, which, of course, was owned by her father. The *Lefthera* would stop in Patras, then proceed to Kithera, until it brought them to Mílos. Captain Rodriguez, who was Spanish, from Salamanca, with Spiro his second in command, welcomed her with a bow, and escorted her to a luxurious private cabin, like a miniature hotel room, complete with flowers, bathroom, kitchenette and a fridge full of champagne. Lefthera told Ben that she was Daddy's favourite. So, when they boarded the ferry in Bari, Lefthera nude, and Ben bare-chested with nipple rings, but with white skirt and white nylons – like a Greek soldier – there were ripples of applause. It was so hot that other ladies, recognising Lefthera, began to strip, some down to their bras and panties, some to panties alone and others to the full nude.

When Ben and Lefthera had settled in their cabin, they went up on deck. Among those ladies who fully stripped off, to lean naked against the guard rail and enjoy the sunshine and breezes of the Ionian Sea, were two teenagers, one a blonde, the other ebony, and both stunning, their breasts casually squashed against the rail, and their big naked bottoms jutting saucily in the air, as though in invitation to dalliance. Both girls wore only crimson calfskin stiletto-heeled shoes, and both had golden nipple rings, with the black girl prettily adorned by a third ring dangling from her big outie navel. The blonde girl, in addition to her nipple rings, had two gold rings at her naked cooze flaps, each flap pierced, and with a ring sitting prettily in the flesh. The satin-smooth skins of their shaven nude bodies sparkled in the Mediterranean sun. Lefthera advanced discreetly, and slapped the black girl hard, on her bare buttocks, covering both big ebony cheeks with one slap, then slapped the blonde girl as well, on her golden buttocks, in the same fashion. Jolted, their breasts bounced, and their rings jangled.

'Neobule! Niobe!' she drawled. 'Have you forgotten your dresses? Your bras? Your panties?'

'Well, we saw your photo in *Paris-Match* magazine,' Neobule replied. 'It seems that, to be fashionable in Europe nowadays, one must be nude. And you know how much we French girls are obsessed with fashion.'

'What a coincidence to find you here! Where are you going?'

'Why, to Mílos, to join the Spartans,' said Neobule, her fingers stroking Niobe's bottom, while the blonde girl simpered.

'I *am* the Spartans,' said Lefthera.

'I know. You were very brave when I whipped and enculed you at the Club Acropolis. A true Spartan.'

'I enjoyed the power it gave me. You understand, Neobule, that I am the *sebastokrator*, the ruler of the Spartan colony on Mílos. If you are accepted as a Spartan officer, you shall be under my command.'

'I want nothing less.'

'The blonde girl Niobe shall be a slave.'

'She already is.'

'I see she has cunt rings now,' Lefthera said. 'They are very pretty.'

'Yes. I pierced her myself,' said Neobule. 'And I also gave her a piercing through the hood of her clito, a little gold rod. That's pretty, too. When I tongue her clito, she comes in seconds. I'm thinking of getting it done myself. A girl with a clito piercing is always trembling on the brink of orgasm. Knowing she is to orgasm keeps a girl submissive.'

'I have further plans for Ben in that direction. The poor lamb doesn't know how painful it will be for him on Mílos. But he is the slave of the Spartans, and must obey. Now, you must join me in my cabin, and have champagne, while you give my boyslave a whipping.'

'But I see you have a Bullworker! May I . . .?'

'Of course.'

Neobule pumped iron, using the compact muscle-building device for several minutes, expertly going through the whole range of exercises, for breasts, back, buttocks, biceps and thighs. Her superb breasts and thighs seemed to Ben to have been enlarged and hardened, in that short space of time. Her nude body gleamed, the heavy muscles pumped up, like a galaxy of blazing stars.

'*Ça, c'est mieux!*' she gasped happily. '*Maintenant, je veux fouetter le beau cul d'un garçon tout nu.*'

Ben shuddered. Neobule wanted to whip a naked boy on his bare! And he was the obvious candidate. It was very hot, and Ben found the air-conditioned cabin a blessing, although, when he was ordered to strip off, and present his bottom for Neobule's rod, he was in some confusion. Just like a girl, he thought. Lefthera presented Neobule with one of her canes, a stinging metre-long willow wand that Ben knew and feared, and Neobule said she thought it would do very well. Having stripped naked, and with his phallus stiffening, in the presence of three cruel, ravishing nude girls – although perhaps the submissive Niobe was, like himself, more the willing victim of cruelty – he was mollified by receiving a small glass of champagne. On the one hand, he longed for his bare arse to smart under Neobule's cane again, and longed to feel her dildo in his arse, as she fucked him. On the other, he was terrified of the pain that would be mixed with his submissive pleasure. Well, he reflected, as lay down on the bunk, and spread his buttocks, I don't have much choice. I'm a slave. Not to be the slave of a girl is unthinkable.

Niobe had her wrists tied behind her back, to stop her masturbating, Neobule said, and was gagged with Ben's panties, to stop her complaining. Her ankles were bound together with cords, and, trussed, the blonde girl sat on his back, to hold him still, and he felt her cooze moisten, as she rubbed her buttocks up and down his spine. Her rings dug into his flesh. Then, his whipping started. *Vip!* Neobule lashed him full across the bare with the cane, and his gorge rose, as tears filled his eyes. *Vip!* The agony was worse than he had ever experienced, for the muscular naked black girl was putting all her strength into his punishment. Punished for what? For the crime of being a slave. Yes, he deserved punishment.

196

Under the increasing wetness of Niobe's cooze crushing his back, he was rigidly erect, and he knew he deserved to be punished for that, too. And for wearing a girl's clothes. There was no end to the punishment he deserved, and craved, from a cruel nude girl! *Vip!* His bare bottom squirmed in agony. The trussed Niobe rocked back and forth on his back, and he knew by the wetness of her cunt that she was masturbating. He felt her stiff clito, and the little bar pierced through its hood, digging into him, as her hot come bathed his skin.

'Yes . . .' he moaned, phallus stiff, as Neobule's cane cuts descended on his helpless bare buttocks. 'Yes . . .'

He took twenty strokes in all, and, when Neobule lifted the masturbating blonde from his come-wet back, she exclaimed that he was still stiff and shameless. Neobule crouched on the bunk, with her buttocks spread.

'Do I have your permission to be enculed by your slave?' she asked Lefthera, and Lefthera, cigarette drooping at her lips, sneered her assent, adding that he was only a miserable slave, and miserable slaves had to obey a lady's command.

'Bugger me,' snapped Neobule. 'Fuck my lovely black arse hard, slave – for you know how boys love a black arse – and give me all your sperm. I want your lovely creamy juice up my rectum. You know you love a black girl's big bottom, my lovely ripe brown avocados, that I know boys like to kiss, and masturbate over. They like to spurt their cream on my thighs. Come on, I want to be flogged on my naked fesses. By you, lovely Ben! Take your revenge.'

Ben looked at the gorgeous black orbs of Neobule's bottom, and his erection throbbed. His flogged arse smarted in agony, yet he felt elated. This superb black girl *wanted* his phallus inside her! Niobe lay groaning and bound on the bunk, her long blonde hair plastered to her breasts with sweat, and Lefthera picked up the cane. While Ben penetrated Neobule's anus pucker, Lefthera began rather casually to cane Niobe on her naked breasts, alternating those strokes with cuts to her bare buttocks. Niobe sobbed and shrieked through her gag, but could only squirm helplessly, as Lefthera flogged her. Lefthera said that on Mílos she would be a helot, like Ben, and must get used to her fate.

Ben thrust, and felt the delicious relaxation of the black girl's sphincter, as her rectum opened fully to his engorged phallus, and he filled her, right to his balls, which slapped against her firm black buttocks, then commenced a powerful buggery. He groaned with pleasure, as he felt Neobule's sphincter squeeze his phallus, increasing the pressure of a rectum that was already deliciously tight. Her slim but massively muscled black thighs – *casse-noisettes*, *nutcrackers*, *like Lefthera's!* – quivered beautifully under his fucking, and he was afraid that they would capture his balls, and never let him go. Or – no – he wanted those superb ebony thighs and fesses to capture him. What was there in life, but to have your balls captured by a girl's thighs? Sperm rose in his scrotum, and he feared that he would come too soon for Neobule's pleasure, for, as Ben buggered her, the black goddess was already enthusiastically masturbating. But he was not enculing her in revenge: he was enculing her in thanks and worship of her gleaming ebony body, writhing, impaled on his stiffly obedient phallus.

Meanwhile, Lefthera, nipple rings jangling, continued to cane Niobe on her breasts and bottom, while the bound girl shrieked and sobbed. Neobule masturbated herself to a powerful orgasm, and then commanded Ben to give her his sperm, into her colon. Gratefully, Ben allowed himself to ejaculate, the honey spurting from his balls, as he gasped in ecstasy. Lefthera, having dealt Niobe two dozen cuts of her cane, wound her hair around her fist, and dragged her like a sack into the bathroom. She ripped out Niobe's gag, and Ben and Neobule watched, as Lefthera squatted over Niobe, and pissed on her breasts and face. The trussed Niobe's lips gasped like a fish mouth, as she swallowed Lefthera's golden fluid.

'Thank you,' she babbled. 'Thank you.'

'I think it is time for luncheon,' Lefthera said. 'Neobule, you and I shall remain nude, and Ben may wear, I think, a white skirt, and pink nylons, with pink shoes – and I think Niobe should be nude too, although I think we can leave her wrists tied behind her back. But I have something which may be useful.'

Lefthera produced, from one of her many cases, a length of wood, with cuffs at each end.

'It is an ankle hobble,' she said. 'Made by my friend Stygia, in Oxford. Neobule, if you will be so kind as to unbind Niobe's feet, we may fit her in this. It is more durable, and more uncomfortable, than mere cord.'

The weeping Niobe, hosed down with an icy spray of water, was soon shuffling in her hobble, her ankles cuffed, and the foot-long length of wood keeping her legs apart, but obliging her to walk like a crab, at an ungainly pace. Her wrists still bound behind her back, and led by Ben, in his pink stockings, pink thong, whose string bit painfully into his whipped arse, and pink court shoes, with bare ringed breasts and a white skirt, Niobe followed her two naked mistresses, Lefthera being nipple-ringed, to luncheon, at Captain Rodriguez's table.

Captain Rodriguez of the *Lefthera*, as a Castilian gentleman, kissed the nude ladies' hands, after inviting them to join him at his table. The dining room was quite full, with a sprinkling of nude ladies being the centre of attention. Lefthera, as the daughter of his boss, was to be shown every honour, as were her companions. And, being Spanish, he served mostly seafood, for the Spanish are obsessed with eating anything that comes out of the sea. There were steaming dishes of cooked crab and mussels, with raw *almejas*, giant clams (eaten alive, with a dash of lemon juice), tiny cooked clams, sliced octopus stewed in its own juice, fried squid and shrimp, pieces of dried salted cod.

Lefthera explained that Ben, as her slave, would not be permitted to join them at table, but would squat on the floor, and accept whatever scraps she chose to give him. Neobule said the same for her own slave, Niobe. Lefthera and Neobule tucked into the feast, under the benevolent eye of Captain Rodriguez. There were Greek wines to drink. Lefthera and Neobule chatted to Captain Rodriguez in Spanish. From time to time, the girls threw their slaves scraps of salt cod, a piece of half-chewed squid, or a clamshell.

'Have you ever eaten octopus, Ben?' Lefthera said, washing down an *almeja*, with lots of pepper and lemon juice, with a glass of white wine.

'No, mistress.'

'Well, you can learn.'

Lefthera rose, and scooped a handful of the sliced octopus, parted her thighs, then rammed the entire dripping handful into her open cunt. She resumed her seat, and ordered Ben to dine from her vagina. Neobule thought this a sound idea, and filled her own cunt with pieces of fried squid, and told Niobe she could dine too. Ben knelt, and began to suck the food from his mistress's cunt, painfully erect, as his lips touched the lips of her vulva. He sucked all the octopus and octopus juice from her overflowing vulva, and it tasted a little bland – not like a meat pie with brown sauce at the Bear Inn – but he didn't mind, for he was tasting her divine cunt. He was a long way from Oxford. But everywhere, really, was a long way from Oxford. Or was it?

The fishy taste of the octopus seemed to marry with the salty sea juices of Lefthera's vulva. Lefthera was busy scooping fresh plump orange mussels from their shells, eating half of them, and putting the rest aside. When Ben had eaten all the octopus from her cooze, she rose again, giggling a little, and shoved a handful of shelled mussels into her anus. Then she sat on Ben's face, ordering him to continue his meal. Ben gasped, for his mistress's naked buttocks, sweatily acrid, were crushing his face, but he was in heaven, as he smelt the divine perfume of her cunt and anus, and sucked the mussels from her filled rectum. Neobule, not to be outdone, packed her own anus with hot tiny clams, and sat on Niobe's face, ordering her to suck the clams from her anus, and shell them with her teeth, before swallowing the morsel of protein within.

Lefthera had her hand on Captain Rodriguez's knee, in his immaculate white uniform. Her fingers crept up his thigh, and began to massage his groin, until his erection bulged in his uniform trousers.

'There is some protein I want,' she drawled.

'I . . .' he stammered.

'Remember, I am the boss's daughter,' drawled Lefthera.

She knelt under the tablecloth, and unzipped Captain Rodríguez, baring his stiff phallus, which she took deep in her throat, and sucked hard. The captain groaned, still smiling at his roomful of luncheon guests, but with his face flushed. Neobule, too, disappeared under the table and, as Lefthera sucked the captain's stiff cock, she had her tongue in Lefthera's cunt. The black girl ordered Niobe to lick her clito, while she licked Lefthera's.

Suddenly, Captain Rodriguez seemed to be alone at his table! He tried not to groan, as he ejaculated in Lefthera's mouth, and she swallowed his load of sperm, while herself shuddering in orgasm, under Neobule's tongue, and Neobule being wanked by Niobe's tongue. Niobe could not masturbate herself, as her hands were bound behind her back, and her legs were hampered by her wooden hobble, but she rubbed her clito on the table leg, and brought herself to climax in that fashion. Ben felt a little left out of things.

'Thank you for a lovely meal, Captain Rodriguez,' Lefthera said, licking his sperm from her lips. 'I shall certainly give you a favourable mention to the boss.'

When they arrived at the port of Patras, a gaggle of fashionable nude ladies stepped off the ship and hailed taxis, to the delight of the taxi drivers of Patras. Lefthera's party stayed on the ship, which would call at Kithera, before depositing them on Mílos, where Lefthera's sister Zenobia would be there to greet them.

'I hear that Timothy Dunton-Smythe is there, too,' she said thoughtfully.

20

Pony Girl of Mílos

Lefthera read:

'Mílos (or Melos), most southwesterly of the major islands of the Greek Cyclades in the Aegean Sea. The greater portion of the 150-square-kilometre island, of geologically recent volcanic origin, is rugged, culminating in the west in Mt Profitis Ilías (751 metres). It has a population of 4,500, not including the nudist Spartan colony of alleged pleasure-seekers, whose numbers are not recorded. Its obsidian exports to Phoenicia helped to make it an important centre of early Aegean civilisation. The bay, 250 metres deep, is a submerged crater created out of a violent volcanic eruption that left an isthmus approximately 2.5 kilometres wide on the south. Mílos, the capital and chief town, lies just north of the chief port, Adhámas. Southwest of the town are catacombs in which early Christians from the Greek mainland sought refuge. On the ancient acropolis of Adamanda the famous *Venus*, or *Aphrodite*, of Milo was found in 1820.

'The British School at Athens, under the direction of Professor Dunton-Smythe, excavated (1896–99) the ancient acropolis of Klima (1000–800 BC) above Mílos, uncovering a palace and a gymnasium and a Roman theatre of later date. The most significant civilisation uncovered on Melos by the British School, however, was that of Phylakopi, a site near Apollonia, the second port of Melos, on the promontory of Pláka. Phylakopi was a flourishing settlement at the time of the late Bronze Age eruption of neighbouring Thera. Evidence discovered at Phylakopi in 1974 tended to reverse earlier assumptions that the eruption had destroyed the island: no break in continuity was established. The oldest city dates from between 2300 and 2000 BC. On the same site a second city rose from 2000 to 1550 BC. The third city (1550–1100), dating largely from the Mycenaean Age, represents the fullest flowering of Melos's Cycladic civilisation. Phylakopi was destroyed about 1100 by Dorian settlers. The Athenian outrage of slaying the entire male population (416) in reprisal for the islanders' neutrality during the Peloponnesian War inspired the playwright Euripides to write and stage before his fellow Athenians his work *Trojan Women*, an anti-war play.

'The historian Thucydides, in his *Melian Dialogue*, preserved the speeches made in negotiations between the Athenians and Melians, which preceded the military action. The Spartan soldier-statesman Lysander (died 395 BC) restored the island to its Dorian possessors, but it never recovered its prosperity. Under Frankish rule the island formed part of the duchy of Naxos. In classical times Melos's sulphur, alum and obsidian mines gave it wide commercial prominence; the Melian earth was used as a pigment by painters. Bentonite, perlite, kaolin, barium, gypsum, millstones and salt are exported, and oranges, olives, grapes, cotton, and barley are cultivated. The island is no longer famous for the ornamental vases and the goldsmiths' art produced in the seventh century BC.'

Lefthera finished her reading from *The Oxford Encyclopaedia of the Mediterranean*. The ship, having stopped briefly at the island of Kíthira, where Captain Rodriguez took on a cargo of the purple dye made since ancient times from the shells of the murex mollusc, was nosing into the harbour of Adhamas.

'So we are here,' she said to Ben, Neobule and Niobe. 'It's amusing, they call us Spartans pleasure seekers. Although we are nude, you will discover that we are anything but pleasure seekers in the usual sense. But I suppose that, if boys and girls are nude, they must be considered by the strait-laced as pleasure seekers, even though they are slaves under the lash, their bare buttocks whipped with olive branches, while they are obliged to crush murex shells with their bare feet, pick olives and oranges, mine salt and chisel obsidian, and perform sacred masturbation at the crossroads at dawn, before a ritual whipping on the bare buttocks.'

'Masturbation at the crossroads at dawn? With a lovely bare-fesse whipping?' said Neobule, licking her lips, and Niobe cringed.

Eventually, it was time to leave the ship. Lefthera offered her friends a last bottle of champagne, while the 'goat-herds' disembarked. When, proudly nude, and brandishing a pigskin whip, she led her equally nude party regally down the gangplank – apart from Ben, who was in his skirt and nylons – there was a chariot of cedar wood and crimson leather waiting for them. Between the polished shafts of the chariot stood a sweating girl, clad only in sandals, blue scalloped nylon bra, scarcely covering her jutting breasts and big plum nipples, and tiny transparent thong panties, like Ben's, which performed just as little service in conceal-ing her shaven cunt hillock; she was fastened by a cowhide harness to the antique spoke-wheeled cart.

Ben gaped: she was ripe of breast and bottom, long-legged, and olive-skinned, with a muscled, narrow waist, almost pencil-thin, and long curly black hair that cascaded over her jutting nipples. In fact, she was the image of Lefthera, although Lefthera was now shaven-headed, and her own mane, cascading over her naked breasts, consisted of the blonde tresses she had shorn from Lucy Parvis. The pony girl's body rippled with muscle, but it was not ripped muscle from bodybuilding. It was muscle installed by hauling a chariot. Her nylon bra and string panties dripped with sweat, making them translucent, and Ben could see every detail of her shaven cunt, through the sliver of nylon gusset that covered her cooze, and the flimsy nylon sheathing her sweat-beaded bare breasts. Whip marks covered her buttocks and back. Under her scanty nylon bra jutted heavy rings, pierced through her big plum nipples.

Without a word, Lefthera climbed into the chariot, and beckoned Neobule to join her on the leather banquette. There was a harness in the chariot, and Lefthera ordered Ben to strip to his thong, then fastened him in the harness, just as he had been harnessed, in the ancient Spartan rite, back at Hereford Hellenic. When he was tethered, she instructed Ben to join the pony girl between the shafts, and held him by reins, fastened to his harness. Niobe, in her ankle hobble, was tied to the back of the chariot by a cord through her nipple rings, and instructed to follow on her bare feet. Lefthera lifted her whip, and lashed a savage stroke to the bare shoulders of the long-haired girl, then followed it with an equally harsh lash to Ben's bared buttocks. His nipple rings jangled, as his buttocks shuddered at his mistress's lash.

'Hurry, you animals! You beastly snails!' Lefthera cried. 'We want to be home in time for tea!'

The chariot took off, at a brisk jog, with Niobe weeping, as she stumbled behind, half running and half pulled, by her savagely wrenched breasts. Lefthera lashed her drivers on, the girl on the back, and Ben on the buttocks. She said to Neobule that she did not wish to spoil the girl's panties, as they were hers, on loan to the slave.

'You have willing slaves,' said Neobule. 'The girl is strong, and pulls the chariot well. Ben likewise.'

'That slut willing? No! That is the most disobedient cow in all Greece. She is my sister, Zenobia.'

Vap! Vap! Lefthera's lash struck the naked bodies of the pony slaves.

'Faster, you snails!' Lefthera cried.

The two slaves increased their pace.

'This is hard,' Ben panted, to the nearly naked girl, sweating beside him in harness.

'We are slaves of the Spartans,' said Zenobia. 'Life is hard.'

'Are you whipped a lot?'

'Of course. My sister Lefthera whips me, of course.'

'Lefthera is your sister?'

'Can't you tell?' she panted, her ringed breasts heaving in their skimpy bra. 'We're twins. But Timothy Dunton-Smythe is the cruellest of whippers, even though he is a slave himself. It is always slaves who are cruellest to other slaves. He whips me, and buggers me. It is my lot, as a girlslave, and I must accept it. His enormous phallus up my bottom, making me cry, but making me come, too! My cunt gets so wet, when I am buggered!

'And I masturbate, as I feel a man's spunk fill my behind! My clito is so stiff – I rub it a few times – and my belly flutters. Masturbating is one of the only pleasures for a girlslave, or a boyslave, too. One of our duties is to masturbate at the crossroads at dawn. We shall be ordered to masturbate together, I'm sure. You see, masturbating is what people, whether girls or boys, really like to do. Being sodomised is painful, but ecstatic, because you can rub your clito at the same time as a man buggers you. And boys really get the most pleasure, not from fucking us, but from wanking off over our breasts and bellies. Or our naked bums. *Looking* at our nude bodies, as we look at theirs! Who better than a boy knows his own phallus, or a girl her own clito?

'I am proud to have my hymen, and remain a cunt virgin, and masturbatress. I see you shave your body. That is good. A nude body is virtue. But we must hurry –' her muscled bare thighs and buttocks pumped as she pulled the chariot '– for if my sister misses her tea, served in the English manner by Timothy Dunton-Smythe, we shall have floggings more severe than you can imagine, from our overladies.'

Vap!

'*Ahh!*' she screamed, as her sister's whip lashed her bare back.

'Faster, you filthy snails!' cried Lefthera.

They ascended a steep hill, and came to the old Venetian palace, in bronze sandstone, that was the headquarters of the Spartan demesne on Mílos. In the fields all around, naked boys and girls laboured, picking cotton, or fruit, under the whips of Spartan girls dressed only in white boots and skirtlets, their ringed breasts heaving, as they lashed the naked slaves on the bare buttocks. Some of the bare boys and girls had, as well as nipple rings, and bars pierced through their earlobes, rings pierced through their central buttocks. This was useful for their overladies to control them, with leash cords looped through their buttock or nipple rings. Under the whips and canes of their overladies, naked girls and boys tramped murex shells in huge wooden vats, the slaves' bare bodies slopped with purple dye, and their naked buttocks striped a lesser shade of purple, too, from the cruel rods of the overseers.

Their journey over, Zenobia was ordered to the stables, where she lodged with pigs and horses and goats, in a stinking chamber with the floor covered in fouled straw.

'I hope we'll meet again,' she whispered. 'I hope you're not sold as a slave.'

'Sold?' Ben gasped.

'You didn't know? There are slave auctions. Women come from all over Asia, Europe and Africa, to buy the choicest boyslaves, and men come to buy the choicest girls. It's a misfortune for you that you are so pretty.'

'But this is the twenty-first century! Slavery! I mean . . .'

'It happens all the time. In Mali, Gambia, Laos or Cambodia, you can buy a girl as your chattel, for a hundred dollars. Enough to get her father out of debt. I'm lucky to be a pony girl. It's the best job here, although it's tough, but it's not as hard as working in the fields, or chiselling obsidian. Slavery is the natural state, for boys or girls, you see. In ancient Athens and Rome, a third of the population were slaves. In Zanzibar and Madagascar, in the old days, over half the population were slaves. Mostly, they were domestic slaves, not field production slaves.

'But a lot of the time young boys and girls sold themselves into slavery, to escape debt. The British outlawed slavery in the nineteenth century and pretty much stamped out the traffic, but it still persists. You see, some of us, especially girls, *want to be slaves*. We pony girls take the merchandise to the port, you see, to be loaded on to the ships, which my father owns. If you're lucky, you'll be made a pony girl – you look strong enough – and you'll have to dress as a girl, wear bra and thong panties, like me.'

'That would please me,' Ben said. 'I want to be the slave of a girl, and to dress as a girl. You see ... it's hard to explain this ... but the reason chaps fall in love with girls is because we worship them, and, secretly, we want to *be* girls. To possess such beauty.'

'Perhaps we could be harnessed together,' Zenobia said coyly, and blushing. 'But here, slaves have to be nude, for shame.'

'It would be no shame for me, Zenobia, to be harnessed in the nude, beside you,' Ben blurted.

Ben was led into the huge airy palace, marvelling at the nude statues, the ornate marble staircase and the tapestries and paintings depicting the male or female nude, which adorned the walls. Lefthera and Neobule led him into a tiled salon, the wall decorated with frescoes, showing mythological scenes of nude Aphrodite, Demeter and Persephone, where they reclined on couches, to receive their tea, a choice of Darjeeling or Lapsang Souchong, while Ben and Niobe had to crouch on the floor. In the corner of the room stood a wooden gibbet, fitted with leather cuffs, for wrists and ankles. Ben shuddered in fear.

'Hello, old chap,' said Timothy Dunton-Smythe. 'We meet again!

Bare to the waist, and barefoot, Timothy wore a pleated white skirtlet that only just covered his naked balls and phallus.

'Sorry I can't offer you tea, it's the best Darjeeling or the Chinese stuff, but it's only for the mistress, you see. Unless she permits you to have a dish. I'm what they call an overseer here, but I'm a slave, just like you. I expect you'll want to see the library, work on some books. We have some fabulous old parchments and papyri here. First editions of Aristarchus of Samothrace, Apollonius Dyscolus, Archilochus, Hyperides, Crates of Millus.'

'It sounds fascinating,' Ben said, from his crouching position, and then cried out as Lefthera's whip lashed his bare back a savage stroke.

'Silence, you helot snail!' she hissed.

Neobule and Lefthera sipped tea from Wedgwood cups, with a floral design, and nibbled imported Parisian *petits fours*.

'There is a punishment to be carried out, mistress,' said Timothy. 'The Armenian pony girl Eudoxia. You know, an undergrad at Lady Margaret Hall? Wants to do postgrad work on the grammarian and poet Philetas of Cos.'

'Founder of the Hellenistic school of poetry,' Lefthera drawled. 'His poem, *Demeter*, describing the wanderings of the nude Earth goddess. Why, we have the only surviving parchment fragment here in our library. I suppose Eudoxia has been working on it. But what is her crime?'

'She soiled her knickers, mistress, pissed in them, in fact, while carrying me to market in a chariot, with a cargo of oranges and obsidian chunks. Of course, she must work off the price of new knickers, by labour, but there is chastisement due. Shall I bring her in, and administer justice?'

'Please do so, Timothy,' said Lefthera. 'It is always amusing for a lady to watch a slave whipped, while she enjoys a proper cup of tea.'

Sobbing, the nude Eudoxia was pulled into the room by her long dark hair. She was petite, slim of frame, but with large conic breasts that seemed almost too big for her slender body. Her big whip-scarred buttocks, too, jutted ripely from her slender, almost obscenely slender waist, that seemed designed to inspire men's lust. Her breasts, topped by pink cherry nipples, quivered, as tears streamed from her eyes.

'Please ...' she whimpered. 'Please no ... are we not whipped enough every day? I didn't mean any harm ... I didn't mean to soil my knickers, but I was doing my best as a pony girl, and Timothy's whip was so fierce ...'

'No excuses, you snivelling Armenian brat!' said Lefthera. 'String her up, Timothy.'

'At once, mistress.'

Timothy dragged the howling girl to the gibbet, and quickly fastened her wrists and ankles into the leather cuffs, suspending her, naked and helpless. Lefthera handed him a long leather cow whip, and ordered him to flog her from long range. He was also to remove his skirt. It was Spartan custom that a whipper should preferably be as nude as the victim, for it righted the cosmic balance. Timothy curtsied, and removed his skirt, revealing his phallus, stirring to erection. Naked, he took up an athlete's whipping stance behind Eudoxia's nude body.

'No ... please, mistress,' whimpered the strung girl. 'Don't whip me ... I promise I'll be good, in future.'

'This will teach you to be good,' snapped Lefthera, as Neobule poured both girls more tea.

Vap!

'Ahh!'

Vap!

'Oh! No!'

Eudoxia's petite naked body writhed in agony under the lash, which descended on her back, and on her clenched, squirming buttocks. *Vap!*

'Ahh!' she screamed.

'More cream and sugar?'

'Yes, please.'

Vap!

'*Ahh! Ahh!*'

At the tenth whiplash, Eudoxia pissed herself, sobbing in shame and pain. A golden stream of acridly perfumed liquid flooded from her cooze, over the tiled floor. Lefthera wrinkled her nose, although Neobule laughed cruelly. Timothy took the girl to twenty strokes, and her arse was crimson with welts, before Lefthera crooked a finger, to order him to halt the flogging. Timothy was fully erect, his massive phallus a hand's breadth from the whipped girl's buttocks.

'Should he ... ?' murmured Neobule.

'Why not?' said Lefthera. 'Soiling her panties! Pissing on my floor! She deserves all the punishment she can take.

Make her lick it up. And Timothy, you may ... you know.'

She nodded to the panting Timothy, who released her from the gibbet, and pushed her to a crouching position on the tiled floor. While Eudoxia licked up the lake of her own piss, Timothy inserted his massively erect tool into her anus, and enculed her, thrusting in, right to his balls, and riding her as if she were a donkey.

'Oh! No! You're too big!' the petite girl squealed.

'Obey, slave!' cried Lefthera. 'Open your beastly arse!'

Both she and Neobule were lazily masturbating, fingers at each other's clito, at the spectacle of the buggered girl from Lady Margaret Hall. Timothy's balls slapped her wealed buttocks, with a pleasing dry sound, as he bummed her. The sobbing Eudoxia licked and swallowed her own piss, before Timothy thrust her face to the floor, and straddled her squirming buttocks, thrusting hard into her anus, while masturbating her clito with his fingers.

'Oh! Don't!' she gasped. 'Oh! No! Yes! Do! Do it harder! Oh, you brute, I'm going to come.'

Within several minutes of heavy buggery, while the girl sobbed, she nevertheless heaved in orgasm three times, as Timothy masturbated her, her face writhing in the pool of her own piss. At length, when Neobule and Lefthera had frigged each other to the brink of climax, Lefthera crooked her finger, giving Timothy permission to spurt, and, wanking his victim to a final orgasm, he ejaculated his sperm into Eudoxia's colon, while Neobule and Lefthera brought each other off, with come flowing down their quivering bare thighs, as their bellies heaved in spasm. Eudoxia was ordered to crawl to Lefthera, and kiss her mistress's feet, while thanking her for her just punishment.

'And that, Eudoxia,' Lefthera said, draining her cup of tea, and snapping her come-wet fingers, for Timothy to light cigarettes for her and Neobule, 'is what a naughty pony girl gets.'

Lefthera said to Timothy that there was a new policy: the pony girls could henceforth be nude for their work, outside as well as inside the Spartan estate. They spoilt far too many bras and knickers, often pissing in them, as they pulled their chariots, and the expense of replacing those items could be saved. Nudity had become respectable in Europe. But nudity could not excuse laziness. Any lazy pony girls were to be whipped and buggered without mercy.

'Very good, mistress,' Timothy purred. 'Is Ben to be a pony girl?'

'Yes, for the meantime,' Lefthera replied.

21

Slave of the Spartans

Ben did not need to use any bodybuilding devices, for his strenuous work as a pony girl built his muscles to rocky hardness. He had to carry loads of the dark glassine obsidian to the port, where one of Lefthera's father's ships would carry them to northern Europe, or America, Mílos obsidian being much prized by certain sculptors. Oranges, too, which were for local consumption in Athens, or clay pots full of purple murex dye, for the designer houses of Paris and Milan. After Lefthera's *diktat*, the pony girls now worked in the full nude, although Ben had to wear a string to cover his phallus. Sometimes, he had to pull the chariot alone, and sometimes, to his pleasure, he was yoked and harnessed with Zenobia or Eudoxia. As they panted, running, he relished the feel of a girl's bare thighs against his own. Always, an overlady or else Timothy sat in the chariot, wielding the whip, and Timothy's whip strokes were hard, although he always said 'sorry, old boy' after lashing Ben, urging him to go faster. Ben once groaned that he could go faster, if he did not have to carry the extra weight of an overseer in the chariot, and that remark earned him further lashes.

'A chariot has a driver. It's the done thing, old boy,' said Timothy, as he whipped Ben's naked buttocks.

His heaviest load was a huge solid block of obsidian, for shipment to Count Scazzo in Venice, to be used for the gigantic sculpture in which he himself would figure. He was proud to see it winched aboard the *Lefthera*. At the obsidian mine, Ben recognised quite a few of the fellows from Oxford, toiling naked, under the whips of their nude overladies, as they chipped at the rock. He also saw girls he knew from St Hilda's or St Hugh's, grimacing, as they trampled the murex shells, which was very painful to their bare feet. Cybele was there, as overlady, nude but for sandals, and Roxanna and Iphigenia too, all the Furies wielding whips – although Roxanna favoured a cane – and administering arbitrary lashes to the naked bottoms of the sweating slaves. There was the chap from Corpus, and the one from Wadham, and the one from Univ. But talking among slaves was forbidden, and they could do no more than exchange sheepish nods, anything more risking a serious flogging with the hippopotamus-hide whip. Among the girlslaves, he recognised Felicity and Abigail, of the Hymen Club, trampling murex shells, and Monica Trencher, and Lucy Parvis, her magnificent blonde tresses now grown back, but soon to be shorn again, for Timothy sneered that she was kept by Lefthera as a 'wig slave' – but again, he could do no more than nod in recognition.

The bodies of the nude slaves, whether male or female, rippled with muscle, from the backbreaking work of mining the obsidian, or loading it – even picking oranges – or, in the case of Ben and the other pony girls, from transporting it. When the pony girls had delivered their cargo to the port, they returned with a load of fish, eggs, tomatoes, onions, cheese, wine, lettuce and bread, which was what the slaves dined on. At night, they all slept together, naked on filthy straw, in one of the various stables or outhouses, roped together by a long cord that passed through their nipple rings, buttock rings, or cunt rings. There could be no sexual touching among the trussed naked slaves, although all of them illicitly masturbated into the straw, which stank of sperm and girl come.

Lefthera and Neobule shared a luxurious bed in the top chamber of the palace, while Niobe was kept chained to the foot of their bed. Ben was roused before dawn, in advance of the others, and fed a breakfast of tea, bread and honey, then escorted to the library, by Cybele or another overlady. In the library, he was set to work in the nude, on a paper he was writing about the grammarian, philologist and critic Aristarchus of Samothrace. Aristarchus was considered the supreme critic, with commentaries on Homer, Aeschylus and Sophocles, and critical editions of Hesiod, Pindar, Archilochus, Alcaeus and Anacreon. Ben's task was to write a commentary on Aristarchus's commentaries. After three hours' work in the library, Iphigenia or Cybele would bring him a cup of strong sweet tea and a cigarette, and then, with the sun risen, he was clad in his thong, and harnessed to the chariot, to begin his day's duty as a pony girl. One day, Cybele was in an expansive, chatty mood, for she boasted she had just flogged a boy from Trinity so hard on his naked buttocks that he had fainted under her lash.

'You're to be given your bum rings tomorrow, Ben, at dawn,' she said. 'Neobule's to do the piercing. Then you shan't go to the library, but to the crossroads, where you'll masturbate to the sunrise, with Zenobia.'

'Yes, mistress,' Ben said, head bowed. 'At your command.'

'You're learning the right words. A boy is only happy when he's learning.'

'I . . . I am happy. I just wonder what it will be like when I go back to Oxford. I mean, I'm so used to being nude, I've almost forgotten what it's like to wear clothes.'

'What makes you think you will go back to Oxford?' Cybele said. 'There is a slave auction at the end of August. A pretty boy like you is sure to be sold. You could end up anywhere on earth. You'll be a slave, and slaves are naked. So, if that's what you want, you'll probably get it. People disappear, Ben. It's easy to make that happen.'

The next day, Ben writhed in a mercifully brief moment of agony, as Neobule pierced the centre of his bare buttocks, and inserted a further pair of bronze rings, from Lefthera's own collection, while Lefthera smoked and watched, her lips curled in pleasure. Then, Ben and Zenobia were harnessed together between the shafts of a chariot, with Lefthera driving, and she whipped them up the hill to the appointed crossroads. Just as the sun rose, each masturbated, Zenobia wanking her clito to several orgasms, while she pinched and squeezed her nipples, their rings dancing, and Ben to just one, spurting his sperm into the dry dust of the roadway. His new buttock rings hurt a little, but he was rather proud of them. They matched his nipple rings! As they pulled the chariot down the hill, Zenobia panted that he looked awfully pretty, and that if she was ever to lose her cunt virginity, although it was a dreadful crime, she wouldn't mind . . .

'Yes?' Ben gasped eagerly.

'I wouldn't mind if you were the first boy in my cunt,' Zenobia said, blushing fiercely.

Ben's new buttock rings tickled a little, whenever he sat down, but the feeling was strangely pleasant, reminding him of the sensitivity of his bottom. Since they matched his nipple rings, he thought of getting an albert pierced into the glans of his phallus, but the idea frightened him. Still, if Lefthera commanded, he had to obey. The point of piercings and rings was to remind you of the delicacy of your body, remind you of parts that you normally didn't think about. Buttocks were not just something you sat on and forgot: they were a source of sensitive pleasure, and, when whipped, the pleasure of pain. Timothy Dunton-Smythe came and admired Ben's new bum rings, then lifted his skirt to show his own bronze buttock rings.

'Lefthera gave me these a long time ago,' he said. 'Fellow's much better off with a few rings. Shows the ladies are in charge, and that's what we like, ain't it? We're just chattels, and can be sold at the slave auction at any time. Concentrates a chap's mind wonderfully, knowing he can be sold as a slave. Keeps him on his toes, as it were. Of course, a pretty boy like you could end up at the far corners of the globe, and no one would know. It happens. The Spartans are cruel ladies.'

It was nearly the end of August. Ben and Zenobia had secreted themselves to cuddle in the hayloft, used for the pigs and goats. The place stank, and their nude bodies

216

were slimed with muck, but the fragrance of Zenobia's naked body overcame the stench of the animals.

'You see,' said Zenobia, 'Lefthera was sent to Oxford, but I was sent to Cambridge.'

'Cambridge?' said Ben. 'Good heavens.'

'Yes, I know. Oxford is for statesmen and scholars, and Cambridge is for spies and comedians. When the late Lord Dacre moved from Oxford to Cambridge, to become Master of Peterhouse, he said that he had a lovely house to live in, though it was a pity the college had to come with it. But Cambridge it was, for me. And I must admit I enjoyed it. Cambridge is like a small Greek village, really, and Clare College, on the Backs, was really nice. I and my girlfriends used to go out at night, and swim nude in the River Cam. Then, in the day, we would punt up the Backs, wearing just bras and panties, or lacy petticoats.

'One June day, when it was very hot, we decided we could take our bras off, and nobody minded. The next day, when it was even hotter, we stripped off our panties and petticoats as well, and poled the whole length of the Backs in the nude. All the fellows cheered. We had a club, like the Hymen Club at Oxford, only we called it the Sappho Club.

'Some of the gross fellows called us the girly wankers' club, and it wasn't far wrong, because that's what we did. We would meet in the nude, to drink tea and masturbate, in celebration of our virginity. Sometimes a girl would masturbate alone, in worship of her cunt, and sometimes we would practise mutual masturbation, worshipping another girl's cunt. But we let boys in, too, boys we could trust, who had vowed to remain virgin and unsullied. Some of them are here now, as helots. The boys would strip off, and we girls would lie down naked, and let the boys spank our bottoms with their hands, or sometimes a slipper, because all girls like that, really, being spanked on their bare bums, I mean, and, after spanking us, they would wank off over our nude bodies. There was no touching, otherwise, except when we felt their hot sperm bathing our breasts and cunt hillocks. You see, for most people, having intercourse is a duty. It's tiresome, and most of us would

217

really prefer to wank off, if there wasn't such foolish prejudice against masturbation. Bodies in reality are messy things, but the image, the platonic ideal of the body, is clean.

'Well, afterwards, when the boys had ejaculated their loads, we would have lots more tea, and meat pies with homemade brown sauce from Mrs Digby's café in Six Mile Bottom, and hot buttered crumpets. We would butter the crumpets, and mix the butter with sperm from the boys' ejaculations. Sperm, saltless Dutch butter and Cambridgeshire brown sauce are a tasty mixture. We would rub it all over ourselves, giggling and slapping each other on the bum, before taking a communal shower. They were lovely times. To be nude, and have nude boys wanking over you, then be all oily and slithery, coated in brown sauce and butter and sperm – it was superb. Everyone likes to be slithery. Now, I am a year older, and I want to recapture those times – and more. It's time for my duty, and yours.'

Ben was achingly erect.

'Are you sure you want to do this?' he said. 'There will be Hades to pay if we are caught.'

'There is always Hades to pay,' Zenobia replied, pressing her lips to his swollen glans, and stroking his tight balls with her gentle fingertips, while her hand strayed over his breast muscles and nipple rings. 'What fabulous pecs!'

She pulled his foreskin fully back, and licked the neck of his glans, running her tongue up and down his frenulum, and making him groan with pleasure.

'Yes, I'm sure I want to do it. We are both virgins, and it is time to defy our overladies. I'm wet for you, and my clito is stiff. Such a lovely big tool! Pardon my French. I'm jealous of Eudoxia, and I don't want *that* Armenian slag taking your virginity. Fuck me in the cunt, not in my bumhole, with that gorgeous hard phallus, Ben. Pump those lovely fesses, fill me with your manhood, crush me with your pecs. Stop me being a cunt virgin. Do it *now*.'

Zenobia lay back, and opened her thighs, using her fingers to part the lips of her cunt. He gazed at her glistening pink slit meat, its succulent fragrance wafting into his nostrils, even as he towered over her. Ben's phallus had never been stiffer. He was going to fuck a girl in her cunt! She handed him a little pot of murex dye, which she had purloined, and told him to coat her in the viscous substance. It would wash off human skin, though not from clothing, but since they were nude, that didn't matter, and she wanted to be slithery when she was fucked. They could rinse in the pig trough. She was already slithery and brown, from the animal slurry that was everywhere, a curious Greek variant on brown sauce, but Ben carefully rubbed the purple dye into every portion of her body, and she ended the operation by tipping the rest of the fluid into her cunt, as if emptying an inkpot.

'Now fuck me,' she gasped, her cunt brimming with purple dye.

She hooked her thumbs in his buttock rings, and pulled him towards her open loins, while her lips fastened on his breast rings, and began to chew his nipples. When his phallus penetrated Zenobia, and her sphincter began to squeeze him, milking him, and she moaned that she wanted all his spunk in her womb, and gasped, '*Fuck me, fuck me, give me your load, come inside me,*' he thought he had never known such ecstasy. He was wanted, and not just as a slave. He fucked her slowly at first, and she gave a cry of pain, as his phallus broke her hymen, but then her hips moved to meet his thrusts, and she urged him to fuck harder and faster. His buttocks clenched, as he slammed into her warm wet slit; he watched his phallus thrust in and out of her heavily juicing cooze, his shaft and balls purple with murex dye, and their nude bodies slithering, slimy brown with slurry of pigs and dotted with currants of goat shit. Watching his phallus fuck Zenobia's purple cunt, he felt curiously disengaged, as though he were watching a puppet drama.

'Yes . . . yes . . . yes . . . !' Zenobia moaned, as their breasts rubbed, and Ben's nipple rings scratched her. 'It's so good. Fuck me! Fill my cunt with that big phallus. Pound me, hurt me. Rub my breasts with yours! I want you, Ben! I want your sperm, your essence.'

Ben obeyed, fucking hard, and it was not long before he felt the sperm well in his balls. He panted to Zenobia that he was going to climax.

'Yes, yes . . .' she moaned. 'Give it to me . . .'

As his ejaculation started, and he felt the shaft of his tool rubbing against her stiff young clito, her muscled belly heaved, and she began to yelp in ecstasy, as she rubbed her rigid nipples.

'Ahh! Ohh! Zeus, yes! *Ahh* . . .'

Ben left his detumescent phallus in Zenobia's cunt. As the new lovers lay clasping each other, after their simultaneous orgasms, Zenobia whispered coyly that her orgasm had been like a volcanic explosion.

'Like lava, flowing from my cunt!' she said.

Suddenly, a shadow darkened their embrace. It was Lefthera, carrying a cane.

'What's this, you beastly slaves?' she rasped. 'You filthy snails! You worms! Lava? *Lava?* Cock in cunt?'

Ben imagined he was hearing Matron Elena Ramsey, at Hereford Hellenic.

'No longer virgin, Ben?' Lefthera sneered. 'No longer a cunt virgin, Zenobia? There will be Hades to pay for this outrage. How lucky that there is a slave auction today. You shall be soundly whipped at dawn, and then put up for auction. And then I shall be rid of you both.'

22

Brown Sauce

'I don't like having to do this, old chap,' said Timothy Dunton-Smythe, as he fastened Ben's wrists to the gibbet, suspending him for his flogging. 'I mean, we're both Oxford men. If you were some Cambridge rotter, I wouldn't have a qualm. But, you know, a mistress must be obeyed. Lefthera is the ruler, here, the *sebastokrator*.'

Ben winced, as he was hoisted and stretched. Beside Ben's naked body, in the twin gibbet, Neobule had already strung Zenobia in the nude. Her arms were painfully wrenched, and her hair was knotted to the crossbar of the whipping frame. Her bare feet, cuffed in leather straps, dangled above the floor. The sun was rising over the blue Aegean, the air was fragrant with flowers and olive trees and orange blossom, and Ben thought that the world was such a beautiful place, yet had such cruel things in it. Watching the spectacle, Lefthera reclined naked on a velvet couch, drinking tea from her favourite rose-patterned Wedgwood teacup – all girls have their favourite teacups – and smoking a cigarette, with Niobe on her lap, while she casually played with the blonde girl's cunt, rubbing her clito, and making Niobe blush. Niobe held Lefthera's Bullworker bodybuilding device, and was pumping iron, as Lefthera frigged her. Her pert breasts were already heavy with hard muscle, and her thighs were broad, like Lefthera's and Neobule's. Cybele, Roxanna and Iphigenia were in attendance, and eagerly awaiting Lefthera's permission to pleasure each other at the spectacle of the fornicants' whipping.

'Let the punishment commence,' Lefthera commanded. 'Flog these worthless slaves to the bone. And, when their skin has been well wealed, they shall be sold at auction. No longer virgin, Ben? Your phallus in my sister's cooze? You disappoint me. No, you disgust me. To be enculed is a small matter, a sacred rite, in fact, but I proudly remain a cunt virgin. My slut of a sister, I expected her to fall by the wayside, but you, Ben – I had higher hopes. You won't mind if I masturbate, as I watch you wriggle in agony, my sweet slave? Masturbation is the sacred duty of the Spartan *sebastokrator*.'

She nodded to her overladies that they, too, might masturbate, once the whipping had commenced, then ordered Neobule to whip Ben, while Timothy was to whip Zenobia. The guilty fornicants were to receive fifty lashes on the buttocks, and fifty on the back. The two whippers raised heavy walrus-hide lashes, from Greenland, two metres long, and took up their stance at long distance. Neobule's gleaming ebony body was naked, and Timothy was also naked, but for one of Lefthera's white thongs, which did little to conceal his stirring erection, as he contemplated the trembling bare buttocks of his victim Zenobia.

'Be brave, Ben,' whispered Zenobia. 'You are special to me.'

'I'll try. For your sake.'

Crack! Ben took the first lash, on the buttocks, from the naked black Spartan, and gasped, at the searing pain. Almost at once, Zenobia moaned, as Timothy's lash whipped her back, high on her shoulders. *Crack! Crack!* The lashes thudded on the naked bodies of the two helpless slaves. Both groaned in agony, as their bodies were covered in welts, for a walrus-hide whip is particularly heavy. Timothy's phallus was fully erect, in his frilly white thong, as he made Zenobia squirm, while Neobule was using only one hand to flog Ben. With the other, she was openly masturbating, and come glistened copiously on her rippling black thighs, trickling down her calves, to bathe her bare toes, and purple-painted toenails. The sun rose over the scene of torment, burning the bare backs of the flogged victims, and adding further torment to that of the whips that lashed them. *Crack! Crack!*

'Uhh ...' Ben gasped, with tears flooding his eyes. *Crack! Crack!*

'Ahh ...' sobbed Zenobia, as her bare body squirmed helplessly, while she wept also.

Iphigenia, Cybele and Roxanna, nude but for sandals and whips coiled around their waists, smiled as they frigged their cunts. Like Neobule, they had rivulets of come trickling down their powerful bare thighs. *Crack! Crack!* The whips rose and fell, torturing the wriggling suspended bodies of Ben and Zenobia, as Lefthera and her sibyls frigged their clitos. Lefthera refreshed herself with sips of tea, as she wanked both herself and the gasping nude Niobe, sitting on her lap. She dipped her fingers in Niobe's cooze, and palmed a portion of her cunt juice, then stirred it into her tea, pronouncing the mixture very refreshing.

She amused herself by wanking Niobe to orgasm after orgasm, in between the blonde girl's sets of exercises with the Bullworker. Lefthera herself wore a new blonde wig, newly shorn from Lucy's head, and the silken tresses brushing her nipples. The sun rose, harsh as the whips that beat the strung victims' naked bodies, until, at last, the hundred lashes had been given. Neobule brought herself off, as she dealt the last lash to Ben's writhing bare, now covered, like Zenobia's, in black and blue welts, and that was the signal for Lefthera to come as well. Their mistress's orgasm meant that the overladies could bring themselves off. Roxanna, Cybele and Iphigenia gasped, giggled and tittered, fingers in one another's cunt, as they wanked one another to climax.

'Now,' said Lefthera, rising, and draining her teacup, 'it is time for the slave auction.'

Ben and his lover were cut down, both trying to hide their tears. Their bare bodies were striped with welts, and they stood shakily. Ben crouched, and kissed Neobule's feet. He licked her toes, while Neobule rubbed her stiff clito, and he felt his phallus rise.

'Thank you, mistress,' he sobbed.

Lefthera glowered, and Ben rushed to kiss her feet, too.

'Mistress, please forgive me for my crime.'

Lefthera was masturbating anew, as Ben took her feet into his mouth, and sucked hard. She stroked the welts on his back and bottom.

'Poor Ben,' she said, as she wanked herself to orgasm. 'such lovely welts, on your lovely girl's body. Ahh! Ahh! Yes!'

'I'm a man, now, mistress,' Ben responded. 'I have fucked your sister in her *cunt*.'

'And for that, you have been well punished, my helot,' she gasped. 'I forgive you for your crime. But still, you and Zenobia must be sold. I cannot have a helot who is no longer virgin.'

The slave auction took place atop Mount Profitis Ilías. The nude pony girls laboured, sweating, to bring the customers up the narrow track, and at the auction plaza, a dusty plain of sand, they had a magnificent view of the turquoise Aegean, and the scent of hyacinth, thyme, lavender and oranges in their nostrils. Ben and Zenobia, to be sold themselves, were yoked to Eudoxia, in a bulky three-pony chariot, to transport wealthy buyers from all over Europe, Africa and Asia. Timothy drove the chariot, with Neobule, Niobe and Lefthera on the passenger couch, beside the prospective buyers. It was a hard uphill journey.

'You fucked her,' panted Eudoxia.

'Yes, and we were both whipped for it.'

'Why didn't you fuck me? I'd have taken a whipping, to have that phallus inside me.'

'I don't know.'

'Boys!' Eudoxia spat. 'They never know. I wanted you, Ben.'

The slave market was a brisk affair. Most, though not all, of the customers were women, some fashionably nude, and draped in gold, some fashionably robed. In that hot summer, the shorter the skirt, the more fashionable; it was customary to wear a skirt so short that the

224

stocking tops and garter straps were visible, and the sliver of panties gusset, or, for many of the ladies, the bare unpantied cunt mound. White and a light pastel shade of pink or lemon were the preferred colours, and the male buyers favoured white linen suits, with panama hats. These were mostly rich buyers looking for pleasure slaves. Selling oneself into slavery, to pay off debts, was a practice as old as slavery itself, and there were few, these days, especially college students, who did not have crippling debts to pay off. The rich pleasure seekers came from India, Australia, Singapore, Brazil, England, France, Belgium and numerous other countries, seeking to purchase submissive concubines. Some, however, wanted production slaves, notably the Greeks, with labour-intensive olive farms. They wanted muscular boys, or, at a pinch, muscular girls.

'All my slaves have muscles,' Lefthera said.

Naked, the boy and girl slaves of Sparta were paraded, roped together by their nipple, buttock or cunt rings, for the bidders to check their young bodies. No indignity was spared them. The boys' cocks were rubbed and felt, the girls' cunts probed, and for both sexes fingers were inserted into their anuses. Some buyers favoured slaves smooth of skin; others, notably the elegant unpantied Brazilian ladies, preferred those well scarred by the whip, as proof that they could endure punishment while working in the coffee plantations, or simply for their own cruel pleasure.

Some expressed a preference for slaves adept at boxing, slave fights being a good source of betting revenue; others, for girl-and-boy couples, the boys with large phalluses, to serve as copulatory entertainment, like the teenage *sphinctriae* of Emperor Tiberius on Capri. Lefthera decreed that Ben and Zenobia should come into this category: sold as a couple, for sex shows. The slaves, in whatever category, were required to perform for the bidders. There were several savage bare-knuckle boxing matches between Oxford men; there were vicious wrestling matches between naked girlslaves, slathered in mud, or purple murex dye, with much gouging, biting, and groin-punching; there were

225

canings of male and female slaves on the naked buttocks, to demonstrate their powers of endurance. It was thought a pretty conceit to present girlslaves dyed in murex from top to toe, and Abigail and Felicity were among those.

Lucy Parvis was not for sale, but was in attendance on Lefthera, with her head cropped to a stubble, and Lefthera wearing a new wig of Lucy's blonde tresses. Finally, Ben and Zenobia were ordered to copulate, in full view of the assembly, lolling under parasols, and sipping champagne, with Neobule acting as mistress of ceremonies, and giving orders to Timothy Dunton-Smythe, clad in yellow peephole bra and thong, allowing his buttock rings to be seen, with sandals, as he served the bidders.

'You mean . . . ?' Ben stammered to Lefthera.

'You did it before. You'll have to do it again, when you're both bought as playthings. Go on, Ben. Fuck her in the cunt. Give my sister a good rogering. But be careful that it lasts a long time. You must make her come, not come yourself. It will get the buyers in a good spending mood.'

Zenobia crouched in doggy style, and presented her whip-scarred buttocks to Ben. Try as he might, he could not prevent his phallus from stiffening, and the appreciative cheers of the crowd faded to dimness as he looked at Zenobia's ripe buttock pears, and swollen cunt lips, dripping wet. He penetrated her wet slit easily, and began to fuck her with long, sure strokes, slamming his helmet to her hard womb neck, and rubbing his shaft against her throbbing clito. His nipple and buttock rings jangled against his skin, as his phallus thrust into her tight warm pouch.

Buttocks rising to meet his thrusts, Zenobia gasped louder and louder, and climaxed after less than a minute's fucking. The crowd roared their applause. Lefthera ordered Ben to withdraw, and fuck Zenobia in the throat. As he did so, Zenobia taking his oily cock shaft right to the back of her throat, and letting her head bob up and down, in a vigorous sucking of his rigid bare phallus, their applause grew louder.

Finally, it was time for Ben to take Zenobia in the anus. Crouching doggy fashion, she held her buttocks wide apart as he penetrated her, filling her rectum, and driving his phallus right to her colon. He fucked hard, as she sobbed and wriggled, wanking her clito, and he soon brought her to another climax. He looked to Lefthera for guidance.

'I think I'm going to spurt, mistress,' he blurted.

'Then spurt in her face,' she ordered curtly.

Ben gave Zenobia's colon a few more hard strokes, then withdrew from her anus, with a squelching plop, as he felt the honey well in his balls, and masturbated into her face. He rubbed his glans, fingers massaging frenulum and corona, and spermed almost at once, splattering her face with a heavy load of cream. The crowd of buyers was most appreciative, with a loud round of applause, as Zenobia licked Ben's sperm from her chin and lips, and swallowed it. Lefthera said to Neobule that the bidding could begin. All bidding was to be in euros, and all purchases paid for in cash, or gold, which would be assayed on the spot by Neobule with a pair of silver scales.

First up was a pretty young fellow from Trinity, with a rather large phallus, which whetted the bidders' appetites, and he eventually went for €6,500, to a Creole lady from Réunion. Next, a girl from Lady Margaret Hall, her large breasts and bottom well bruised by cane strokes, who went to a gentleman from Argentina, for €7,000. The naked slaves sweated in the sun, as the heat grew more intense, along with the bidding, and Timothy Dunton-Smythe plied the guests with more champagne, and plates of squid and octopus, onions, tomatoes and olives. It was not the best champagne – Lefthera was always cost-conscious – but it was certainly moreish.

A sold slave was tagged with the new owner's name, and sent to a holding compound, guarded by the Furies, to await transportation, while the new owner opened her handbag, or his wallet, and shelled out the price in shiny €500 notes. From time to time, as a diversion, a girlslave or boyslave was chosen at random, strung to a gibbet, and flogged a couple of dozen strokes with a bullwhip or olive-branch cane, either by Neobule or by submissive blonde Niobe, who proved surprisingly adept at the flagellant art, and glad to have a respite from her submission. Another marketing device, at the demand of the ladies, was to oblige a boy to masturbate openly, and spray his sperm, so that the ladies could judge the creaming capacity of his balls.

The spectacle of boys wanking off, and the sight of flagellation, caused many ladies to commence masturbating themselves, especially when it was a boy's bare buttocks squirming. They cooed, blushed and gazed with rapture, as a naked boy was reduced to tears by Neobule's vicious cane strokes to his bare. Neobule's superb black body, in the nude, rippling with muscle, as she caned, caused many erections among the white-suited gentlemen, and many wet cunts, with much frigging, among the ladies.

Another diversion was that Timothy stripped and fucked Niobe in the anus, thrusting savagely, as he grasped her hips, and she sobbed in agony, which was a popular spectacle. Some of the Brazilian ladies had their hands under their skirts, and were discreetly masturbating, while the nude ladies frigged their clitos quite openly. Lefthera was adamant in her doctrine that slavery was about sexuality.

Many slaves had been sold, Oxford men and girls who would never see their colleges again. The moment came when Ben and Zenobia were put on the block. Bidding was fierce, and went up to €20,000 for the pair, then €30,000, when, suddenly, the proceedings were interrupted by the arrival of a huge dark-blue Mercedes-Benz 680S roadster, the 1929 model, from which stepped a nude lady, smoking a cigarette in a holder of silver and blue amethyst. The car had been abandoned by a retreating Waffen-SS officer in 1944. Her lips were painted blue, like her car. Lefthera fell to her knees, and kissed her feet. A male in a white linen suit remained in the shade of the car, with his chauffeur, a pretty miniskirted girl, bare-legged, clad in a dark-blue bra and thong panties. Dark blue is the colour of Oxford. The chauffeur was Dr Sarah Mountjoy.

'High Priestess . . .' Lefthera babbled.

'What is the meaning of this?' snapped the naked Dr Rosalynn Demande. 'Why is Ben on the auction block? Don't you know he has important work to do for me, an essay on Philetas of Cos, the grammarian, and his pupil Zenodotus of Ephesus? I need him back in Christ Church at the end of the summer vac.'

'An auction is an auction!' cried a Brazilian lady, bare-breasted, and wearing only a white miniskirt and white nylons and shoes. Her golden nipple rings jangled in wrath, on her bare brown breasts. 'My bid for this pair of slaves stands!'

'And what is your bid?' drawled Rosalynn.

'Forty thousand euros!'

'Let me say, then, fifty thousand. I want these slaves for myself.'

The Brazilian lady opened her purse, and brandished a sheaf of banknotes.

'I have the cash,' she snarled. 'Where is yours?'

'As High Sibyl, I have the power to stop this auction,' Rosalynn said quietly. 'But, as an English lady, I must play by the rules.'

'High Priestess,' said Lefthera, 'I must ask, do you have the cash?'

'*Cash*, you whore?' snarled Rosalynn. '*Cash?* I have more than cash. *I have your father.*'

Lefthera gasped as she looked closely at the white-suited man in the 1929 Benz roadster.

'Father,' she babbled. 'I'm sorry, I didn't realise –'

'Who do you think has been fucking me throughout the summer vac?' said Rosalynn, in triumph.

Ben and Zenobia were promptly sold to Rosalynn, who proceeded to exert her authority as High Sibyl of the Spartans. First, Ben was ordered to fuck Lefthera in her cunt.

'No! please, mistress!' Lefthera blurted. 'I am a cunt virgin! It is too shameful . . .'

'You do not find it shameful to sell my best scholar into slavery, in a distant land?' drawled Rosalynn. 'Bend over, slut, and let Ben take your virginity.'

Ben was erect at the sight of Lefthera's naked brown bottom. He had deflowered her sister, Zenobia, and now he would deflower her. It seemed like poetic justice, or the continuity of the world, the *one*, as taught by Parmenides. He grasped Lefthera by the hips, and penetrated her, thrusting hard. He heard her cry out, as her hymen broke, and then gasp in a staccato howl, as his stiff phallus brought her to a shuddering orgasm. She ordered him to withdraw, without coming, and keep his phallus stiff. Next, on Rosalynn's orders, it was Timothy's turn to be fucked. He obeyed her, and knelt, with his knickers off, and bare arse spread. Niobe took an olive branch, and whipped his bare arse thirty strokes, making him weep, while Neobule donned a strap-on of cedar wood, then, after his flogging had left him squirming and crying, plunged the giant dildo into the boy's anus.

'No, please . . .' he sobbed. 'It hurts.'

'It's supposed to hurt, you filthy boy,' Rosalynn snapped.

Timothy writhed under his enculement by Neobule, who was masturbating hard, as her buttocks thrust the dildo into his rectum. His phallus was stiff, and, after five minutes of savage buggery, he moaned, ejaculating his sperm into the sand.

'Now,' said Rosalynn, 'the summer vac is almost over, and we all have work to do. The cooling Aegean breeze, so pleasant in summer, becomes a freezing wind in winter. Those girls and boys who have not been sold into slavery may accompany me back to England on the *Lefthera*, which is to sail tomorrow for Miami, where Lefthera's father winters, with one of his many mistresses, but calling at Venice and Southampton on the way.'

Rosalynn sneered at Lefthera.

'Your father has already paid for Count Scazzo's excellent sculptures, my dear. We shall take delivery of them in Venice. They show you, Ben and Nicola . . . shall we say, in compromising poses. You being buggered by Ben, while Nicola wanks and pees on your writhing bodies! Then, Ben buggered by Nicola with a strap-on. But it is all art. In case you're wondering, I have had sex with Nicola, too. Her and Count Scazzo. I sucked Nicola's breasts and cooze, and Count Scazzo's quite tasty phallus. Both of them, in their different ways, are very good.'

Lefthera started to cry, and Rosalynn patted her bare bum, then put her finger in her anus, which made the Greek girl sigh with pleasure.

'Cheer up, old girl,' Rosalynn said. 'It's not that bad.'

23

New Term

It was the first day of Michaelmas term, and Ben, dressed in grey flannels and a brown sports coat, with his old school tie, was greeted at the gate lodge by Perkins. He saw Neobule and Niobe, dressed in French maids' uniforms, with flesh-coloured nylon stockings, sweeping the quad, in their new jobs as college servants.

'Have a good summer vac, sir?' said Perkins. 'You have a bit of a suntan, if I may say so.'

'Yes, it was jolly good. Greece, you know. Spent most of my time in the library, gnoming.'

'Well, that's what scholars are good at, sir. I've never been further than Abingdon, myself. We've two new statues in the quad, sir, if you'd like to take a look. A white one in Carrara marble, and a black one, in Greek obsidian. Quite an adornment to the college, in my view. Of course, stuffy people might think them a bit naughty, but it's art, isn't it, and that's what we're all here for. Classical, you know. In fact, if you'll forgive me, one of the figures, chap with no clothes on, looks a bit like you. Probably a trick of the light. As long as you enjoyed your vac, and got some studying done, that's the main thing.'

'Yes, of course,' Ben said. 'But do you know what the best thing about the summer vac was? It was getting back to Oxford, and going into the Bear Inn for a pint of ale and a meat pie, covered in brown sauce.'

He leant close to Perkins, and murmured in his ear.

'You can't beat a pint of good English ale, and brown sauce on a meat pie.'

'Very sound reasoning, sir,' said Perkins. 'Worthy of Parmenides, if I may say so. He was the greatest member of the Eleatic school, apart from Pyrrhon the Sceptic. Socrates once heard him speak. Parmenides argued for the existence of absolute being, the nonexistence of which Parmenides declared to be inconceivable, but the nature of which he admitted to be equally inconceivable, since absolute being is dissociated from every limitation under which human beings think. Parmenides held that the phenomena of nature are only apparent and due to human error; they seem to exist, but have no real existence. He also held that reality, true being, is not known to the senses but is to be found only in reason. Parmenides's theory that being cannot arise from nonbeing, and that being neither arises nor passes away, was applied to matter by his successors Empedocles and Democritus, who made it the foundation of their materialistic explanations of the universe. I think there is something eternally true about a good meat pie. The meat pie the earth, and the brown sauce the sea enfolding it. Of course, that's just my viewpoint, and what do I know? I'm just a humble college porter, like my father and grandfather before me.'

Dr Rosalynn Demande passed through the lodge, dressed in shorts and halter, braless and unpantied, on her way back from the gymnasium Phiditia. Behind her, on a leash around their bare waists, she led Louella Potts and Eudoxia, both rippling with muscle, wearing only lemon-yellow bra and panties, and carrying new Bullworker bodybuilding devices. Ben nodded to Louella, admiring her superbly muscled thighs, and got a sheepish grin in return.

'Ben!' Rosalynn cried. 'What are you doing, dressed in such an ugly manner? And with brown sauce dripping from your lips? You deserve a whipping, young man. Follow me at once, and we'll get you caned, and properly kitted in a decent girl's dress and nylons. I'm not sure I shan't give your bum some attention with one of my nice new *godemichés* from that Italian place in Mestre. You're one of those unruly scholars who need to be enculed by a woman.

233

'And then we have to go to these awful weddings. Lucy Parvis is to be married to Lefthera's father, and Lefthera is to be married to Timothy Dunton-Smythe. He's had Stygia fit him with an albert, a bloody great cock ring through his glans! Lefthera couldn't resist that. She does love being buggered. And, do you know, the girls are going to be married in the nude! I have to make speeches and things. So I'll have to be in the nude too. Truly, a woman's work is never done. Well, you can jolly well help me. And a good caning on the bare will get your mind right. Go up to my chambers, and get your knickers down!'

'Yes, mistress,' Ben said, quavering.

'By the way,' snapped Rosalynn, 'have you ever thought of getting married?'

'No,' Ben stammered, 'I can't say I have. I'm a bit too young to think of marriage, I suppose.'

Rosalynn sighed.

'Boys are always a bit too young to think of anything. Well, you can marry *me*, then. I'll be nude, and you can wear a lovely pink wedding dress, with pink nylon stockings and perhaps white court shoes, but I'll think about that. We'll get married in Hereford, and Elena Ramsey will be bridesmaid, in the Cathedral Church of the Blessed Virgin Mary and St Aethelbert, which exemplifies all architectural styles from Norman to Perpendicular. The see was detached from that of Lichfield in 676, Putta being its first bishop. After the body of Aethelbert, a slain English leader, had been brought to the site, a superior church was reconstructed in 1030, but this was burnt by the Welsh, and building began again in 1079; it was completed only in 1148. The cathedral's main features include a fifty-metre central tower in decorated style and a north porch in rich Perpendicular style. There is a noted organ, a large chained library and a collection of rare manuscripts, early printed books and relics. We must get married, Ben, for we both have important books to write. So we *shall* get married. I decree it.'

'Is that an order?' Ben said. 'That I must marry you?'

'Of course it's an order!' Rosalynn hissed. 'I am High Sibyl of the Spartans, you snail!'

'Then I must obey,' Ben said.

'Now get upstairs for your bare-bum whipping, husband.'

'Yes, mistress.'

'May you enjoy your new term, and your next meat pie, sir,' said Perkins, 'and have many of them. I think Parmenides would have liked a pint of good Oxfordshire ale, and a meat pie, with Bicester brown sauce.'

The leading publisher of fetish and adult fiction

TELL US WHAT YOU THINK!

Readers' ideas and opinions matter to us. Take a few minutes to fill in the questionnaire below and you'll be entered into a prize draw to win a year's worth of Nexus books (36 titles)

Terms and conditions apply – see end of questionnaire.

1. Sex: Are you male ☐ female ☐ a couple ☐?

2. Age: Under 21 ☐ 21–30 ☐ 31–40 ☐ 41–50 ☐ 51–60 ☐ over 60 ☐

3. Where do you buy your Nexus books from?
☐ A chain book shop. If so, which one(s)?

_____

☐ An independent book shop. If so, which one(s)?

_____

☐ A used book shop/charity shop
☐ Online book store. If so, which one(s)?

_____

4. How did you find out about Nexus books?
☐ Browsing in a book shop
☐ A review in a magazine
☐ Online
☐ Recommendation
☐ Other _____

5. In terms of settings, which do you prefer? (Tick as many as you like)
☐ Down to earth and as realistic as possible
☐ Historical settings. If so, which period do you prefer?

_____

☐ Fantasy settings – barbarian worlds

- ☐ Completely escapist/surreal fantasy
- ☐ Institutional or secret academy
- ☐ Futuristic/sci fi
- ☐ Escapist but still believable
- ☐ Any settings you dislike?

- ☐ Where would you like to see an adult novel set?

---

6. In terms of storylines, would you prefer:

- ☐ Simple stories that concentrate on adult interests?
- ☐ More plot and character-driven stories with less explicit adult activity?
- ☐ We value your ideas, so give us your opinion of this book:

---

7. In terms of your adult interests, what do you like to read about? (Tick as many as you like)

- ☐ Traditional corporal punishment (CP)
- ☐ Modern corporal punishment
- ☐ Spanking
- ☐ Restraint/bondage
- ☐ Rope bondage
- ☐ Latex/rubber
- ☐ Leather
- ☐ Female domination and male submission
- ☐ Female domination and female submission
- ☐ Male domination and female submission
- ☐ Willing captivity
- ☐ Uniforms
- ☐ Lingerie/underwear/hosiery/footwear (boots and high heels)
- ☐ Sex rituals
- ☐ Vanilla sex
- ☐ Swinging
- ☐ Cross-dressing/TV

☐ Enforced feminisation
☐ Others – tell us what you don't see enough of in adult fiction:

_____

_____

_____

8. Would you prefer books with a more specialised approach to your interests, i.e. a novel specifically about uniforms? If so, which subject(s) would you like to read a Nexus novel about?

_____

_____

_____

9. Would you like to read true stories in Nexus books? For instance, the true story of a submissive woman, or a male slave? Tell us which true revelations you would most like to read about:

_____

_____

_____

10. What do you like best about Nexus books?

_____

_____

11. What do you like least about Nexus books?

_____

_____

12. Which are your favourite titles?

_____

_____

13. Who are your favourite authors?

_____

_____

14. Which covers do you prefer? Those featuring:
(tick as many as you like)

- ☐ Fetish outfits
- ☐ More nudity
- ☐ Two models
- ☐ Unusual models or settings
- ☐ Classic erotic photography
- ☐ More contemporary images and poses
- ☐ A blank/non-erotic cover
- ☐ What would your ideal cover look like?

_____

15. Describe your ideal Nexus novel in the space provided:

_____

_____

_____

_____

16. Which celebrity would feature in one of your Nexus-style fantasies?
We'll post the best suggestions on our website – anonymously!

_____

THANKS FOR YOUR TIME

Now simply write the title of this book in the space below and cut out the questionnaire pages. Post to: Nexus, Marketing Dept., Thames Wharf Studios, Rainville Rd, London W6 9HA

Book title: _____

TERMS AND CONDITIONS

NEXUS NEW BOOKS

To be published in December 2006

SILKEN EMBRACE
Christina Shelly

The Bigger Picture is a radical and powerful organisation of dominant women intent on turning young men into ultra-glamorous she-males to become housemaids that serve wealthy women and demanding men. Shelly manages to escape the strict training programme and shelters with Mrs Ambrose, a beautiful and glamorous widow who runs a rival academy. But it's not long before the beautiful and severe agents of The Bigger Picture track her down and return her to captivity, where her erotic torments and re-education continue, with an even greater creativity and extremity than ever before.

£6.99   ISBN 0 352 34081 9

WHALEBONE STRICT
Lady Alice McCloud

Petticoats, corsets, frilly knickers, lace, and canes – all part of the Imperial world inhabited by Thrift; a young and naive foreign office agent sent on special missions on behalf of the empire. In *Whalebone Strict*, Thrift Moncrieff's assignment for the British Imperial Diplomatic Service takes her to the North American colonies, where she is supposed to compromise the position of a politician. In this she is rather more successful than she had planned, leading her ever deeper into difficulties that more often than not lead to the opening of her ankle-length corset and elaborate underwear, either for the entertainment of a string of lecherous men, or to have a hand applied to her delectable buttocks.

£6.99   ISBN 0 352 34082 7

IN FOR A PENNY
Penny Birch

Penny Birch is back, as naughty as ever. *In for a Penny* continues the story of her outrageous sex life and also the equally rude behaviour of her friends. From stories of old-fashioned spankings, through strip-wrestling in baked beans, to a girl with unusual breasts, it's all there. Each scene is described in loving detail, with no holding back and a level of realism that comes from a great deal of practical experience.

£6.99   ISBN 0 352 34083 5

If you would like more information about Nexus titles, please visit our website at www.nexus-books.co.uk, or send a large stamped addressed envelope to:
  Nexus, Thames Wharf Studios,
  Rainville Road, London W6 9HA

This information is correct at time of printing. For up-to-date information, please visit our website at www.nexus-books.co.uk

All books are priced at £6.99 unless another price is given.

ABANDONED ALICE	Adriana Arden 0 352 33969 1	☐
ALICE IN CHAINS	Adriana Arden 0 352 33908 X	☐
AMAZON SLAVE	Lisette Ashton 0 352 33916 0	☐
ANGEL	Lindsay Gordon 0 352 34009 6	☐
AQUA DOMINATION	William Doughty 0 352 34020 7	☐
THE ART OF CORRECTION	Tara Black 0 352 33895 4	☐
THE ART OF SURRENDER	Madeline Bastinado 0 352 34013 4	☐
AT THE END OF HER TETHER	G.C. Scott 0 352 33857 1	☐
BELINDA BARES UP	Yolanda Celbridge 0 352 33926 8	☐
BENCH MARKS	Tara Black 0 352 33797 4	☐
BIDDING TO SIN	Rosita Varón 0 352 34063 0	☐
BINDING PROMISES	G.C. Scott 0 352 34014 2	☐
THE BLACK GARTER	Lisette Ashton 0 352 33919 5	☐
THE BLACK MASQUE	Lisette Ashton 0 352 33977 2	☐
THE BLACK ROOM	Lisette Ashton 0 352 33914 4	☐
THE BLACK WIDOW	Lisette Ashton 0 352 33973 X	☐
THE BOND	Lindsay Gordon 0 352 33996 9	☐

----------✂----------------------------

Please send me the books I have ticked above.

Name   ....

Address   ....

....

....

.... Post code ....

Send to: **Virgin Books Cash Sales, Thames Wharf Studios, Rainville Road, London W6 9HA**

US customers: for prices and details of how to order books for delivery by mail, call 888-330-8477.

Please enclose a cheque or postal order, made payable to **Nexus Books Ltd**, to the value of the books you have ordered plus postage and packing costs as follows:

UK and BFPO – £1.00 for the first book, 50p for each subsequent book.

Overseas (including Republic of Ireland) – £2.00 for the first book, £1.00 for each subsequent book.

If you would prefer to pay by VISA, ACCESS/MASTERCARD, AMEX, DINERS CLUB or SWITCH, please write your card number and expiry date here:

....

Please allow up to 28 days for delivery.

Signature   ....

Our privacy policy

We will not disclose information you supply us to any other parties. We will not disclose any information which identifies you personally to any person without your express consent.

From time to time we may send out information about Nexus books and special offers. Please tick here if you do *not* wish to receive Nexus information.   ☐

----------✂----------------------------